Growing Up

Growing Up

Martha Marie

The Second Irish Novel

PATJAC

About the Author

The second eldest of ten children (one of whom is now a very well known Irish comedian) Martha Marie was born and went to primary school in Dublin. She immigrated to London in the late 1950s after the clothing factory where she had worked since she was fourteen closed. She is now seventy three, a widow of nearly two years, three grown sons, two teenage sons, eight living siblings and a few dozen nieces and nephews; studied with The Open University and gained a BA in 1984.

As a form teacher in a multicultural state school she was responsible for teaching the personal social and health course to her pupils. Many of the discussions she had with them involved talking about different cultures and families. During lessons she was constantly pressed to talk about growing up in Ireland, and what it was like to be one of twelve living in one house. It was through telling these stories about her own life and the life of her friends also from large families that she decided to write a book.

Growing Up is the second of several! Move Over is the first of The Irish Novels.

Chapter One

The office was on the ground floor of an old three-storey building in a street near the main Phibsboro Road on the north side of Dublin City. Rain dribbled down the dirty window while Joan finished typing the last specification on the house Peter had asked her to do before she went home. She shoved her spectacles up on her nose, pushed her chair back, walked over to the door and turned the key in the lock.

It was getting on for five so Joan decided she would change into her jeans. Even if the rain stopped within the next half hour the pavements would still be wet, and she didn't want to get the bottoms of her good trousers splashed.

She went into the back room that was furnished with a table, four chairs, a small sink in the corner, and an electric kettle for making coffee. Most of the floor on the far wall was covered with old brown paper wallet files, piled up, waiting to go into storage in Peter's garage. She turned on the gas fire and went out through another door to the toilet.

Returning from the cold toilet, Joan stood in front of the fire and removed her trousers.

'Very nice,' a husky male voice leered. 'I wonder you don't have pneumonia from those little things,' he said, pointing to Joan's bikini pants.

Joan recognised the voice of Peter's father before she turned round and saw a big tall fat man with a red round face. 'How

did you get in?' she gasped, while she stretched her hand out
to get her trousers off the chair.

The old fat man leered and said, 'Peter might have the business now, but I still own the building.' John Cunningham tossed
a bunch of keys in the air, but he never bothered to catch them
because he walked over to Joan and grabbed her trousers.

Barely five-feet-two and weighing only eight stone, Joan
put all her strength into wrestling with the heavy man after he
had shoved her down on the pile of folders. As fast as she freed
herself from his strong arms, she slipped on the pile of papers.
When he pulled her pants down to her ankles she brought her
knees up and caught him under his chin.

'You little bitch,' John swore, slapping her hard across her
face.

Chapter Two

Church bells clanged out the evening angelus when Joan felt cold water running down her face.

'Joan, Joan,' Peter Cunningham repeated as he patted the sides of her face. He lifted her shoulders and inserted another towel under her head.

Joan opened her eyes, raised her head and looked down at her feet. Her legs were covered with a man's jacket. 'Where is he?' she asked.

'Did he rape you?' Peter asked, bringing his hand up to his mouth. His stomach had settled, but he could still see the lower part of Joan's body with her knees up and her legs parted. But he had to ask her.

'I don't know,' Joan said, making to sit up but she slipped on the papers she was lying on. 'I punched him with my knee, then he hit me.' She rolled on her side towards Peter who was crouched on his hunkers beside her. 'Is he still here?' she asked again.

'He is in the office slumped over my desk,' Peter replied standing to give her space to move. 'I will phone the police, and an ambulance.'

Joan got up on her elbows and said, 'I don't need to go to hospital, and I don't want the police.' She flapped her hands around the papers to find her glasses. 'I'll be all right.'

Peter found her glasses and gave them to her.

'I didn't mean to hurt him,' Joan said. She held the jacket

around her waist and tried to stand, but she found her panties were around one of her ankles. 'I only wanted to get him off me,' she said hastily, 'but he held my shoulders down.' All she wanted to do right now was to soak in a bath. She looked around for her trousers as she said, 'I'll get a mini cab home.'

Peter wiped his hands over his face as though he could wipe his thoughts away. He knew a crime had been committed and should be reported. At the same time he also knew that the only one that would suffer would be Joan. 'I'll phone your mammy and send a cab for her to come down for you.'

In the space of the few seconds while he watched the sadness in his young secretary's eyes, images of his mother, his wife, and young daughters flashed into Peter's mind. His worried thoughts went on to think that maybe, just maybe his father hadn't raped Joan at all. After all the man was nearly seventy and most of the time he was drunk. Besides, Peter went on to think, a woman would know if she was raped. But Joan wasn't a woman. The girl was only seventeen and most of the time she only looked fifteen with her small body and mousy straight hair. He had never seen her wearing make up. 'I'll leave you to get your clothes on,' he said, backing out the door into the office.

Still holding Peter's jacket around her Joan said, 'Will you phone my Aunt Sue?'

Chapter Three

On the Sunday morning after Sue Ryan had brought her young niece home to her own house she was driving slowly past the church on her way to visit her sister Sheila in Ballyglass on the north side of Dublin city.

The rain that had drenched Dublin City on the Saturday was now pouring over the Irish Sea. But it left the Dublin air as cold and damp as Sue's temper when she pulled up outside her sister's house.

Wearing her dressing gown, Cathy opened the door to her aunt then withdrew into the hall. 'Sue,' she said, surprised to see her.

Two years younger than Joan, Cathy is an opposite of her sister in every way. She is tall, with a pleasant round face, and thick, dark, brown hair.

'Is your mammy in?' Sue asked, following Cathy into the living room.

'She's in bed,' Cathy sniffed, wiped her nose on the back of her hand, then knelt down at the fire and struck a match.

After Cathy struck the third match Sue took them out of her hand. It was obvious that Cathy was putting the flame to the sticks and not the paper. Her eyes were watering so much that she couldn't see what she was doing. 'You go back to bed,' she said.

'I will be warmer down here,' Cathy said, wiping her eyes with a tissue. 'It's only a cold.'

Sue was walking along the lobby from the back door with a bucket full of coal when Cathy came out of the kitchen with a hot water bottle in her hand. She nodded approval at the hot water bottle and said, 'Go into the living room and get warm. I'll bring you in a cup of tea when I come back from talking to your mammy.' She walked into the living room with the coal.

Cathy put the water bottle on the stairs and said, 'Will yeh bring that up to her?'

Faced with three closed doors at the top of the stairs and not knowing which of the bedrooms her sister was in, Sue called out, 'Sheila.' On hearing a light thump from the small bedroom at the back of the house, she knocked and opened the door.

Barely big enough for a double bed, a bedside cabinet, and enough space to open the wardrobe, the small room was a cold room.

'The fire is lighting downstairs,' Sue said, while she pulled the curtain back on the small window. The thud she had heard had come from a small plate that had fallen on the floor. She picked up the plate. It had smears of butter and toasted breadcrumbs and it was warm. 'Cathy has a bad cold,' she said, turning back to the door.

Sheila Malone raised her head off the pillow and closed her eyes at her sister. She was curious to know why Sue was here but she was not going to ask because she never asked her about anything. Expecting her sister would tell her, she stretched her arm over to the bedside cabinet and picked up a half-full cup of tea.

In her early sixties, and four years older than Susan, Sheila had never been close to her sister. Until four years ago she had bullied and manipulated Susan like she had her ten children. She looked at the small clock on the cabinet. 'I gave her a couple of Anadin when she brought me the tea and toast,' she said.

Furious with her sister for allowing Cathy to make her

breakfast, Sue took the cup out of Sheila's hand and walked out of the bedroom.

Walking downstairs, Sue heard Cathy coughing. She went into the living room and put more coal on the fire. 'Get dressed, Cathy,' she said. 'It will be warmer down here than upstairs but you will be better with your clothes on.' She opened her handbag and checked she had money in her purse. 'Is there anything you need in the shops?'

'Cigarettes,' Cathy smiled.

Cough, or not, Sue decided this wasn't the time to nag her young niece about her smoking. Besides if she didn't get them Cathy would only cough her way into the village to get them herself. 'Is there any special cough mixture you like?'

'I can't remember ever havin' te take any before,' Cathy said, taking her last cigarette out of the packet. 'Get what yeh think yerself.'

Chapter Four

Five months after Cathy had recovered from her cold and a month after Joan had moved to England, Sheila Malone stirred the embers in the grate, expecting to find a few red pieces that would bring the rest alive with some rolled-up newspapers. It soon became obvious that the fire hadn't been lit the previous evening.

The hollow sound in the tin container when she inserted a shilling into gas meter told her it had been emptied recently. She couldn't remember finding any money when she came home last night, or the night before, so she suspected that Cathy had kept the rebate. She went into the small kitchen and lit the grill to make toast. She also lit two of the rings on the cooker. They gave off better heat than the two-bar electric fire, which she was too lazy to fetch from the living room.

A small table, and two old wooden stools faced the door in the middle of the small kitchen. To the right there was a butler sink under a small window at the front of the house. On the left of the sink there was a wooden draining board and on the right the gas cooker.

While she waited for her bread to brown under the grill, Sheila stared out of the window. But unlike some of her neighbours she wasn't interested in what was going on out on the road, so she didn't move the net curtain, or stand on her toes so she could see who was talking outside the front gate.

Other than the roof of the house across the road, Sheila was never able to see anything from the window in the kitchen. She was only five-feet-two. She stared at the clouds and decided she wouldn't ask Cathy if the gas meter had been emptied. With Joan gone now, she had only her youngest daughter living with her. She worried that Cathy would leave for England or Canada like her other five daughters.

Marmalade killed the taste on the edges of the burnt toast, and Sheila never ate the crusts anyway. She shoved the plate away and lit a cigarette. She was dropping the burning match into the sink when she heard the front gate rattle. She stood on her toes and stretched her neck to see if she had a visitor. A tall blond hair man was walking up the path.

'Good morning, Mrs Malone,' Peter Cunningham said to the small grey-haired woman who opened the door. He didn't need to ask if she was Joan's mother because he could see the resemblance in the small eyes, nose and thin lips. 'I'm Peter Cunningham.'

Sheila bowed her head like she was a lady responding to her butler, then tilted it back so she could look into the tall man's face.

As the small cold blue eyes bored into him, Peter wondered if Joan's mother knew the real reason why her daughter was in England, even though Joan and her Aunt Sue had said that she wasn't to be told.

Sheila raised her hand to the neck of her housecoat and said, 'I hope the sun comes out for the afternoon.' She didn't really care, but she expected the man to know that she wasn't going to ask him into the house.

Peter withdrew a white envelope from the inside pocket of his tweed jacket and held it out to her. 'Joan asked me to give you this.' He watched her comb her untidy short hair with one hand while she took the envelope with the other. Snippets of conversations he had overheard between Joan and her Aunt Sue shot into his thoughts like bullets fired from a gun as he watched Sheila feel the envelope with her finger and thumb. 'I would like you to count it,' he said.

After she counted four five-pound notes Sheila said, 'It's all here.'

'I will be up again at the same time in two weeks,' Peter said then walked back down the garden.

Chapter Five

He counted three bags in the boot of his car before he lowered the top and banged it shut. It wasn't Jack Byrnes' habit, or temperament to bang doors, but this time he was closing the door on his thoughts. He knew in his heart that he should be going to Ireland with his wife and two young sons. He had lied to Una when he had said that he didn't like weddings. He couldn't tell her he was jealous of her family. They were always fighting, but they were honest and they loved each other. He also knew he would have to stay with his ma and da.

Walking up the short front garden path of his home in Dagenham, Jack could hear the voices of his boys coming from the front room. Shea and Liam were counting their money. Their mammy made them two small string bags, a green one for their Irish money and a blue one for their English.

It always annoyed Jack when he had to change his notes and coins when he went to Ireland, but he smiled as he listened to his sons adding up the few pence they would save because the English money bought more than the Irish. Shea was ten, had nearly finished his second year in junior school so he was well able to add up the pennies he would save. His brother Liam would start school in another year but he could do his sums. Jack was very proud of his boys.

'Do you two want anything to eat before you go?' Jack called into the front room while he opened the fridge.

'We will be having something to eat with our mammy's brother when we get to Dublin,' Liam called back.

Which brother? Jack wondered. She has four of them. He ran his eyes over the pork pies, cold potatoes, packets of ham, sausages, bacon, bread and rolls that Una had filled the small fridge with. With his mind on food, he went on to think that he would have the perfect wife if Una learned to cook. He felt some shame while he closed the fridge door gently because he was comparing Una with her older sister, and Josie was a wonderful cook. He also knew there was no such thing as the perfect wife, but Una came close.

It was Una Malone's red hair that Jack first noticed when she moved into a house on the same road where he was living with his parents and sister over fifteen years ago. Una was one of three teenage girls in the large family. There were two younger girls. Two years later when the Malones moved to another house on an adjoining estate, Una had five sisters.

When Jack had brought Una to London he never imagined that she would miss her siblings as much as she had done. He assumed that because he was pleased to get away from his own family that Una would be too, especially as she was always fighting with her mother. There were times when he saw tears in her eyes when she talked about her siblings, but the only time he had heard her cry was when she had learned her young sister Joan had been in England and she hadn't gotten in touch.

Light footsteps on the ceiling told Jack his wife was running around the bedrooms. He prayed she had packed everything she wanted to bring with her. They would be late leaving if he had to bring her bag in from the car if she had forgotten something. He dreaded what she would do if she missed her plane. She needed to go home to see her family, and it wasn't only so she could enjoy a wedding.

Chapter Six

There was only one photograph in Una's album that needed a full page, and Una stared at it while she whispered, 'It's been six years.' She had asked her younger sister Maura a few times for a smaller one but it never came. All her spoilt and pretty young sister sent her was a Christmas card every year. She continued to turn the pages so she could find a photograph of Joan.

Still hurting because she had so little communication from Maura since she had last seen her, Una continued to talk to herself, 'In six years we have had one wedding, one divorce, one death and five more children.' She turned back a few pages in her album to find a photograph of her quiet young sister Joan. Finding one that was taken two years earlier she moaned, 'God Almighty, she looks about twelve, not eighteen.'

'The cases are in the car, Mammy,' Shea called up from the hall.

Snapping her album shut Una called back, 'I'm on my way down,' She didn't need to go through all the photographs because she knew every one of them. Jack had given her the album for her birthday the first year they were married. She rubbed her fingers along the two embossed words that read, "My Family" on the front cover before she dropped it into the bottom drawer of her bedside cabinet. While she was taking her makeup bag off her dressing table she noticed the photograph of her two boys sitting beside a swimming pool. She recalled how much her sons had enjoyed their holiday at Pontins while she wondered if they should have gone home instead of going to the holiday camp last summer.

'Are you ready, Una?' Jack shouted up the stairs.

'I'm coming, I'm coming.' Una closed her handbag, and shut her mind on her worries. She prayed that she was wrong in thinking that perhaps her family assumed that because she had decided not to go home for the last two years that she didn't want to know them any more. And that was probably why Joan hadn't bothered to get in touch with her.

Families grow apart, Jack had told Una the day after Joan's letter came. She knew it was true because she had worked with people who never heard from their brothers or sisters. At the same time she believed that it only happened in small families. Large families like hers were always much closer. They had more weddings, funerals and christenings to go to.

'Do you have your tickets?' Jack asked when she was at the bottom of the stairs.

Una opened her bag and showed Jack her tickets. She smiled into his small blue eyes and said, 'You're right to make me check.' She returned the ticket to her handbag and walked down the narrow hallway and out the hall door in front of her husband.

Chapter Seven

Una counted three boarding cards before she turned round from the checking-in desk. Her heart skipped a beat when she saw her eldest son Shea was still holding his daddy's hand. She didn't know what she would say, or do if Shea said he didn't want to come with her. She looked round for her younger son Liam.

'He's right beside you,' Jack said, letting go of Shea's hand. He raised his arm and looked at his watch, then nodded towards the large blue sign that read departures and said, 'Enjoy your weekend.'

'We will,' Una said, forcing a smile, wondering again if she could have said, or done anything different that would have encouraged her husband to come with them. She lowered her eyes from his face to his leather jacket and asked, 'Any message for your ma or da?'

'Nope,' Jack replied, although he wanted to tell her to tell his da not to bully the children. He put his arm around her shoulder, pulled her towards him, kissed her and said, 'Give my best to Joan.'

Passengers with children were allowed to board the aeroplane first so Una lead the procession with her two sons across the tarmac. 'Take your time,' she called out to Liam when her four-year old son started to climb the metal steps.

It was because they were travelling by aeroplane that Liam was very excited. Shea would have been more than happy to be going on the car ferry again if his daddy was coming with them. When his daddy said that he was definitely not coming he was relieved to come by plane because his mammy had only passed her driving test a week before she booked the tickets. The drive to Holyhead was nearly eight hours when they went two years earlier.

Shea loved Ireland but he didn't like staying in his Granddad Byrne's house. He was always cold, and he never saw other children. His Granny Byrne never did anything without asking his granddad if it was time to do it. He didn't like his food because his granny put brown sauce on everything. His Granny Byrne's name was Betty but his granddad always called her Ma. And she always called him Da. He didn't like that because he got confused with his own mammy and daddy.

Even though he was always getting the names of his aunts and uncles mixed up, Shea liked his mammy's family. With the exception of Josie, he could never remember who was his mammy's sister or her brother, or who was married to her sister, or to her brother. But it didn't matter when he was with them because they all knew him. He had never been to a wedding and he didn't understand why he was coming to Ireland for this one, while at the same time he wouldn't be going it.

When the plane began to gently roll and rock as it moved down the runway, Una felt tiny shivers in her stomach, her mouth, and her eyes. Now that she was on her way, she started to worry about her family.

From as far back as Una could remember, Una had fought with her older sister Josie. But whether it was a big row or a tiff she had never felt anxious about meeting her again. She also fought with her mammy and she had never been afraid of her either. It was her younger sister Joan she was worried about meeting. Other than with Josie, she never fought with her siblings. Nobody ever fought or argued with Joan.

Even with the engines roaring, Una always felt a frightening stillness in the aeroplane before it lifted off the runway. It was the only time she imagined that the plane would crash. And the sensation made her think about all things that she hadn't done. She wondered again if she should have swallowed her pride and written to Joan to ask her why she hadn't let her know she had been in England.

'Are you two all right?' Una called over the aisle to her two sons.

'It's noisy,' Liam whined.

'I know, I know,' Una said, nodding her head in agreement. 'It's not so bad when we get airborne. And we'll be there in an hour.' The noise from the engines became a loud buzzing sound when the plane was airborne. Una showed her sons how to hold their nose and pop their ears.

'That makes the noise louder,' Liam moaned.

'It's no worse than the tubes,' Shea asserted, 'and the plane isn't rattling so you won't get a headache.'

Imagining she was growing a headache from the loud buzzing coming from the engines, Una closed her eyes and rested her head on the back of her seat. She had never been plagued with headaches like her Aunt Sue, but she had suffered her share of pain with her teeth. And it was because of her teeth that she hadn't come home for her aunt's funeral a couple of months after Cathy had stayed with her. She was asleep in the dentist surgery when Jack had taken the phone call from Mike to tell them that Sue had died and Jack didn't tell her until the next day.

The day after Cathy had told her that Sue had been in London, Una phoned Josie. Although she was twenty miles away, at the other end of the phone she could picture the blank face of her sister when Josie hesitated before she had said that she hadn't seen their aunt. She was further convinced that Josie had been lying when she started talking about how busy her business was. Josie always changed the conversation when she didn't want to answer a question.

As the plane took her nearer to her home city Una became more anxious because after she had asked about Joan all Josie wanted to talk about was how pleased their mammy was to have their sister back home again. She sighed and thought, typical Josie, she never answers a question when there is something unpleasant going on. Her thoughts went on to when she had finally heard from Joan.

Expecting the letter would be for Jack because the envelope was long and the address was typed Una was putting it on the small shelf beside the radio when she noticed the Irish stamp. She read the letter before she made a cup of tea. On reading the letter the third time and counting the weeks twice, she phoned Josie.

After she had told her older sister that Joan was getting married in less than six weeks, Una worried why Joan offered to send her the money for her ticket. She read the letter again trying to find a hint that would tell her why the wedding was taking place so quickly.

The cold coffee in the plastic cup the hostess had served brought Una's thoughts back to when Sue died and because the last of her teeth had been removed and she could only manage cold drinks. She wondered if Joan offered to send her money for her ticket because she thought she hadn't come home for their Aunt Sue's funeral because she didn't have the money.

'Will all your sisters be coming home for the wedding mammy?' Shea asked, recalling the last time he had come to Ireland for a weekend with his mammy when his daddy didn't come with them. He was only four at the time and he had stayed with his Granny Byrne. 'Like the time when we came for the party?' he added.

Surprised that her son remembered, Una said, 'That was six years ago.'

'I remember coming on the boat, and the day we went into

town with your brother Liam and your sister Pauline,' he said. He laughed: 'We walked from O'Connell Street up to Grafton Street.'

Una remembered the day like it was yesterday. Less than an hour before they were rushing back into town, her youngest brother Liam told her that he was going to leave home. He was only sixteen at the time. 'No Shea, my two sisters that are in Canada won't be here this time.'

'Will Josie be?'

'She will,' Una knew, and replied, nodding her head. Josie's husband was also coming home. She didn't know what she would say if her son asked why his daddy wasn't with them.

'Daddy won't be home yet?' Shea said, wriggling his hand so that the cuff of his jacket would show his watch.

'He has to go his meeting first,' Liam informed his brother.

'That's right,' Una agreed. She smiled at her older son again. 'Your daddy's meetings are always important.

Liam was less than half his brother's age, and Una was constantly amazed at how sharp he was. She nodded her head to Shea: 'I think that your daddy didn't come for such a short holiday because he wanted to go to his meeting.' When Shea started to smile she added, 'And he has another one tomorrow.'

Chapter Eight

Coming through the arrivals in Dublin Airport with all the other passengers, Una and her two sons faced a crowd of people behind railings.

'Is this the wedding?' Liam asked, when they were close to the barrier and the people started waving and calling out. Una was about to answer him when she caught sight of her brother Sean and his wife Flo in the middle of the crowd.

'Teh b–boys have grown,' Una's eldest brother Sean said to his wife as he moved his stocky body nearer to the railing that was holding back the crowd of people so the passengers that were on the plane could come out of the arrivals gate.

'Stay where yeh are, Sean,' his wife said. At five-feet-three Flo was just an inch shorter than her husband so she couldn't see over the heads of the people that were in front of them either. She waved at the crowd, then ran her hands down her short straight hair while and said, 'Una has seen us, and teh main thing is that she is here.'

'Yer r–right,' Sean said. He never argued with his wife. He placed his arm around her small shoulders and eased her back from the crowd and waited for his sister.

'There yeh are, Una,' Flo said, moving her wide grin from her sister-in-law's face to Una's two blond-haired sons and asked, 'Well what d–did yez think of teh ride on teh aeroplane?'

'It was very noisy, and the windows were so small that we couldn't see anything only clouds,' Liam complained.

'It's g-great that yer here, and yeh look s-mashin,' Sean said.

I hope so Una thought, noticing he had said it was great that she was here. He usually said it was great to see her. She wondered if he thought that she wouldn't come.

Shea's feelings of sadness about leaving his daddy on his own faded when he heard his uncle laughing. He thought about a coloured picture of a happy moon when he saw his uncle's light, rusty, curly hair and bright blue, laughing eyes.

Settled in her brother's car Una asked, 'Where to first?'

The days of sleeping three or four to a bed in the family home in Ballyglass ceased when the three eldest girls left. But there were still only three bedrooms and all the family were adults now. Una didn't want to stay with the Byrnes so she was delighted when her brother's wife Maeve asked her to stay with them.

'I promised Joan I would b-bring yeh straight out te Plunkett Road,' Sean called over his shoulder while he eased his car out of the parking spot.

'She's de-lig-hted that yer here,' Flo said, swinging her arm across Sean's seat so she could lean into the back of the car. Like Joan and Sean she was relieved that Jack hadn't come. But at the same time she thought that he should have come for Una's sake. 'It's a pity Jack had to work, Una,' she said.

'He couldn't come,' Liam answered; 'he has a meeting to go to.'

'And another one tomorrow,' Shea said. He knew how his daddy always went to his meetings. He sometimes changed his shifts so that he could go to them.

Although there was nothing to see in the dark except cars passing, or making good speed going the other way, they all looked out of the car windows. Sean chatted away about the extensions to the airport and the new roads as he drove at a moderate speed along the main road until he turned into a wide lane that would take them to their family home in Bal-lyglass.

Una didn't know half of the roads they turned into. 'It's hard to believe that there's still farming going on around here,' she called out when Sean eased the car into part of a cottage driveway so a tractor that was coming the other way could pass them. Her eyes were now adjusted to the darkness so she could see the outlines of half-built houses and other buildings on both sides of the narrow road.

'Sure it's g-gradually all g-goin',' Sean said, winding down the window. He then poked his head out of the open space so he could watch the tractor that was growling along the road. When the dirty noisy machine was almost scraping the side of his car he shouted, 'D-don't let t-teh tractors fool yeh though.' He rolled the window up again and said, 'T-they're usin' them on teh buildin' most of teh time now.'

'Teh factories are takin' over most of teh land these days,' Flo said. She grew up in the area they were driving through, and although she never voiced an opinion about what should be built on any of the land she enjoyed watching the estates developing.

'What are they making in the factories?' Una asked. With the exception of foods, like bread, cakes and biscuits, and drinks like milk, stout and whiskey, and some small factories that made clothes she never thought about Ireland as being a country that made anything. It was because there were so few jobs in factories that Jack went to England in the first place.

'Everythin', e-everythin',' Sean bellowed. 'There's a lot m-more jobs goin now than there was t-ten years ago. We have a lot of foreign companies openin' factories and warehouses.'

'My daddy works in a factory,' Liam said, 'but he doesn't make everything.'

'Is that so?' Flo said, smiling at the bright blue eyes shining at her. 'What does he make then?'

'Motor cars,' Liam said, raising his head to show his aunt how proud he was of his daddy.

'He works for Ford's,' Shea added proudly, 'and he is a shop steward as well.'

Una passed her hand over Liam's hair. 'Our daddy is one of the best electricians in Ford's,' she said while she wondered if Jack would move back to Ireland to live. She thought that if there were jobs there would be more workers, and they would need more unions.

Chapter Nine

When Sean was turning his car towards the Ballyglass housing estate his brother Maurice was sitting in a low armless easy chair in the living room of his family home. It is a large room that runs the width of the house with a window at the back overlooking a large untended back garden, and a window at the front looking out on a neater front garden that was as long as the width of the house.

He smiled at his sister Josie's two children that kept moving their eyes curiously between him and the television. Eileen is seven and her brother Rory is five.

Maurice doesn't know Josie's children because he hasn't spent any time with them. Josie is the eldest of his six sisters and she lives in England with her husband Mike. She had been home for a week now to help with the preparations for Joan's wedding. He was uncomfortable because his chair was too low for his long legs. With his knees level with his chest, his elbows resting on them, and his lower arms dangling to his feet he looked like a folded-up loopy-loo doll.

His mammy was sitting in her favourite easy chair beside the fireplace facing the television that was in the opposite corner near the back window. She had her back to the front window and her son. She was as engrossed with the film on the television as if it was an ordinary Friday evening.

Alongside feeling apprehensive over his young sister Joan's wedding, Maurice was nursing his usual anguish over his mammy ignoring him again. He watched her roll the hem of her apron and wondered what she was thinking about, but he wasn't going to ask her.

Tiny tremors would dance around Maurice's stomach whenever he thought about the day when he had asked his mammy what she was thinking about. It was six years ago now and whenever he read his electricity bill he would recall the football match that he nearly didn't get to see. It was easier for him to think about his football than to believe that his mammy had lied to him.

Shamrock Rovers were playing that day and he didn't have a ticket for the match so he was up an hour earlier than usual when he wasn't working overtime. When he walked into the cold living room with his bowl of cornflakes his mammy was sitting at the table opening letters. He knew from the colour of the envelopes, and the small pictures in the corners that they were bills. He sat down at the table and said, 'Yeh'ed better tell Cathy that we're nearly out of cornflakes.'

If Maurice had remembered that nobody ever told his mammy that she 'should do anything' he might have enjoyed his cornflakes. The only heat in the room came from a two-bar electric fire at his mammy's feet. He thought that she had turned it off when she tightened her dressing gown around her neck and stared hard at him, then stared into the cold fire grate. 'I'll call Cathy before I go out,' he said, 'and she can light teh fire fer yeh,'

'I don't need the fire lit right now,' Sheila Malone had retorted sharply. She selected one of her letters and said, 'I was thinking.'

'What about?' Maurice had said, then added quickly, 'I thought yeh were cold.'

'I was thinking about how I could get this paid before the E.S.B. closes today,' she said, handing her son the electricity bill.

The red print on the letter was enough to tell Maurice it

was the electricity bill, and if it weren't paid then the electricity would be cut off again. He passed his eyes over the date, and the amount of the bill. 'What time do they close at?' he asked ,seeing a way of leaving. 'I can pay it fer yeh. I have te stop off in town anyway.'

'I can't remember if it's twelve or one,' his mammy had said as she stood. She was walking towards the door when she added, 'You had better get in for twelve just in case.'

'Will do,' Maurice said, sliding the letter back into its envelope. 'Give me teh money and I'll get it done fer yeh.'

'I don't have the money,' Sheila Malone had called out from the hall, then walked down the lobby to the toilet.

Maurice had paid the bill with some hope in his heart that his mammy would be grateful enough to show him some affection. Right now, while he sat in his uncomfortable chair and recalled the day, he would have settled for some attention.

With a round face, bright blue eyes and mass of light ginger curly hair, Maurice looked like his daddy used to when his mammy had married him, but Maurice had never reminded her of Terry. Maurice seldom laughed.

Josie came into the room, nodded her head to her brother then sat down at the table with her back to the door.

With his old feeling of resentment towards his eldest sister nagging at his heart, Maurice said, 'I think it's a great idea fer te hire weddin' dresses.' He returned Josie's nod, then looked back to his mammy and added, 'After all, yeh only wear them once.'

'I quite agree with you, Maurice,' Josie lied. She was willing to agree with everything any of her siblings said to avoid any arguments. She then stretched her hand across the table and pulled the evening paper over towards her and ran her eyes over the front page.

It annoyed Maurice that Josie had answered. He closed his eyes at her as if it would make her go away and looked at his

mammy again, hoping she would say something. But she continued to keep her eyes on the television, and roll the hem of
her apron.

'The problem is getting the one you like in your size,' Joan
said from the doorway. She heard him talking from the kitchen
where she had been tidying out units that were already clean
and orderly. She was nervous about meeting Una. She also
wanted to avoid sitting with Josie and her mammy because she
didn't want to discuss any of the arrangements for her wedding. She walked to the other side of the table and sat down
facing Josie and her brother.

'Does Una have much to do to teh dress then?' Maurice
asked, thinking Joan looked too small and thin to be getting
married. He was surprised she was able to get a wedding dress
to fit her at all.

'I hope not, Maurice,' Joan said coughing to stop herself
from laughing when she saw how awkward he looked sitting
in the low chair. 'Just a few tucks at the waist so that it will
hang better.'

'Let's hope that Una isn't miffed because she wasn't asked
to make the dress in the first place,' Josie said, swiping her hand
over the newspaper as if she was cleaning it.

Will they ever change, Maurice thought? He watched his
handsome eldest sister turn the pages of the newspaper. Josie
looked smart in her knitted trousers and high-necked jumper.
He was always proud of his sisters, but Josie was always noticed.
At five feet-eight inches she is the tallest. She is slim and has
straight, light brown hair like Joan, but hers was thick and silky
where Joan's was thin and dull.

Reflecting on what Josie had said about Una, Maurice's
resentment towards his three older sisters began to bubble in
his chest. He always believed if Josie, Una and Pauline hadn't
been so bossy when they were living at home then his mammy
would have done more cooking and housework when he was

growing up. Especially Una and Josie, and they were always fighting with each other. Maurice always saw his older sisters and his mammy with his eyes wide shut.

If Maurice knew now what his older brother Sean had arranged for later in the evening, he wouldn't be pleased that Una was coming home for the wedding, but he didn't, so he looked over at Joan and said, 'It's great that Una is coming.'

Joan nodded nervously back at him. 'I'm looking forward to seeing her,' she lied. It was only half a lie because she always pleased to see Una, but this time she wasn't looking forward to facing her.

The third time Josie tried to read the same article in the newspaper she scowled at the black print as though blaming the newspaper for what she had just said about her sister. Una was a good dressmaker, and for as far back as Josie could remember until now she had made all the special clothes for all the family. She recalled all the clothes that Una had made for all the other weddings, and for her two younger sisters' communion and confirmation. She always made them with a great heart, and nothing was ever too much work or trouble.

'I imagine that Jack would have phoned if she had missed her plane,' Joan said to Maurice.

'I suppose so,' Josie said, smiling weakly at Joan. Then by way of making amends for what she had said about Una being miffed, she added, 'And you're right, Maurice. We are all pleased that Una is coming.'

Not used to being told he was right about anything, Maurice smiled at Josie.

'I have plenty of time to give her a perm if she wants one,' Josie said, sitting up straight and swinging her head from her brother's feet towards Joan, and then to her mammy a few times as though she was expecting them to applaud.

Joan smiled knowingly at Maurice. She was too young to have known her eldest sister before Josie had left home to live in England. The few memories she had were all about doing things to please their mammy. During the four months she had lived with Josie she grew to love her while at the same time she had to use all the patience she could muster to cope with her.

Maurice returned Joan's smile, and their mammy continued to watch the television. He had never before shown any interest in how often his sisters that were living in England saw each other, and he wasn't really interested now. Encouraged by Josie saying he was right about Una, he said, 'How long is it since yeh have seen Una?' He was also curious to know if Josie had told her about why Joan had been in England last year. When Josie glared at him like she was saying, "it's none of your business", he pulled his feet back towards the seat of his chair to move away from her hard stare. He didn't know why Josie had scowled at him and he thought he was being friendly when he asked, 'Do yez live far from each other over there?'

Josie hated the expression, 'over there,' for living in England. She liked living in England. People minded their own business and the schools were very good. 'We live where we have always lived since we moved to England,' she said. To prevent him asking any more question about England, or her relationship with Una, she said, 'You go and get the girls now. It might be better if they're all here when Una comes.'

Chapter Ten

When Maurice had left to go over to his mother-in-laws house to bring his wife Maeve and two daughters Patsy who was four and Emir three Joan pulled the newspaper over towards. She spread the week's entertainment page out on the table. She was scanning over all the films that were going to be shown in town during the following week when she heard her mammy fart.

As usual her mammy didn't claim responsibility for the hard sharp noise but Joan enjoyed listening to Eileen and Rory giggling. The brief moment of good humour helped her to feel less worried about meeting Una. Her wedding was turning out to be a bigger affair than she wanted. She just wanted to be married to Tony. She hadn't been to any weddings outside the family but she remembered all the preparations and arguments that had gone on when Josie, Una, Pauline, and Maurice were married. She also remembered that when Sean and Maeve were married at eight o'clock one morning very few people knew about it until they came back from a weekend holiday in Galway.

Joan knew she wouldn't be able share any of the arrangements for her wedding with her mammy. And it had nothing to do with the months when she had been in England last year. Her mammy had never done anything for her but use her to cook, clean and give her money. She brooded for a week about how she could get married very quietly before she talked to her uncle Fred. And Fred had been right. After a week her mammy started to talk to her again.

The second burst of noise was louder, and it rolled like a balloon that was losing air while being stretched at the neck. Joan was laughing loudly with Eileen and Rory when her mammy farted a third time. The newspaper covered the table and she turned the pages over quickly like she was looking for something

'There's nothing interesting in the paper,' Josie said, 'I've already looked through it.'

'There never is on a Friday,' Joan said, continuing to turn the pages of the newspaper. A photograph of a grey-haired man sitting in a car brought her mind to her Uncle Fred again. He was probably too old to be a father, but she hoped he would marry again.

'Will yeh take yer time?' Maurice shouted from the hall.

'You can save your breath,' Joan whispered while she giggled with Eileen.

'Will yeh take yer time?' Maurice repeated from the hall.

'I'm not runnin',' the young voice of Emir called back to her daddy.

'God,' Josie mumbled, scowled at the clock, then pressed her hand on the table and stood.

Afraid Josie was going to keep Emir and Patsy in the hall so that their mammy would be able to watch her television, Joan shot out of her chair and was at the door while Josie was smoothing the knees of her trousers. She decided that if her mammy didn't know there was a family wedding tomorrow then it was about time that she found out.

'How are yeh doin', Joan?' Maeve said when she walked into the room in front of her daughters. She cast a quick glance at the side of her mother-in-law's face as she said, 'We just got teh weather on teh radio in me ma's and it's goin te be great. No April showers or anythin'.' She nodded hello to Josie then called out, 'Hello mammy. I see yer bearin' up with all teh excitement.'

Sheila turned her head away from the television, looked at Josie, then closed her eyes.

If Josie were to be asked why her mammy never showed any pleasure in seeing any of her grandchildren she would ask another question. It was a technique she learned from her mammy when she was a child. And she used it when she couldn't, or wouldn't answer any question she was asked. To cloud her embarrassment with her mammy for ignoring Maeve and the children she said, 'What time did you get the weather report at?'

Maeve knew Josie asked about the weather to take attention away from her mammy. She also knew the only excitement her mother-in-law was suffering was that Joan would not be home after tomorrow. She didn't like Josie, but she felt sorry for her so she said, 'Half past six.'

Josie was relieved from commenting further on the weather when Emir walked into the room.

'We won't be stayin',' Emir said to Josie, then walked over to her granny and rested her hand on her granny's knee.

Given a choice Josie would have preferred the children were not there at all. While she waited for her brother to do something to keep his children quiet so that her mammy could continue to watch her television, she gave her attention to Maeve. After a few seconds she decided Maeve's fringe was too long for her small eyes and it also covered her neat and tidy eyebrows. She also thought that Maeve should wear her long hair high on her head for the wedding because it suited her short neck and plump face. Also at five-feet-four Maeve could do with the added height.

'Yeh do know that Shea and Liam are comin' home with us,' Emir said to her granny.

When Joan saw her mammy press her head against the back

of her chair so she could continue to watch the television she stooped and hugged her smart little niece. 'We all know,' She said turning Emir away from her mammy towards Eileen. 'They will be here in a few minutes.' A power cut right now she thought wouldn't get her mammy out of her chair, but it would turn off the television.

Emir raised her head and pointed her chin at her cousin and shouted, 'They're not stayin' here.'

'We know, we know,' Joan said, hugging the little girl again.

'Have yeh been busy all day as well?' Emir asked turning back to her granny. She ran her hands over her granny's knees, and smoothed out the bottom of her granny's apron and continued, 'We haven't stopped all day fer te get everythin' ready.' She held a lump of fabric from the sides of her corduroy trousers in both of her hands turned round to Maeve and said, 'Haven't we, Mammy?' She hooshed up her trousers but they dropped back down when she took her hands away.

Her granny continued to watch the television as if Emir was talking to someone else.

Like all her siblings, but to different degrees, Joan had learned to endure her mammy's moods, tantrums and tempers. She was not surprised her mammy was not pleased that she was getting married, and she braced herself for anything her mammy was going to do the spoil the wedding. However, she was disgusted with her ignoring Emir. 'Are you not going to take your hat off?' she asked Emir to distract her away from her mammy. She laughed into Emir's round face, bright blue eyes, and the small wisp of dark brown hair hanging over her forehead.

'I'm comforable,' Emir said, touching her crochet cap with one hand and hooshed up her trousers with the other. 'Cathy gave it to me.'

Joan put her hand on Emir's head and guided her away from her mammy over to her daddy and her sister Patsy.

For two minutes Josie continued to smile for a camera that

wasn't there. She was also disgusted with her mammy but her way of coping was to ignore the child. She watched rather than listened to Joan telling Maeve about her dress. Even though she knew the noise would grow she prayed that Una would come soon. She expected they would stay about twenty minutes, then leave with Maurice, Maeve and their daughters.

When the nine o'clock news came on the television, Sheila picked up her handbag and left the room.

Josie followed her mammy. She was walking into the kitchen when she heard the small bolt snap shut in the small bathroom.

Chapter Eleven

The aroma from burning turf hit Una's nostrils like a whiff of perfume when she walked into the hall of her family home. She was used to oil and gas heaters to warm her house and as a consequence she had grown used to the smell of them.

Josie came out of the kitchen and looked down the lobby. It was over ten minutes since her mammy had gone into the toilet. She worried that someone would want to use the small room straight away after their journey. She always did. 'Mammy is the toilet,' she said as if Una had just come in from work or from shopping.

Surprised that her mammy was home, Una raised her eyebrows as though Josie had told her the house was flooded, smiled and said, 'I will still have a cup of tea.' She pushed in the door of the living room.

Curious to witness how Una would greet Joan, Josie followed Una into the room.

Una was so stunned at how thin her young sister was she wondered where Joan had the energy to squeeze her so tightly. She choked back her tears and looked around the room to find something to talk about.

'The whole house has been done up,' Maurice informed Una when he saw her smiling at the walls.

'Very nice,' Una lied, wondering how her mammy had allowed the chimneybreast to be painted orange.

'Cathy picked out the colours for this room,' Josie said, apologetically and closed her eyes at the gold star painted on the wall over the mirror. 'The boys decorated the whole house before Christmas.' She turned to go back out to the kitchen to get Una's tea.

'Stay w-where yeh are, Josie,' Sean said, walking in with two mugs in his hands. He put mugs of coffee on the table and continued, 'Yeh are teh best cook we have but we are all able te make coffee.' He nodded a smile at Joan, then turned back to Josie. 'Is the c-cherry cake fer somethin' special or can we h-have a bit now?'

'As far as I know there is only one cake,' Josie said.

'I took it out of the tin,' Joan confessed, 'I remember you saying that you made it for Una.'

'And so I did,' Josie said, sitting down.

'She's not goin' te eat a whole cake on her own, is she?' Maurice chuckled.

'Not all at the same time,' Una said, turning round to her brother. Although she was looking at a young man of twenty-six, she saw a boy of four years folded up on the low armchair. She recalled when he was a small boy he used to pinch a carrot, or a few peas from off one of his sibling's dinner plates. We were all hungry, she thought, moving her eyes from her brother's clean-shaven handsome face to his curly hair. But we weren't all greedy. 'Thank you Josie,' she said smiling, 'but we are all here for a family celebration and I'm sure that Josie won't be annoyed with me if I let you all have one slice each.'

'I only meant that we could keep it until you got here,' Josie explained.

So Josie has been worried as well, Una thought, sitting down in the chair she had moved. Josie always cooked when she was worried. She never gained any joy when Josie was worried so she patted her sister's hand and said, 'We all know that Josie's cooking is worth walking three miles for.' Another pat on her sister's hand, 'So Sean you can cut half of the cake for now.'

'There'll be no need fer any walkin',' Flo called out from the doorway. She nodded her head to Maurice and said, 'Will yeh bring in yer mammy's tea?' She placed another mug of coffee and a plate with slices of cake on it on the table. 'She is on her way in. I have just seen her goin' into the bathroom to wash her hands.'

Sheila wasn't washing her hands. She was applying black mascara on her on her grey thin eyebrows like she had seen Cathy and her friends do. She then ran the hot water and used the lid of Cathy's lacquer tin to pour water down her skirt and into her slippers.

When Maurice was crossing the hall to go into the kitchen his mammy came out of the bathroom. It was dark now so the small window in the back door didn't give enough light for him to see anything different about his mammy's face or clothes. He waited until she had walked up the short lobby to say, 'Una is here.'

Sheila closed her eyes and lowered her head to her feet. When she looked up again, expecting her boring son to comment on her wet slippers Maurice had walked into the kitchen.

Maurice waited in the kitchen until his mammy passed the door. He worried about his mammy's tea getting cold but he had no intention of bringing it into the living room until Una had greeted her. He didn't know whether his mammy wasn't pleased about the wedding, or that Joan was getting married. If he allowed himself to think back he would recall that his mammy had not been pleased when any of her children were getting married. But he preferred to keep his eyes wide shut. He felt cold on his feet and thinking that Sean had not closed the hall door properly and knowing that his mammy hated any cold to blow into the living room he left the kitchen.

As he had expected the hall door was wide open. He closed it and went back into the kitchen, picked up his mammy's cup of cold tea and brought it into the living room. Una's Liam and Emir were sitting in his mammy's easy chair. Shea and Patsy were looking out the front window. Patsy was showing Shea the house across the road where her Granny Dolan lived. His sisters, Maeve, and Flo were sitting around the table talking and Sean was standing in front of the television watching the end of the weather forecast. He also noticed there was no cake left on the plate.

'Where is Mammy?' Maurice asked.

'In the toilet,' Josie said.

'She is at the front gate,' Patsy said, pulling back the net curtain so that her aunt could see out the window.

Maurice looked at Josie. Josie looked at Una. Una looked at Joan. Joan looked at Maurice. It was no surprise to any of them that their mammy was out in the front garden. It was another one of her tactics to annoy her children.

'She probably wants some fresh air,' Una said, smiling at Flo.

Realising he had closed the hall door and his mammy was outside, Maurice wanted to drop the cup of tea on the floor and go home. He put the cup on the table and walked over to the back window at the other end of the room. He didn't want to open the hall door to let his mammy back in.

Josie stayed sitting and stared over at the window. 'At least it's not raining,' she said.

Pity, Una thought, but she knew that wouldn't stop her mammy. She smiled, recalling the Saturday morning years ago when she had closed the hall door after her mammy had walked out then went out to the back garden to hang out the washing so she wouldn't hear her mammy knocking on the door. 'Mammy never goes out in the rain,' she said.

'Yer right, Maeve,' Sean said, turning round from the television. 'We will have a fine day tomorrow.'

'Of course we will,' Una said and stood. 'Let's try on the dress, Joan, and we will get out of your way.' She didn't want to start her weekend with having a row with her mammy. She didn't want to know why her mammy was playing her stupid games.

Joan nodded to Maeve and they left the room. Both of them noticed the hall door was closed when they were in the hall. Maeve was afraid to open the door, and Joan didn't care if her mammy stayed out in the garden all night so they climbed the stairs.

Chapter Twelve

Maurice followed Sean into the kitchen. 'What's up?' he asked, taking a slice of cake off the plate that was on the table.

'It's about w-what happened te Joan l-last year,' Sean said, shoving his hands into the pockets of his trousers and raising his shoulders. He knew that Maurice wouldn't be happy about what he was going to say so he wished his brother Donal or Liam were with them before he continued. 'We are g-goin' to tell Una this evenin'.'

Maurice glared at Sean as though he had been asked him for a million pounds. He moved his hand across his face and down the back of his neck to ease the heat that was crawling up his back. 'Can't it wait until after teh weddin'?' he asked.

'N-no it can't,' Sean said, firmly pausing to control his temper. He was sure that Maurice was, or had been embarrassed when he had been told what had happened to Joan before she had gone to England. 'Joan w-wants Una te know b-before temarra,' he continued, 'and I agree with her. Una should have been be told when it all happened.'

No, Maurice's thoughts screamed at him. Una didn't have to know. His body shivered with resentment towards his older sister while he examined the new wall cabinets over the table. He couldn't think of any reason why Una had to be told, or should be told. Why should she be told when his mammy wasn't? And anyway Joan was better. She was home again and getting married. He thought that the family should be grateful that she was getting married so soon after everything. For a second he was sorry he had eaten Una's cherry cake. 'Why should Una be told?' he asked.

'Joan is worried that Una will ask her why she didn't get in touch with her when she was in England,' Sean said impatiently. 'And she doesn't want te t-tell any more lies.'

Maurice held his mug of tea out from his face like he was going to propose a toast. He imagined it would take them about five minutes to tell Una, and she would rant and rave for another fifteen. But there was nothing she would be able to do to change anything. He swallowed a good gulp of his tea and asked his brother, 'What are yeh thinking of?'

Food always appealed to Maurice. It was three hours since he had enjoyed his dinner and the slice of cherry cake had only whetted his appetite. He rocked his head gently in agreement while Sean explained he would go for a pint and bring back fish and chips. Maurice agreed to take the children home, put them to bed and wait until Flo Maeve and Una came from seeing Joan in her dress. He was relieved that his brother hadn't included Josie. He didn't ask why in case Sean had forgotten and he might still ask her. 'I'll go now,' he said. He wanted to be gone when his mammy came back into the house.

Chapter Thirteen

S heila Malone was standing under the concrete shelf over the hall door when four of her grandchildren burst out of the house.

'We are goin home to 'er house, Granny,' Emir said, 'but we will be back in teh mornin'.'

Maurice walked out after the children in front of Sean. He turned round to Sean and said, 'Leave the door open fer Mammy.'

'I'll leave it on the catch and close it over,' Sean said. 'It's startin' te g-et colder now.' He thought his mammy's tantrum had gone far enough. He followed Maurice down the path. He turned back at the gate and called up to his mammy, 'See yeh temarra.'

Sheila looked down on her cold wet feet. When she raised her head, her sons and grandchildren were getting into their cars.

An uneasy silence like cold mist hung in the room when Sean, Maurice and the children had left. Una was getting angry because her mammy still hadn't come in to say hello to her. Joan worried that Una would go out and drag her in. Josie thought about going out to the kitchen to make a cake.

Cooking was Josie's refuge. She was fourteen when a neighbour gave her two broken eggs, and told her to beat them up, add a cup of flour and half a cup of sugar, then bake it in the oven until it doubled in size and turned light brown.

She didn't have a cake tin so she used the lid of the potato pot. When she removed the cake from the oven Sean helped her to scrape the cooked mixture out of the improvised cake tin. She had made her first cake and her brothers and sisters ate every crumb. Since that time whenever she wanted to please her family she would make a cake.

When she was living at home other than washing up after meals when she had to, Josie avoided housework. And like her mammy, she could ignore all the cleaning that needed doing, because she knew that her sisters Una, Pauline and her daddy would do it.

Josie never developed a special relationship with any of her siblings. She was five when Sean was born. Five years later when Maurice was a year old and Donal was an infant, she shared her bed with one or two of her young siblings. By the time Cathy was born, Josie was used to moving over for another baby.

Seven of Josie's siblings were still going to school when she went to England. Although she had come home once or twice a year, she had continued to treat her younger siblings like the children they had been when she had left. She had never felt they resented her bullying and as a consequence she was now finding it difficult to see them as teenagers and adults with their own opinions and needs. Una believed that, like Maurice, Josie saw her family with her eyes wide shut.

Josie avoided thinking back. Unlike Una, she could never find anything funny with dividing eight sausages by ten. Also she had trained her mind to forget about yesterday and look forward to tomorrow. This evening she struggled not to remember why Joan was in England last year. And at the same time she tried not to think about Una being told because she dreaded tomorrow. She expected Una would be round early in the morning and confront their mammy.

The last person Josie wanted to look back, or forward about was her mammy. The only time she had seen her mammy smile or laugh since she had come home this time was when Cathy was talking about the antics she and her friends got up to in the factory where they worked even though her young sister had held Eileen and Rory spellbound.

Serves them all right when they had to work overtime on the Saturday before last, Josie thought, pulling the cuff of her jumper down to polish the table. Cathy and her friends deserved to be punished for putting the wrong coloured lining in the jackets on the Friday.

Jealousy was a new emotion for Josie. Until a few years ago she had never had occasion to be jealous of any of her siblings to get her mammy's attention. At that time she was competing with her sister Maura who had come home from Canada with her new husband. Now she was competing with Cathy, and with her eyes wide shut she still refused to see that her mammy was manipulating them.

'Are you all right, Josie?' Una asked when she noticed her sister was staring dreamily at the television.

'I was thinking about Sue,' Josie lied and began to shove back the skin around the nails on of her fingers.

Even though her mammy's sister had cared more about all of them than her mammy had, Una was always envious of the preference their aunt used to show for Josie. 'Did you know she had been very sick?' she asked.

'No, but Mike did,' Josie said and continued to fight with her fingers. 'Fred told him when he was sure that she wasn't going to get better.'

'When did Fred tell Mike?'

Panic, mixed with waves of memories, swept over Josie. She wiped the table with her hands as though she could erase her memory clean of when Sue had come over to Kent. It was when Joan had gone into hospital, and Una hasn't been told. All she could think about was when they were children Una telling her that it was expensive to tell a lie because it only led to telling more to cover up. She imagined she saw Joan's face in the polished surface of the table and recalled her sister saying 'no more lies'. She raised her face from the table and she was telling the truth when she said, 'I don't know, Una.'

Una had often seen Josie looking sad, but this was the first time seeing her looking almost devastated. She also knew that Josie would miss their aunt more than the rest of the family. She decided this was not the time to ask about Sue being in England so she said, 'We all miss her.'

Josie nodded her head and continued, 'Sue went into the Mater for some tests because she was having her headaches again.' She picked a small piece of white paper off the table and started to fold it. 'They found she had a brain tumour and she died three weeks later.' After a few seconds she raised her eyes from the paper she was squeezing with her fingers and said, 'That's all I know.'

Chapter Fourteen

Una wanted to cry when Joan walked into the living room wearing a long white dress. Her young sister looked about fourteen years old – the same age Una was when Joan was born. At that time Pauline was kept home from school to mind the new baby because Una had started working when Joan was only two months old. She hadn't nursed the new baby as often she had Maurice, and Donal but she still felt a fondness for her like she was her own child.

The simple dress was made from light, small-patterned voile that young girls were wearing to music festivals. The narrow frill on the band at the neck, and the slightly raised gathers of the sleeves on the shoulders framed Joan's face like an angel in a holy picture. It was clear the dress needed to be lifted on the shoulders and tucked in under the bust. While she was putting some pins under the bust Joan was looking at the front window. The door opened and her mammy walked in.

'Mammy's tea must be cold now,' Josie said, getting up and retrieving the cup from the mantle piece.

'Wait until she comes in,' Una said turning round.

Josie was already walking out the door.

'Hello Mammy,' Una said. She doubted the broad smile her mammy gave her was because she was pleased to see her. She managed to convert her expression of shock to a return smile and said, 'You were in the toilet when I arrived.'

Sheila bowed her head as if she was accepting an apology and walked over to her easy chair and sat down.

Una winked at Flo, then turned back to Joan. 'Turn round and let me see the back,' she said. 'What do you think, Maeve?'

'Perfect,' Maeve returned.

Josie came in with her mammy's cup of tea.

'And you Josie?' Una called over her shoulder.

'I quite agree.' Josie said, raising her eyes from the hearth where she thought she saw her mammy's slippers emitting a light wave of steam. She cleared a space on the mantelpiece for the cup of tea. To avoid looking at her mammy's face she lowered her eyes to the hearth where the steam from her mammy's slippers was so strong now it was making its way up the chimney. 'Is it raining, Mammy?' she asked.

'I don't think so,' Sheila returned, wiping the front of her wet skirt and looking down smugly at her steaming slippers.

'And you, Mammy?' Flo called out. She didn't care what her mother-in-law thought, but she expected it would please Josie if she were asked. Josie was so downcast that Flo began to worry that she might want to come round to Maurice's with them just to get away from her mammy. She was used to her mother-in-law plastering her face with make-up, going out in the rain without a coat, coming home from town with a stone of potatoes, or four large yellow turnips. She couldn't make up her mind if her mother-in-law was trying to get pneumonia, break her arm, or encourage her children to believe she was suffering from Altziemers.

'Una always knows what to do,' Sheila said, closing her eyes and resting her head on the back of her chair as though she was exhausted. When she opened her eyes again Josie was walking out of the room.

'Fer now can yeh manage teh do teh dress?' Flo asked.

'Not now,' Una said. 'It only needs to be tacked and it will take less than twenty minutes. 'I'll do it tomorrow before she goes to the church.'

Will yeh be able te get the stitches out fer before yeh go back?' Maeve asked. She was going to bring the dress back to the shop where Joan had hired it on the Monday because Joan and Tony were going away on Sunday for a short honeymoon.

'That will take about two minutes,' Una said, moving behind Joan to see the dress from the back. She was now facing her mammy who was watching the television even though there was hardly any sound coming from it. 'I think that will do, Joan,' she said.

Joan was struggling not to laugh at her mammy's black eyebrows. She coughed a giggle into Una's shoulder when she hugged her and said, 'Thank you, Una.'

'Don't say anything about the eyebrows,' Una whispered in Joan's ear. The whisper wasn't low enough for Eileen and Rory not to hear.

The two children looked at each other and giggled.

When Una winked at the children, Eileen shrunk her curly head into her neck as though she had been caught doing something she was not allowed to do. Rory brought his hands up to his face and wiped them across his eyebrows by way of telling Una what they were laughing at. Una nodded her head to show she understood and that it was all right.

When Joan and Maeve went upstairs again Una sat in the low chair under the front window. She was behind her mammy who was still watching the television with no sound. Eileen and Rory were sitting in the corner diagonally opposite to her like two silent rabbits. It was gone ten and she was surprised Josie had allowed them to stay up so late.

The room was so silent Una could hear Flo moving her hand down the newspaper. She spoke loudly so her mammy would hear her and asked, 'What's the arrangements for tomorrow?'

Sheila opened her handbag and pulled out a bunch of envelopes.

Una glanced at Flo, then raised her voice and said, 'Did you hear me, Mammy?'

Like all bullies, Sheila was easy to bully. She knew from experience that when Una raised her voice her temper was rising so she said quickly, 'All the women and Fred are leaving from here.'

'How is Fred?' Una asked.

'He's fine,' her mammy replied into her handbag where she was removing a small coloured bag.

Una knew what her mammy had in her coloured bag and she didn't want to sit and watch her remove her selection of cosmetics so she stood and said, 'We will move off now and let you all get to bed.'

Flo also knew what her mother-in-law was going to do with her coloured bag. She had also seen the steam coming from the slippers, and she knew where the water had come from because she had known her mother-in-law to do the same thing before. She felt sorry for Josie and Joan because they would have to cope with what her mother-in-law would do when Una, Maeve and herself left. To distract attention from her mother-in-law she said, 'You will be busy tomorrow, Josie, with getting all the hairs set.'

'Una and meself will wash and set our hairs in rollers in my place and come around here fer Josie te comb out and touch up. Maeve said, 'I'm goin' teh leave teh girls over with me ma first. They want to see Joan leavin' teh house.'

'My two are goin' straight te teh church,' Flo said. 'I don't want them up here. I'm looking forward te havin' a full day without them. We'll leave them off at me mam's on the way up.' She moved her chair so she would be looking at Una and asked, 'Is Jack's mother still takin teh boys to teh church?'

'She said she would,' Una said, thinking how different Betty Burn was to her mammy. She had never known her mammy to look after anyone else's children. 'Anyhow she wants to go for herself. You know how she likes to keep up with all the goings on in the parish.' She said, 'She's a nosey awl bitch at the best of times, but she'll mind the boys for the day.'

'We're going to the church,' Eileen said, her voice barely above a whisper, but it was loud enough to wake Una, Maeve and Flo up to the fact that she was still in the room.

'What's going on in the parish?' Josie asked as though she had just woken up from a sleep, and in a way she was because she had been deep in thought as to why her mammy's slippers were so wet.

'Neighbours goin' te weddins,' Flo said.

'It's nice though,' Maeve said smiling at Eileen. 'I was delighted te see all teh neighbours at teh gate when I came out of teh house on my day.'

'I'll never forget mine,' Una said. She heard Josie sniff, then glance from Maeve to Flo. She remembered how embarrassed Josie was at the time but she continued, 'I think all the neighbours were there, but they weren't there for me.'

'Then what were they doin' there?' Flo asked. She didn't know the Malones when Una was married.

'Half of them were waiting to see Alice next door,' Joan said. 'Alice was married on the same day.'

'They still gave me a good clap though,' Una shouted over to Eileen who was now rocking with silent laughing. She had never seen her niece laugh so heartily.

To entertain Eileen, Una told some more stories about other weddings. Eileen had tears rolling down her face because she was laughing so much when Una told her about Maeve's car going to Cabra instead of Ballyglass. Flo and Sean had been married very quietly and it was never talked about.

When the laughing had died down Josie reminded them all

about Daddy not being at Maurice's wedding, and now Sue wouldn't be here for Joan's.

As if she realised she wasn't going to have an audience, Sheila Malone returned her small bottles and tubes to her coloured bag, then glanced at Josie and began to roll the hem of her apron.

Josie had gone back to staring at the wet slippers so she didn't see her mammy. But Joan did so she said. 'If you girls don't mind I'll finish my ironing upstairs.' She also didn't want Josie to talk about their Aunt Sue now.

'In that case we'll get out of yer way,' Flo said, 'I'm sure Josie is dyin' teh get teh kids te bed and get some rest before temarra.'

Chapter Fifteen

I t was getting on for half past ten when Una, Flo and Maeve left Plunkett Road for the fifteen-minute walk around to Maurice and Maeve's house.

The air was crisp and clear and it was so quiet they heard a hall door close eight houses down the road.

The difference between Plunkett Road and the road she lived on in Dagenham seemed more stark to Una. It felt new to her, and yet it was the same as she would pull out of her memory when she thought about her family in Dublin. She wondered what her life would be like now if she hadn't left Ireland, and if she would adjust if Jack decided to move back.

The three girls walked silently three abreast, their arms linked together with Una in the middle. The same worry binding them like a halo of mist. What will Sheila do next to spoil or stop Joan's wedding?

'Let's hope yer weatherman is right about us havin' no rain until we all get to teh hotel temerra,' Flo called over to Maeve.

The weather was the last thing on Una's mind but she nodded her head in agreement and continued to listen to the click-clack sounds the three pairs of heavy, wide-heeled shoes made on the concrete pavement. She cleared her mind about her worry over Joan being pregnant and wondered why her mammy had stayed at home on a Friday evening.

'I suppose we can always blame me ma if it rains,' Maeve suggested, 'She always swears by the weatherman on teh radio in teh evenin's.' She giggled and continued, 'She looks so happy when she is listenin' to his posh voice that I think she fancies him.'

What a treat it would be to see her mammy happy, Una mused, though her mind was still on returning to Dublin to live as she surveyed the wide space between the houses. The narrow roads with only enough room for two cars to pass on most of the housing estates wouldn't bother Una. She would love a long garden. The long gardens on both sides of the road made a noise insulator for the houses and the pedestrians. She was reminded again of the contrast with her own home in Dagenham where the roads were three cars wide, but she only had a little over three feet from the front window to the pavement for a front garden.

'What are yeh lookin' fer, Una?' Maeve asked when she saw Una was jerking her head around and looking from one side of the road to the other, and up and down at the houses.

'Listen.' Una stopped walking, then squeezed her elbows to her waist so that Flo and Maeve would also stop.

'I can't hear anythin'.' Maeve tightened her grip on Una's arm.

'Not even one sound from one television,' Una said, smiling down at Maeve's upturned freckled face. 'If you walk along my road in Dagenham you'll hear every television set that's turned on in every house as you go by.'

'Would you come home to live?' Maeve asked, thinking that if Una came home for good, Cathy would have some help with their mammy.

They were walking towards a lamppost and the yellow light from the bulb made all their faces look grey and dirty but Una could see the brightness in Maeve's eyes. She knew that Maeve would tell Maurice what she said, and Maurice would tell their mammy so she said, 'I'm thinking about it.'

Chapter Sixteen

Maeve had never felt smart. Girls like her whose mothers had always done cleaning jobs never were. She was an average child at school, and she had never nursed a desire to stay on and do her leaving certificate. Her ambition was to become a hairdresser. This folded three months into her apprenticeship when she had walked out of the salon.

Sorting the curlers, topping up the shampoo bottles, folding and stacking the towels, and checking the stocks of perm lotions was tedious and boring. And Maeve hadn't enjoyed sweeping the floors or washing the sinks either. But she had accepted that she had to do them as part of her training.

One afternoon she had refused to wash the wall after her boss had sprayed it with hair dye when she had shaken a bottle that didn't have a lid on it.

'Loyalty, my ars,' Maeve had shouted after the bus she had stepped down from. She still never forgot the way the woman had spat the word "loyalty" at her. She only had an idea of what the word meant so she looked it up in the dictionary when she was home. She decided that hairdressing wasn't a cause, a country, or a sovereign. She let her tears roll down her face and drop onto the dictionary before she had closed the book.

Though only sixteen at the time, Maeve was determined she would never do cleaning jobs like her mammy. She forgot about her ambition to become a hairdresser when she started working in a department store. Her money was better, the job was cleaner, and she had more friends her own age.

She was two years past her teens when she had married Maurice, and Maeve still never felt smart, and she didn't feel she needed to be because Maurice knew about everything. When she started going out with Maurice, and she was with the family, Josie always made her feel silly and stupid, but Una was not like a sister. She also knew if Una came home she would help Cathy to cope with her mammy. She tightened her grip on Una's arm again and stretched her legs a bit more so that she could stay in step with her sister-in-law's longer strides.

Chapter Seventeen

The apprehension Maurice was feeling about telling Una, or even talking about why Joan had been in England hadn't prevented him from making his home a warm and welcoming place. The grate was full of briquettes burning in the hearth. He turned off the television when he heard the voices walking up the garden path. When he met the three women in the hall he wore a warm smile, and he raised his hand and waved it at the ceiling while he said, 'They're not asleep but they're in bed.'

Furniture polish, fish, vinegar, and deep fried chips mixed together emit a sickening odour. But it wasn't the smell that was coming off the small table that was making Una's stomach turn as if everything she had eaten for the last week was rotating in her stomach is if it were in a washing machine.

The briquettes made a soft thud when they collapsed in the grate. It had taken Sean less than ten minutes to tell his sister Joan had been raped by her boss's father over a year earlier, in the office where she had worked. And three months later discovered she was pregnant.

Alongside the horror of what had happened to Joan, Una was also devastated because she hadn't known, and that Joan had been in England to have the baby. 'God almighty,' she said, 'it's like something you hear on the news, read in the papers, or see in a film. But I still don't understand why I wasn't told.'

Until now Sean hadn't talked about what had happened

to his young sister. He had often doubted his aunt's reasons for Una not to be told but right now this wasn't the time to talk about it so he continued, 'Sue a-arranged fer J-Joan te stay with J-Josie and Mike te have teh b-baby, and teh baby was goin te b-be adopted. Sue's main concern at teh time was t-that Joan would go off te some b-back street old nurse and g-get herself cut up.'

So that's why she wasn't told, Una thought, nodding her head and bringing her hands up to her neck as if her head would fall off from the shock of what her brother had said. She sat forward in her chair and said accusingly, 'Sue thought that I would take Joan to a clinic so that she could get an abortion.'

Flo had also doubted Sue's reasons for Una not to be told but right now thought a prayer for Sue before she said, 'Sue said Joan was afraid Jack's mother would tell everyone in the neighbourhood. Yeh know yerself how Jack's mother talks. Sue said Mrs Byrne just might get te know through you without yeh even knowin' about it, and nobody would believe Joan had been raped.'

Imagining she could see Betty Byrne standing outside the church telling the latest gossip about her family to the neighbours they used to know when they had lived in Ballymore, Una nodded her head as though in agreement. At the same time she felt hurt that her family believed that Jack would have told his ma. 'What about the police?' she asked.

Maurice looked at Sean with terror in his eyes. He dreaded that Una would march them all off to the police station now.

'When P-peter found t-them, Joan was just comin r-round. His father had had a heart attack. Joan didn't want to go to the hospital. She asked Peter to get Sue. By teh time Sue and Fred had arrived teh father was already on teh way te teh hospital. Peter told teh ambulance men that he would follow in his car, but he never did. He phoned his wife and mother and stayed with Joan until Sue came,' Sean said.

Una had no intention of going anywhere. She was finding it so difficult to believe what her brothers had told her she thought she was living in a film. 'Why was Joan coming round?' she asked, frowning.

Sean unfolded his arms, rested his elbows on his knees, joined his hands, and linked his fingers. He felt very uneasy in his mind because he had allowed his aunt to make all the decisions. He kept his eyes on his fingers and said, 'At t-teh time it happened w-we were told t-that she had been pushed when some b-blokes had a fight in one of teh p-pubs where she was d-doin a gig on teh S-Saturday night.'

Una could see Sean was struggling and she felt sorry for him but she wanted to know what had happened so she asked again, 'Why was Joan coming round?'

'The man had hit her,' Flo said. 'He d-died two hours after he arrived at teh hospital,' she added.

Una didn't feel, or show any sympathy for the man. She tried to keep her tone soft when she asked, 'Was there an enquiry or anything about how he died?'

'N-not that we know of,' Sean answered. 'Yeh have te bear in m-mind Una that it was only S-sue and Fred that had k-known anythin about Joan b-bein' attacked on teh d-day it happened.'

Una felt she just lived a year during the last hour. 'I knew there was something going on,' she said covering her ears with her hands to stop more questions from shooting into her head. 'Am I the only one in the family who hasn't been told?'

'No,' Sean said, 't-they don't know in Canada.'

'What about Mammy and Cathy?' she asked.

'Are yeh sure yeh don't want a cup of tea, or coffee, Flo?' Maurice asked. He was prepared to make tea or coffee for all his neighbours just to stay in the kitchen until Una was told about his mammy.

'No thank you, Maurice,' Flo said, and continued to tell

Una about the Sunday morning after Joan had been assaulted when Sue had come up to teh house to tell her sister. 'She was so disgusted with yer mammy in bed waiting for Cathy to light the fire, and that Cathy also had a cold that she changed her mind.'

Until now Maeve had been silent because she was afraid to say anything in front of her husband. 'Cathy told me she didn't know why but yer mammy and Sue hadn't been gettin' on since teh last time yeh were all home,' she said.

Una knew why but she wasn't going to talk about that now so she said, 'Poor Joan.'

'And then when Joan found that she was pregnant,' Flo said, 'Sue was adamant that yer mammy wasn't te be told. She said that if Joan had a baby she would be stuck with livin' with yer mammy fer teh rest of her life. She told us that Joan knew that as well and that was why Sue was afraid that Joan would get desperate and get herself cut up with havin' a secret abortion.'

'When all this first happened teh office was closed fer teh week fer the father's funeral,' Sean said. 'We didn't know about Joan at the time.'

'We really didn't know, Una,' Flo agreed. 'Joan went back home on teh Tuesday evenin' after she had been told that Cathy had teh chest infection from the cold she had. Although she was very quiet we all thought that it was because her face was hurtin' her. Yeh know yerself, Una, that Joan is quiet any-way, and we had no reason te think that she was lyin'.'

Maurice came in with coffee for Una and Maeve than sat down again. He had heard them talking and was satisfied that Una knew why their mammy hadn't been told. He folded his arms across his chest and said, 'Sue went te England and talked with Josie and Mike.' He then uncrossed his arms and rubbed his hands together as if to say 'now you know everything'.

Flo had recalled so much of what Sue had told them while she was telling Una what had happened to Joan that she was now very suspicious about some of Sue's motives. At the same time she was sure that Sue was thinking about Joan. 'Sue thought about goin' te you, Una, but she decided that Jack's mother was too big a risk. She knew that you would all find out eventually, and she was sure that if Josie was not one of teh first to know she would cause teh most trouble fer Joan.'

'So Joan stayed with Josie until she had the baby?' Una said, counting months and running her mind back to the times she had been down with Josie and she never saw Joan there.

'No, not all the time,' Sean said. 'She she s-stayed with a friend of Peter Cunningham's fer teh first few months. Teh s-story was that Joan w-was goin' fer s-six months te learn about teh way that teh house b-buyin' was done in England. As it t-turned out, she d-did because she w-worked fer this friend while she was t-there.'

Una closed her eyes, rested her head on the back of her chair and allowed her tears to run down her face.

Chapter Eighteen

When yeh start makin' yer fortune with yer own business Sean yer te buy a car with one of them automatic heaters,' Flo ordered while she tightened the collar of her jacket under her chin.

'I've told yeh before yeh just have teh wait a few minutes,' Sean smiled, and thought about the orders that had started to come in for new porches since Joan had given out a few of his cards.

'I'm talkin' about one where yeh can turn teh heater on five minutes before yeh even get inte teh car,' Flo said, glancing down at the heater switch.

'What are y-yeh talkin' about? There's n-no such thing,' Sean replied, expelling his first chuckle in four hours. He knew his wife was making fun of him and he was pleased to go along with her because he also felt lighter in his heart now that Una knew all about Joan.

'They have them in America,' Flo continued, 'Liam told me they're on teh way over here.' She hadn't believed Liam but the thought of having the car nice and warm before she got into it made her want it to be true.

'I wouldn't be a b–bit surprised if teh Americans are t-thinkin' about it even if they haven't t-told Liam yet,' Sean replied. 'He always seems te k-know things b-before anyone else.'

'We are all lookin' forward te seein' him,' Flo said, snuggling into her jacket.

Sean waved to Maurice as he eased his car away from the kerb. 'When we were g–goin' over about Joan I was r–remem-berin' him tellin' me that S–sue intended te k–keep teh baby fer herself,' he said, 'I think I laughed at t–teh time.'

'I think Liam was right,' Flo said, thinking back to when Sue had argued against Una being told about when Joan was pregnant. She closed her eyes. It was time to block out the memory of that awful time. 'That old man,' she said, 'has caused so much sadness in the family that I find it very hard to pray fer his soul.'

Sean turned the corner at the end of Plunkett Road and glanced up as if he would be able to see his family home. 'I expect they are all in bed now,' he said. 'We should have a good day tomorrow now that all the worry about telling Una is over.

'We will,' Flo encouraged. She decided not to spoil her hus-band's optimism with telling him about his mammy's black eyebrows and wet feet.

Chapter Nineteen

Half an hour after Una, Flo and Maeve had left Plunkett Road, Josie was climbing the stairs. She pushed in the door to the big bedroom. 'I thought you were packing?' she said and looked over Joan's shoulder at the cases on the bed against the far wall.

'I have done as much as I can until morning,' Joan said, closing the book she was reading from, and moving off the bottom of the double bed that Eileen and Rory were sharing. She kissed Eileen on the side of her face before she placed the book on the chair beside the bed and said, 'Cathy will finish it.'

'Mike has already read that book to her twice,' Josie said, smiling at her daughter while she inserted the plug for the radio into the socket.

'I thought as much,' Joan said, giggling at her niece. She smiled at Josie as she said, 'She told me all about the chapters before I started to read them.'

'What about him?' Josie asked, nodding her head over to the small body that was curled up with his hands under his chin, and smiled fondly at her son.

'One sentence is like a bang on his head,' Joan giggled again.

When she heard some music without any cackling sounds on the radio, Josie stopped twisting the button. 'If you are finished packing for now,' she said, 'I'll go to bed myself when I have warmed Mammy's milk.'

'Get into bed now,' Joan said walking towards the door, 'I'll warm Mammy's milk.

'Josie is gone to bed,' Joan informed the side of her mammy's face while she was closing the door after she had walked into the living room. She wasn't expecting her mammy to answer her so she asked, 'Is it too soon to warm your milk?'

Sheila turned her face to the fire and started to scratch her eyebrows. The mascara was itching.

Tempting though it was to demand an answer from her mammy, Joan swallowed her temper and said, 'I'm off to bed myself.'

Alone in the living room Sheila stared into the fire until she couldn't stand the itching on her eyebrows any longer. She went into the bathroom and washed off the mascara. Her temper was higher than Joan's when she went into the cold kitchen and took a small tumbler out of the new press over the small table, and went back into the living room. She sat down in her chair, took a small bottle out of her handbag, emptied it into the tumbler, drank half of it, stared at the television and thought about the letter in her handbag. After five minutes she washed two sleeping tablets down her throat with the rest of the whiskey, returned the empty bottle to her handbag, then went to bed.

Chapter Twenty

Nobody had told Josie that her daddy had ducked to avoid the brass-covered hearth brush that her mammy had thrown at him, but she never forgot the slapping sound when it had hit her on the shoulder before she fell to the floor.

It was a Saturday afternoon and she was sitting on her little stool at the small table that her daddy had made for her and her two sisters. She had been showing Una how to draw some of the letters of the alphabet she had learned in school.

The pain in her shoulder had gone when Josie had left the hospital but a bitter smell stayed with her for weeks. Her mammy's friend Ena took her to the hospital again six weeks later and a man wearing a snow-white coat cut the hard plaster jacket away. By the time her brother Sean was born a year later she was using her arm again and she rarely thought about the pain. But she never forgot how loudly her mammy had been shouting at her daddy before something had hit her sharply on her shoulder. She had no memory of her time in the hospital, but she never forgot the sound of the hearth brush hitting the wall after she had felt the pain in her shoulder. She was reminded of that sound now when she heard the door to her mammy's bedroom slam shut.

Josie woke early on the Saturday morning. She lay back and stared at the white freshly painted ceiling and thought about the day ahead of her. She decided she would dye her mammy's eyebrows so the silly woman wouldn't put the mascara on again before they left for the church. It would only take her about fifteen minutes. She didn't allocate any more time to the rest of her chores because she knew that she would get them all done. She always did. So she listened to the hollow thumps, creaks, and squeaks coming from the house next door. She welcomed the sound of the slam of a hall door. She didn't like silence. When she was growing up her family were always around her so there was always plenty of noise. She preferred to hear a baby crying than to listen to dead silence. When she first went to London she used to leave her radio on all night. She still woke up to a radio because Mike was always awake before her and he turned it on.

Silence encouraged Josie to think and remember. Silence was Josie's nightmare in school, and the worst times were when the class was silent. She used to worry about her pencils. Were they all sharpened? Did she still have the red and blue one or did Una borrow it again and not give it back to her? Did she have enough pages left in her jotter?

Besides, silence made Josie think back and she never wanted to do that. When she was in school and they were doing their sums, or writing, the teacher used to walk up and down the passages between the desks with the cane in her hand. Josie could hear every swish the awful woman made as she flapped it on the sides of the small desks. She used to hear, and feel her own heart beat when the teacher slapped the cane on the top of a desk and tell one of the girls to stand up in front of the class.

Because she was tall, Josie dreaded the day when it would be her turn to have to stand and wait until the teacher asked her to spell some words or recite her tables in front of the other forty girls. And then get caned for every mistake she made. She could never understand why all the other girls in her class didn't learn their spellings and tables so they could avoid the humiliation.

When she started her apprenticeship, as a hairdresser, Josie didn't mind the low pay or that she worked on a Saturday because she loved the environment of the salon. The noise of the hairdryers, the smell from the lotions, the heat from the perming machine and people talking all the time never bothered her at all as she swept the floor, filled the different bottles, sorted the towels and washed the sinks. She was busy all the time and she never had to worry about getting slapped or being asked about anything.

Even though everything had to be done again and again, Josie was content to work with all the sounds and smells around her. Her training began when she started doing the shampoos for the two hairdressers she worked for. She was always gentle and considerate of the customers. Before she moved on to learning about cutting hair the money she was getting for tips was seldom less than her weekly wage. With her large family to practise her newly acquired cutting skills on she made some extra money with cutting hairs for Una, and Pauline's friends.

Josie had four years' experience at hairdressing when she was eighteen. She was also very happy because she was pleasing everyone. She had her own special customers and she was always busy. Her wages were also much higher and she was giving it all to her mammy because her tips were more than enough for everything she needed.

When the new cold perms replaced the hot iron clamps that had been used when she had started her apprenticeship Josie was able to do perms at home on her afternoons off, and on Sundays. Everyone was happy. Una and Pauline's friends, and many of the neighbours in Ballymore were sweet to Josie because they got their hair permed at reduced rates, and Josie loved the respect she was always shown.

With doing perms, cuts and sets at home or in other people's houses on her days off, Josie didn't do much housework. This used to infuriate Una. When she could manage it on Sundays

Una used to start to vacuum the stairs when Josie was getting her lotions and curlers packed. There was a bag attachment for the vacuum cleaner that could be used as a hairdryer so Josie had to wait until Una had finished cleaning the stairs. Una stopped making her sister wait for the vacuum cleaner when Josie made Maurice or Donal follow her with the machine.

From the day she started work and with her eyes wide shut, Josie saw herself as he mammy's favourite child. And she was because she was always generous with her money. As she lay in her bed staring at the ceiling now she had no control on where her mind was wandering so she started to think back to Monday evening when Donal and Joan met her at the airport. She understood that her mammy wasn't there as well because of the room in the car for them all but she tasted disappointed when she found that her mammy wasn't in the house when she arrived home.

Chimes form the empty milk bottles coming from the street didn't break the silence for Josie because her memory was on a roll. She also knew it was the milkman walking up the path with the fresh milk. She continued to brood over how quiet her mammy had been on Tuesday when she had taken her into town. And her mammy didn't show any excitement about the outfit she bought her for the wedding.

It was the Wednesday after she was home that Josie was mostly smarting about. She started to breathe in time with the gentle grating sounds of Eileen snoring while she thought about Wednesday again. Mammy stayed in bed and she had asked Josie to keep the children quiet because she wanted sleep off a headache. It was a sunny day so she brought the children into the village. When she arrived home her mammy was out. She knew her mammy had had a bath because talcum powder, and damp towels were on the floor in the bathroom.

As usual Josie searched her memory for an excuse for her mammy's behaviour. The milkman was halfway down the road when she decided that it was probably the dinner that her mammy hadn't wanted to be at home for. Tony was coming up for dinner that evening, and maybe her mammy didn't like Tony. She started nodding her head in agreement with her thoughts and whispered, 'And I can't say I blame Mammy for that.' All the arrangements for the wedding had been made down in Tony's house, or in The Beggars Lodge.

Chapter Twenty-one

Expecting to see one of her sisters, Josie glanced into the kitchen when she was at the bottom of the stairs. 'It's you,' she said to her mammy, 'I thought it was Joan.'

Sheila pulled on her cigarette, walked over to the sink and looked out the window.

'Go back up to bed and I'll bring you up some tea and toast,' Josie said. She didn't want to start her day with her mammy sulking while she made her children's breakfast.

'I'll have it down here,' Sheila returned, pulling the front of her dressing gown around her neck as if she was cold, smiled and said, 'I don't want to waken the children.'

'Go inside then and I'll bring it in,' Josie suggested. She assumed because her mammy was up so early, and she didn't want to go back to bed that she wanted to talk to her about why she had been so miserable all the week. She put her hand on her mammy's shoulder and ushered her towards the door as she said, 'It is warmer in the living room.'

The first time Josie came into the living room with something for the table her mammy was sitting in her easy chair by the fireplace fumbling in her handbag.

Out in the kitchen waiting for the bread to brown, Josie searched her thoughts for something her mammy would want to talk about, but she couldn't think of anything. When she brought in the toast her mammy was staring out the back window as though she was in a daze. She was fondling a white envelope.

'Just the tea to bring in,' Josie sang and returned to the kitchen.

Sheila continued to stare out of the window until Josie appeared in the doorway with the teapot.

'Over you come now, Mammy,?' Josie said. She filled the two cups with tea while her mammy rose from her chair and made her way over to the table with the white envelope in her hands. Josie returned to the kitchen with the teapot and rested carefully on the gas ring so that the tea would keep hot but not boil. During her mind searching about what her mammy was worried about, she had decided it must be her youngest sister. With Joan gone after today her mammy would be on her own with Cathy. She expected her mammy was having trouble with keeping Cathy under control.

Now nearly eighteen, and the youngest of Sheila's children, Cathy had left school three years earlier. She started working straight away and this calmed down all the objections from the family about her leaving school without trying to pass some examinations. Una was Cathy's best supporter when she had said that at least she wouldn't be hanging around the streets and getting into trouble if she was working.

Cathy getting into trouble was a dread for all the older Malone children since Liam was caught for shop lifting a few months after their daddy had died. Although they saw the funny side of four youngsters each taking a plastic bag full of special offer pot washers from the local supermarket for the fun of it, one of the youngsters should not have been a Malone. It happened during the summer holidays when Liam was hanging around with other youngsters from the estate during the summer holidays.

Cathy worked in one of the new modern factories on the housing estate that made jackets and skirts for export. They employed mostly women, and the majority of these were young girls who either failed school, or were encouraged to go to work to earn some money to help their family.

At first mammy had wavered about showing her approval about Cathy going to work. She had reasoned that Cathy would be out of the house all day, and there wouldn't be any school holidays so she would do less housework. But then as Cathy kept reminding her mammy, she would be giving her some money every week. Sheila Malone's money had gone up and down since her children started working, leaving home, and getting married. No matter how good things were, she always wanted more. She went for the money.

None of the Malone children, not even Josie, or Maurice would be flattered at being told they were like their mammy. And apart from some physical resemblances none of them were except Cathy. Cathy liked her own money, and, like her mammy, she spent it as fast as it came into her purse. She spent it on clothes; make-up, cigarettes, the pictures, and although she frequented the pubs at the weekends she rarely drank more than a pint of beer. She went for the music and comedians.

Cathy and two of her friends borrowed money from one of their mothers' Credit Union and went to Una in London for a week's holiday shortly after Joan came back from England. When she didn't talk about wanting to live in England her mammy began spoiling her. Cathy soon learned how to manipulate her mammy so that she could get her own way. She lied to her mammy, and her mammy lied to her. They both knew it, accepted it, and together they lied to everyone else. They used each other.

'I think I have thought of everything,' Josie said, smiling at her mammy. She fiddled nervously with the neck of her housecoat and asked, 'Have you enough room there with the table against the wall?'

'Plenty,' Sheila Malone replied, stretching her hand into the table for some toast.

'I hope Eileen and Rory don't wake up until I have eaten this,' Josie said before she bit into her toast.

Desperate now to encourage her mammy into a better mood, Josie recalled that her mammy was always happy whenever Ireland was praised over England so she said, 'I don't care what anyone says the Irish bread and butter is better to what we get in England.' She held her piece of toast out to her mammy as though her mammy would know what bread was like and added, 'It has a lot more taste to it. This toast is lovely.'

'Toast is always at its best straight off the grill,' Sheila said, raising her head as though she was going to talk to the ceiling, looked down her nose at her daughter, then picked up her white envelope, opened it, removed a white sheet of paper and placed it on the table beside her.

The radio poured out popular music while Josie and her mammy buttered and ate more toast.

Josie forced herself to listen to the sounds pumping from the radio and stirred her tea every time she took a sip. The dull chimes her spoon made in her cup sounded like the clanging of church bells. She looked around, hoping to find something to comment on just to talk before she said anything about Cathy. She noticed the ceiling was starting to turn yellow over the fireplace but she decided not to comment on the smoking. She also noticed the bookshelves had more books than the usual clutter of papers and magazines. She closed her eyes at a hook in the wall over the back window near the ceiling.

While she followed an imagined line across the ceiling to the wall facing the hook she imagined she could see damp clothes hanging down from the rope that used to join the two hooks. She moved her bum on her chair and shut her mind to the memory of how the line used to block out the light when it was full of clothes. Especially the nappies, there were always nappies. She continued her quest for a topic of conversation and noticed the photographs on the wall under the clock and over the bookshelves. With her mind flitting between how much the batch of family photographs had grown, nappies drying on the line across that room, and parties, and not wanting to talk about any of them Josie blurted out, 'It's grand not having any babies with us this time.' She listed all the paraphernalia she could think of like, pushchair, bottles, nappies, and toys that needed space.

Sheila smiled gratefully at her daughter as though Josie had paid her a compliment.

Encouraged by her mammy's smile, Josie continued, 'I suppose that will all start again with Joan before long, and I dare say Cathy will follow soon enough.'

Sheila smiled again.

'Does Cathy have a boyfriend?' Josie asked.

'Not as far as I know,' Sheila lied and smiled again.

'What time did she come in at last night?' Josie asked, 'I didn't hear her come in.'

Neither did Sheila, but she wasn't going to tell Josie. Cathy might find out and she had more important things on her mind. 'Do you think Cathy is spoilt, Josie?' she asked, picking up her letter. She read it again and returned it to the table beside her elbow.

Usually Josie would be curious about why her mammy read a letter twice but she was so stunned by the question about Cathy she hardly noticed what her mammy was doing. Of course she thought Cathy was spoilt. She was also selfish and irresponsible. At least compared to herself and her other sisters but she wasn't going to say that to her mammy. She folded her arms across her waist and looked over to the window and tried to remember something her young sister might have done to upset her mammy.

Sheila smiled smugly as though she had been playing poker with her boring daughter, had opened her hand of cards and found she had four aces.

Josie remembered Cathy had been to Dagenham for a holiday and Una had probably complained about their young sister's behaviour. Una always spoke her mind no matter what anyone thought or whom she was speaking to. Joan wouldn't complain about anyone and the boys only cared about themselves. 'Did Una say that?' she asked.

Sheila Malone turned her body so that her legs came to the side of the table and eased her body up on her feet. She took two steps towards her daughter, rested her hand on Josie's shoulder and said, 'I'll get us more tea.'

For Josie, these were two friendly gestures from her mammy: patting her on the shoulder, and getting up from the table to get the tea. She felt back in favour with her mammy again. She wondered what Una had said about their young sister, and she had just begun to make a mental list about her own complaints when she heard a crash and sprang up from the table. 'God,' she moaned while walking towards the door. She knew the sound; after all she grew up with it. They never had six matching plates, cups or saucers for more than three days. When she reached the hall she found her mammy standing in the kitchen with her back to the doorway.

'Josie I'm sorry I have dropped the lovely plates you bought me last year,' Sheila said turning round and smiling sadly, her eyes alive with glitter. She lowered her face to the shards of broken plates that were on the floor and around her slippers.

'Never mind the plates,' Josie shouted, still shaking from the scream of the plates crashing. 'Come over here,' she coaxed, holding out her hand for her mammy to walk towards her.

Sheila hesitated a few seconds, then smiled gratefully and held out her hand.

Chapter Twenty-two

Joan was lying in bed listening to Cathy snoring when she heard the crash. She thought a window had been broken so she swung her legs out of the bed, grabbed her dressing gown and raced out of the room. 'What happened?' she called down to Josie who was helping their mammy to cross the hall into the living room like the small woman was a fragile china doll.

'It's all right, it's all right,' Josie returned, moving her body in front of Joan to stop her sister from going into the kitchen while she panted, 'Mammy broke a couple of plates, that's all.'

Joan moved backwards a few steps up the stairs.

'Get her another pair of slippers,' Josie snapped.

Her dressing gown half-buttoned, Joan continued to stand on the fourth stair riser as though her feet were glued to the carpet and stared at the coloured pieces of crockery decorating the new lino in the kitchen. They had been lovely plates and herself and Cathy had always been careful with them when they were washing up.

'Just get the slippers and don't worry about the plates,' Josie repeated.

'I don't really care about the plates,' Joan whispered to the floor. She stole another glance into the kitchen and wondered what her mammy was doing with dinner plates at half past nine on a Saturday morning. She became no wiser when she could neither see, nor smell any signs that anyone was cooking a fry. She was still thinking about her mammy and the dinner plates when she was halfway down the stairs with a pair of her own slippers when Josie burst out of the living room.

'You can go back to bed,' Josie said, shooting her hand up towards her sister for the slippers.

'I'm up now,' Joan said, and continued to descend the stairs. Her foot was on the third last step when Josie swiped the slippers from her hand and went back into the living room. She was tying the belt on her housecoat when Josie came back out into the hall again.

Josie tossed her head back and opened her mouth to deliver another order when Joan held her hand up and said, 'Josie, you go back inside and sit with Mammy. I'll clear up the kitchen.' She then nodded her head to the floor: 'They were lovely plates.'

Josie sounded frantic as she snapped, 'You go in and sit with Mammy while I clear up.' She moved back to the door into the living room and pushed it open. 'I'll make some fresh tea and you can go back to bed with yours.'

Joan closed her eyes.

Expecting to be obeyed, Josie walked down the lobby and opened the small door of the cupboard under the stairs. She was determined to find out what Una had said to her mammy about Cathy. She was coming back up the lobby with a pan and hand brush when she saw Joan's foot sticking out at the bottom of the stairs. 'Go on,' she said, 'Mammy is on her own in there.' She then bent down to the mess on the floor.

The last thing Joan wanted to do today was to sit with her mammy. She sat down on the bottom of the stairs, and covered her ears with her hands to block out the sound of the broken plates scraping on the kitchen floor.

'Don't worry about the plates, she only broke three,' Josie sang, coming out of the kitchen with the pan full of the broken crockery, then started down the lobby.

Joan held her head in her hands and listened to her sister fighting with the bolts on the back door. She contemplated going back to bed to get away from her. She hugged her legs tighter and rested her forehead on her knees and she told herself again that Josie had a good heart. 'Josie, Josie, Josie,' she whispered into her lap, 'how generous and cruel you can be at the same time. There was no need for you to come home so soon. I told you it was going to be a small wedding and that Liam and Donal were giving me all the help I needed.' She raised her head when she heard the gentle tone of her alarm clock. She decided it was time that Cathy was up anyhow so she let it ring.

'Are you still there?' Josie demanded when she scuttled back up the lobby.

Joan raised her face from her lap and thought a prayer for patience.

'When do the bins go out?' Josie asked, dropping down on her knees to fill the pan with more of the broken crockery.

'Monday,' Joan said, turning to see Josie's hair hanging over her face like it was a curtain. 'Why?'

'Because they're nearly full, that's why,' Josie retorted, standing up straight and tossing her hair back. 'Are you going to sit there all day?'

'There's a spare bin down at the bottom of the garden,' Joan said, knowing her sister wouldn't make her way down the overgrown land.

'We'll need it,' Josie said, tossing her hair away from her face again, then jerked her head towards the sink and ordered, 'Put the kettle on before you go into Mammy.' She stopped at the door and looked into the tray of broken plates she was holding and said, 'You needn't worry about these. There's enough room in the bin for now.'

While the water was flowing into the kettle, Joan looked out of the kitchen window. She saw her friend Angie scuttle up her garden path, put her key in the lock of her door, then heard her gate bang. Joan always hated the way people let their garden gates close over by themselves like that, but she would never tell Angie off over it, because Joan would never tell Angie off over anything. She plugged in the kettle, then bent down to shove the grill back in. The smell of toast from the crumbs of bread in the bottom of the tray teased her so much that she contemplated making toast for herself and Cathy. She then wondered if her young sister would want to eat anything after her evening at the Beggars Lodge. On hearing Josie closing the back door on her way back into the lobby, she shoved the grill tray back in again.

'It was full of cardboard and paper, and I shoved most of it down,' Josie declared from the doorway of the kitchen. She nodded her head towards the crackling sounds of the kettle. 'That will take another couple of minutes to boil, so off you go now into Mammy, I'll just nip into the loo.'

If Joan had known that Josie wanted to get her out of the way so that she could talk to her mammy about Cathy, she would have made herself toast and a boiled egg, then brought it into the living room, sat down and ate it. Her good sense told her she had to humour Josie for the rest of the day so decided to join her mammy. Like all her siblings, she loved her eldest sister, but she had never liked her until she lived with her last summer. As she crossing the hall she thought that her mammy could wait another couple of minutes so she sat down on the stairs again. She knew that the man's voice she could hear in the living room was coming from the radio, but it made her think about the time when she was living with Josie. Every room in Josie's flat had a radio on all day. She thought about the months she had stayed in Kent.

Chapter Twenty-three

Peter Cunningham was the last person Joan wanted to think about today, but, while she sat on the stairs and draped her dressing gown over her knees, she wondered again how she would have managed if he hadn't insisted on paying all the expenses when she had gone to England. He threatened to go to the police if she and Sue didn't accept his money. "It is the only thing I can do," he had pleaded. He begged them to see that where none of the incident was Joan's fault that it wasn't his either. However, it was his father and he had some responsibility.

Every time Joan's thoughts wandered over the last sixteen months of her life, she mostly dwelled on Mike's kindness and caring. He had more than made up to her for Josie not knowing how to cope when she stayed with them. While Josie rattled on about the nutritional benefits of the foods she cooked, Joan made herself eat some of all the meals to please Mike.

Dinner or supper, Joan didn't care what they called the evening meal in England. In Ireland they called it tea. Josie's cooking was easier to swallow when Mike was with them for the evening meal. While she sat on the stairs willing her heart to have patience with Josie, Joan now wondered if Mike had read magazines all day so that he would have plenty to talk about. She also wondered if he had talked so much to prevent Josie from saying anything about their mammy. She wanted to cry at the memory of how kind he had been to her.

Every time Josie had mentioned their mammy Joan had found an excuse to leave the room. She was terrified at the thoughts of having a baby, and all Josie seemed to be worried about was how her mammy was managing. She loved sport, but football on the television wasn't able to hold Joan's interest on the evening Mike was going over the accounts for Josie's salon. She wasn't interested in Josie's business but she was learning how to do accounting for her job so she listened.

At the time Josie's takings were down because of the power cuts and other shortages brought about by the three-day week and the miners' strike in England. Joan heard Mike explaining to her sister how he included the money she sent to her mammy in the wages they paid to the staff. She had been furious when she learned her sister had sent their mammy extra money. She didn't want to say anything in front of Mike so the next day when she was in the kitchen helping Josie with the dinner she said, 'When you phone mammy tonight will you ask her if she is still getting my money from Peter?'

Josie had stopped slicing her mushrooms and asked, 'What money?'

'I made arrangements with Peter to give her my usual money every two weeks while I am away,' Joan said. She watched Josie return to slicing her mushrooms for a few seconds before she said, 'I know she likes her money on the dot every week, but she will have to put up with a two-week payment until I get back. At least she's getting it in advance.' She walked out of the kitchen and left Josie to her mushrooms, and her thoughts.

A cold breeze pulled Joan's thoughts away from her sister. When she raised her head to the hall door in answer to the sound of tin rattling, she watched a pile of white and pale coloured envelopes tumble to the floor as they spewed from the letterbox. The letters gave Joan a brisk reminder of what she was doing today. She doubled her resolve not to upset Josie, then made the few steps over to the door and picked up

the cards before Josie came back from the toilet. She inhaled
deeply after she tucked the cards under her arm and went into
the living room.

Chapter Twenty-four

Compared to the hall, and the kitchen, the living room was warm. It always was when the fire had been burning the day before. Joan found her mammy sitting by the fireplace smoking a cigarette. 'Are you all right, Mammy?' she asked, picking up the slippers she had brought down for her off the low chair where Josie had left them and sat down. 'Are you cut?' she continued. When her mammy still didn't reply, Joan wanted to swipe her around the ear with the slippers but she dropped them on the floor beside her mammy's feet and asked, 'What happened?'

'I'm not cut,' Sheila Malone said, looking down her nose at the slippers. She bent the top of her body over, and stretched her hand down and rubbed one of the slippers with her fingers. 'I got a fright, that's all,' she said, picking a hair off the fur that was around the other slipper. 'You go back to bed, and I'll get Josie to bring you up a cup of tea.' She didn't say anything about what had happened with the plates in the kitchen. With unnecessary heaving and panting, she managed to get her feet into the new slippers.

Joan made no effort to help her mammy. She recalled how she used to chase her slippers with her feet around her bedroom because she couldn't see them. And she couldn't bend over to put them on when she was sitting down. Five hours she thought, when the radio pumped out soft sweet pips to tell everyone who was listening, and who might be interested that it was ten o'clock. Her new home for a while would be with Tony and his grandmother Bella. Joan liked Bella and Tony loved her. She envied Tony's love for his grandmother. She wished she could love her own mother half as much and it worried her. 'What happened with the plates, Mammy?' she asked again.

Sheila Malone fumbled around her feet for her handbag.

Joan closed her eyes, prayed for patience, and the courage, for once, to demand an answer. She suspected her mammy had broken the plates deliberately and she was curious to know why. When she opened them again, her mammy was walking over to the hot press in the corner beside the back window. With her mammy's body no longer blocking her view, she could see the photographs on the wall beside the hot press.

The photographs were a mixed and haphazard collection of all the family. Some of them in single frames; there were a couple of large frames that had eight different snaps in them. Joan remembered Una buying the frames the first year she had come home after she was married, and she and Cathy helped her to arrange them. They made her think of Una and how her sister had behaved when their brother had told her about why she had been in England last year.

Una and Pauline had always looked after the photographs. Joan remembered Una had cut away the curled-up corners on some of their old school pictures because the film part had peeled away from being fastened on the wall with draw-ing pins for months. She smiled at the memory of Una saying the snaps were shrivelled so much they reminded her of Betty Byrne's face.

Alongside remembering the fun the three of them had enjoyed for the whole day it had taken them to frame the photographs, Joan prayed that Una would understand why she hadn't gone to see her when she was in London last year. She forgot about her sister when her eyes rested on the photograph of her youngest brother Liam in his uniform. 'I wonder if Liam got in all right?' she said.

Sheila Malone opened the hot press, then closed it again. She looked at the floor as though she needed to be careful where she placed her new slippers while she made her way back to her armchair.

'If who got in all right?' Josie called from the doorway. She nodded her head in approval at the new slippers on her mammy's feet. She cleared a space on the table for the teapot and repeated, 'if who got in?'

When Sheila saw Joan uncross her legs she said quickly, 'Donal was to pick him up at the airport last night.' She didn't want Joan to leave her on her own with Josie. Joan was standing when she said, 'I expect we would have heard if he hadn't come.'

Josie knew her mammy was referring to Liam. She didn't know why, but she believed that her mammy was afraid of her youngest son. Every time Josie mentioned Liam's name during the week her mammy abruptly walked out of the room as though Josie had threatened her. 'I wouldn't be so sure,' she snapped smiling conspiratorially at her mammy. 'The boy's never tell us anything until the last minute,' she added nodding her head as if she had given her mammy important information by letting her know that she didn't like Liam either. She picked the old slippers up off the floor and said, 'I'll put these things in the bin.'

And quite right too, Joan thought. They know how to save themselves a lot of bother. She was following Josie out of the room to go back to bed when she heard a beep from the horn of a car out on the road so she looked out the window. She recognised the two young girls running down the path on the far side of the road. She also knew where they were going when they climbed into the car beside two other girls. The woman behind the wheel of the car gave another light beep to the horn before she drove the four young girls into the village for their dancing lessons.

Looking out of the living room window in Plunkett Road was often the same as looking at the clock. On a Saturday morning nearly all the neighbours did the same thing at the same time. Joan knew that she would miss the neighbours because they had always been very kind to her. She was nearly sixteen when she ceased to be embarrassed because her mammy always crossed the road so that she could avoid returning the greetings the neighbours always offered her.

Joan had been surprised and delighted when Grace had given her four thick exercise books for a Saint Patrick's day present when she was fourteen. She felt awkward when Nancy had given her two new pairs of white socks for no reason at all. She had been so pleased with her gifts that she hadn't cared if they all knew that she gave her mammy most of the money they had given her for baby-sitting.

'It looks like the rain might hold off,' Joan called out to her mammy.

Sheila picked her handbag up off the floor.

Joan wasn't worried about the weather, but it was something to say because she wanted to stay at the window and absorb the memories of her life in Plunkett Road. For a second she wondered if any of her neighbours knew the real reason why she had been in England last year. But she wasn't worried because she knew that they would understand. Some of the warmth she was feeling for her neighbours seeped over to Josie, and she started to think about her four older sisters.

How they must miss the friendliness of their own home Joan thought, recalling how lonely she had felt when she had been in England.

'It will be the same in an hour,' Josie called over.

Even though she wouldn't be looking at the houses across the road so often Joan knew would still see all her neighbours because she wouldn't be moving far away. Tony agreed that when they bought their own house it would be near Ballyglass. She vowed again that she would be a good wife for Tony. She also prayed that he was doing the right thing today. She straightened the net curtains, turned round and asked, 'What will?'

'The view from that window,' Josie said, scooping two spoons of sugar into her mammy's teacup. 'I left yours on the table in the kitchen,' she said to Joan.

Joan knew that the view from the window wouldn't be the same in an hour but she wasn't going to argue. She was still holding the pile of cards against the top of her leg when she moved away from the window. She allowed her temper a rare moment of freedom when she stretched her arm out and yanked the door open. She forgot she was angry when she saw Eileen standing in the hall. The little girl smiled shyly at her. While she thought how lovely the little girl was Joan also saw how well Jose cared for her children. 'Don't you look lovely,' she called out. Then because she was still holding her cards she was only able to use one of her arms to hug Eileen. The light pressure of the little girl's arms around her neck squeezed the temper out of her heart so quickly that she smiled at Josie when she turned back into the room and called out, 'Guess who's here?'

Josie nearly cried when her young daughter walked slowly into the room then.

While Josie was suffering deep disappointment because her friendly chat with her mammy was cancelled again, Joan whispered, 'Oups,' She steadied her hand and watched a few drops of her tea drip onto the carpet, then climbed the stairs. Unlike Cathy, and her mammy, Joan was always very careful about spilling liquids on the carpets. She looked back down the stairs to admire the wallpaper again. She imagined the little white cameos on the blue background were smiling at her and was reminded of her brothers, and how great they had been to her when she had come back home from England. As part of her determination to leave her tragedy behind and look to her future after she was home, Joan decorated the bedrooms. Sean, Donal and Maurice encouraged and helped her.

It had all seemed so easy to Cathy; with help from her brothers she decorated the rooms downstairs and within a month the whole house was painted and papered. Joan smiled at the wallpaper again and whispered, 'Well at least Cathy will have a lovely clean house.'

Chapter Twenty-five

Four years after Liam joined the English Air Force there were spare beds in 34 Plunkett Road. Maurice's bed was the first to become vacant when he married Angie Dolan's youngest daughter Maeve a little over a year after all the family had been home for Maura's twenty-first birthday party.

Donal's move out of the family home was gradual. He started sleeping odd nights in the Beggars Lodge where he worked, then after some months he stopped coming home to sleep at all. When Liam came home on leave now he stayed with Donal.

Both Cathy and Joan saw Donal as the man of the house and they contacted him when they blew an electric fuse, the sink was blocked, or grass on the front lawn needed cutting. Although he did nothing other than hold a spanner, or get in his best friend's way, Tony Murphy always accompanied Donal on the emergencies to Plunkett Road.

Tony Murphy was a month old when his mother had left him with her mother and returned to England. When her grandson was a year old Bella bought an insurance policy for him so that he would have enough money to buy his own house when he was getting married.

Fortunately for Tony the endowment paid him enough money to buy a half-share in the old Ballyglass village pub. The Beggars Lodge was run down when Tony became half owner, and manager.

The old good sturdy building that Liam and his friend Brian walked past on the day that Brian was having his photograph taken six years earlier still hadn't had a coat of varnish or paint when Tony invested his money in it. He renovated, altered and improved it to suit the younger people that were now going to pubs for their evening entertainment.

Before he painted the walls, Tony started providing music at the weekends. He encouraged the local hopefuls to bang out tunes on guitars, sing, and tell jokes. They brought their friends and within a year he was making money. After two years he borrowed more money and bought out his partner.

As a boy all Tony's energies went into football. He was hopeless at all kinds of manual work and he thought that clerical and shop jobs were for women. He settled with working in a pub after trying an assortment of driving and warehouse jobs.

The ideas for the renovations to the Beggars Lodge were a mixture from Tony, Liam, and Brian Farley. Liam's ideas were all grand. Brian didn't have any ideas but he always stressed the importance for keeping all the old and early parts of the building. Tony's ideas were all on what would bring in customers and get them to spend their money.

When all the ideas were mixed up and sketches of the designs were ready, Tony needed Donal's carpentry skills to see that the work and changes were done properly. Donal borrowed the money for the renovations and became Tony's partner in the business. He gave up his full-time job on the building sites. He worked all sorts of odd hours and it was seldom that either he or Tony weren't in the Beggars Lodge during the day or evening.

When Tony first went into the partnership the deal included a caretaker barman that lived above the pub. After two years the caretaker left and Donal renovated the rooms and made them his home.

Chapter Twenty-six

With the curtains pulled over, the light in the bed-room was poor but Joan saw a long bundle with a dark mop of hair turn over in the bed towards the wall when she came into her bedroom. 'Come on, Cathy, wake up,' she called out, pulling back the curtains. She took a sip of her tea, then put the mug down on the windowsill.

Cathy raised her head up off the pillow. 'It's you,' she said, 'I thought it was bossy boots.'

'Josie's downstairs with Mammy,' Joan said, turning round from the window. 'Mammy broke three plates.'

'That's a pity,' Cathy said, pulling the covers up to her chin. 'Still it should cheer Josie up fer a few hours with goin' out and buyin' her another lot.'

'I never thought about that,' Joan giggled. 'I hope she doesn't go running into town before she has done our hairs.'

'Don't yeh worry about that,' Cathy said, poking her head out from under the blankets. 'I'll do yer hair fer yeh.'

No thanks, Joan thought, smiling because she mused that Cathy would want to dye her hair purple. 'I know you would,' she said, 'and you're right about Josie buying more plates.'

Since her eldest sister had been home this time Cathy had gotten to know a different Josie. She hadn't started school when Josie went to England, so she had few memories of her doing anything other than cutting her hair. And when Josie was living at home she was very seldom in because she was off dancing, or perming someone's hair. Cathy had never liked her eldest sister because Josie was always telling her what to do. Especially when Josie wanted her do something to please their mammy.

Cathy didn't know or care why Josie spoilt their mammy, but she resented the way her sister expected the rest of the family to obey their mammy's every whim. She saw Josie as being as big a bully as their mammy. Reflecting on the week since Josie had been home, Cathy felt both angry with and sorry for Josie. 'Mammy has been givin' Josie a hard time this week,' she said.

'She still is,' Joan replied.

Cathy turned on her back, stretched her legs and said, 'Liam and Donal will be here soon.' She decided not to say anything about Liam's hair.

'How would you know that?' Joan asked, closing her eyes and thinking, thank God. She knew her mammy was right when she had said that they would have heard if Liam hadn't come in. At the same time she suspected that Donal wouldn't have phoned her because he wouldn't have wanted her to worry. She turned round from opening the top window wider and asked, 'Did you see him yourself?'

'I was talkin' te them last night, and Donal brought me home,' Cathy said, slapping her arms on the quilt beside her legs and moaned, 'and he waited outside till I shut teh door if yeh don't mind.' She pulled her knees up and smiled at the bright white ceiling and hissed, 'The way he goes on yeh'ed think I was still only fourteen.'

'He means well,' Joan said, wondering again if she should have told Cathy about why she had been in England. She wanted to a number of times, and she often believed that they might be closer now if she had. It wasn't Cathy's fault that she didn't want her mammy to know. Maybe when she came back from her holiday. 'There's only Mike to come in now,' she said sitting down on the side of the bed. She wanted to tell her sister how wonderful Josie's husband is but she knew that she would also have to tell her why she knew so she said, 'Eileen is looking forward to seeing her daddy.'

'We had a great time though,' Cathy continued. 'Liam bought us all drinks, and Tony sent us over chicken and chips.'

'I'll have to have a talk with Tony about that. I can't have him spending the profits so recklessly,' Joan said, leaning over to the windowsill and picking up her mug of tea.

'Yer not tellin' me that yeh would begrudge yer poor hungry sister a meal?' Cathy pretended to moan.

'I don't have a poor, or a hungry sister,' Joan replied and brought her mug up to her mouth. 'I have a very pretty and cheeky sister though.' She knew she needed to make sure that Cathy was awake before she asked her to have patience with Josie so she put her mug of tea on the small table then removed her slippers. She withdrew a small pair of scissors from the little drawer in the table, moved the pillows on her side of the bed, then sat up on them. She then pulled one of her feet up towards her stomach and began to cut her toenails.

When the first bit of white crust shot up into the air Joan said, 'I think you had better sit up straight if you don't want some of this stuff in your eye.'

Light dizziness hit Cathy when she sat up. 'Oh God, I smoked too much last night,' she said and lay back on the propped-up pillows.

'You usually do,' Joan said, brushing bits of her toenails off the bed, then added quickly, 'We all do most of the time.' She didn't want Cathy to think she was moaning at her.

'Except Josie,' Cathy said and sat up again, then stretched her hands down her legs towards her toes. 'I don't know why she bothers te light them at all. Most of teh time she leaves them burnin' away in teh ashtray.'

'I agree,' Joan said. 'I think she tries to smoke to be like everyone else.' She put her hand on her sister's knee and said, 'Cathy could you be patient with Josie today?' She rocked Cathy's knee as if to make sure her sister heard her and added, 'For my sake,'

Fer Josie's sake, Cathy wanted to say. She knew the mind game her mammy was playing with Josie because she has read the letter in the white envelope her mammy was carrying around. Her mammy had played the same games with herself and Joan. 'Can I have a sup ev yer tea?' she asked.

Joan picked her mug of tea off the table, drank a sip, then handed the mug over to Cathy. 'No you can't have a cigarette to go with it,' she said, 'not in my bed.'

'It'll be mine in, let me see, one, two, seven hours and that's given yeh an hour te be late.'

'Your hair,' Joan said, holding her hand out to take the mug back again. Cathy's side of the bed was against the wall so she had nowhere to put it.

Cathy sat up in the bed, rested her chin on her knees and hugged her legs. She cast her eyes around the walls. 'What way do yeh want me to have me have me hair done?'

'Cathy, I'm so pleased that you are going to be with me that I'll be happy with whatever you want,' Joan said, returning the mug to the small cabinet while Cathy moved over to the edge of the bed.

'Yeh could have had any of us,' Cathy teased. She had never known any of her friends or cousins to have an older, or married sister for a bridesmaid but she added, 'Even Josie'ed make a lovely matron ev honour.'

'I know, I know, but I want you. And not because you're the best-looking but because I love you the most.'

'If I ever get married I'm goin' te have Eileen, Patsy and Emir,' Cathy said, folding her arms. She threw her head back and added, 'Like I said, if I get married. I might decide te just have children.'

Delighted that Cathy didn't argue over having patience with Josie and infected with her young sister's good humour Joan said, 'I couldn't have Una for a bridesmaid.' She waved her head, raised her voice and repeated, 'I just could not have Una.'

'What's wrong with Una fer god's sake,' Cathy asked.

'The union,' Joan said softly and looked behind her as though Una might be standing in the doorway. She nodded her head at the blank face of Cathy and whispered, 'We would all have had to join a union.' She giggled into Cathy's gaping expression and added, 'Even Mammy would have to join a union.'

'If yer talkin' about a workers' union,' Cathy said, 'then yeh wouldn't get te yer weddin' because none ev the unions would have her. And anyway yer thinkin' of Jack.'

Joan wiped her eyes with a tissue, then blew her nose and said, 'Una is as bad.'

Cathy realised she hadn't seen Joan laugh, or tell a joke since she came back from England. 'How do yeh know? I never heard Una talking much about teh union.'

'Mike told me,' Joan said. She was so enjoying her joke about Una she forgot about not wanting to talk about Mike right now. She wished again she had the time to sit and tell her sister what a very good man Josie's husband was. But it was something else to tell Cathy about so she said, 'Do you think you will be able to fill your head up with patience for Josie before you go downstairs?'

Cathy wrapped her arms around her Joan's small shoulders and said, 'Josie deserves me patience fer all teh lovely dinners she gave me this week.' She moved to the edge of the bed. 'I think it's a good job that yeh bought me a loose fittin' dress because I think I've put on a few pounds.'

Joan struggled to hold back her tears while she returned Cathy's hug.

Chapter Twenty-seven

Cathy kept her promise and did everything she could not to annoy Josie. Josie responded by thanking Cathy for something almost every ten minutes. Joan smiled constantly at the pair of them, while their mammy screwed up her face as tight as a dried prune and rolled the hem of her apron.

Cathy was walking by the front window when she heard cars stopping outside the house. 'They're here,' she called out ,pulling back the curtain so she could see her favourite brother.

'Who?' Josie asked glancing at the clock. As Cathy was opening the hall door she walked over to the window to see for herself. She saw Liam taking a large white cardboard box from the back of a new dark red Ford Escort Estate. She also saw Donal talking to a neighbour while he was locking the driver's door of a new dark blue Ford Escort Estate. 'Who owns the new cars?' she asked.

'Do they have the flowers with them?' Joan asked from the far side of the room where she was sitting at the table with a towel around her shoulders and half of her hair in rollers.

Before Josie had started doing her mammy's hair, Joan moved the table to the far end of the room close to the hot press and back window. 'This will give you better light be-cause you will be nearer the window,' she insisted when Josie objected. But the main reason why Joan wanted Josie in the corner was that it would get her out from the centre of the room where she wouldn't be able to keep telling the rest of them what to do all the time.

'Just pull it out from the window and the hot press so we can get a couple of chairs in behind it,' Joan said when Josie frowned for the third time.

Josie wasn't used to being told what to do but she was so depressed with her mammy that she would have moved the table out to the hall rather than argue. Besides, as she was enjoying the attention from her younger sisters she thought she would please them.

'I think so,' Josie said, walking back towards the table. She picked up her tail comb, then shoved her Joan's head down so far that her chin was resting in the top of her chest. 'They've come in two lovely new cars,' she said, taking a roller from Eileen's hand. She then looked down at her mammy and asked, 'Does Donal have a new car?'

'Donal always has a nice car,' Sheila returned coldly.

'Yes Josie,' Joan said, 'Tony and Donal have new cars.'

Sheila squeezed her face into a tighter prune, shoved her chair back, and turned it towards the door as though she was expecting the queen to walk in and she didn't want to miss her when the door opened.

Cathy jutted her head into the room and called out, 'Joan, teh flowers are here. I'll put them up on er bed fer now, is that all right?'

'I suppose so,' Josie answered, 'we still need to use the bathroom.'

'All right,' Donal said, walking into room. He wasn't asking his mammy if she was tired, and he wasn't asking Josie if she had enough rollers to set all his sisters' hairs. It was his way of saying 'hello' and his usual smile was broad and warm.

Josie looked up from parting Joan's hair and nodded a greeting at her quiet brother as though he had walked in with a shovel of coal for the fire.

Sheila Malone picked her handbag off the floor at her feet and opened it like she was going to give her son something out of it.

Used to a weak greeting from his mammy and eldest sister, Donal shuffled the bundle of pastel-coloured envelopes he was holding and asked, 'Where do yeh want these? They came in the post this morning to the Beggars Lodge.'

'I'll take them here,' Joan said, quickly holding her hand out towards an immaculately polished pair of shoes. She could only see her brother's feet because her head was still folded over towards her knees.

'They have to go to the best man,' Josie, said inserting the hairpin in the last roller on Joan's hair. She smiled at her brother when she saw him hesitate about giving the cards to Joan; she was sure the expression on his face was saying; 'Sorry Josie I didn't know.'

Joan pulled the envelopes from Donal's hand and tucked them under her arm.

'Did you hear me?' Josie said, walking round to the front of Joan to put a hair net on her head so that the rollers would stay in.

'I heard you,' Joan replied, gripping the envelopes tighter.

Expecting to be obeyed, Josie draped the net over the front of Joan's head, then moved to the back of the chair, and instead of taking the ends of the net to tie them at the back of Joan's neck she moved back so that her sister could hand the cards back to her brother. She nodded at Donal's wide smile, then ran her eyes over his thin, light brown hair and waited.

Donal thought Josie was panting because her arms were tired. Then when he watched her move her head between himself and his mammy a couple of times, he moved back a couple of steps, because he thought she was trying to make up her mind whether she should shout at him or his mammy.

'Don't worry, he'll get them in good time,' Joan said. She

tucked the cards under her chin, then took the ends of the hairnet to tie them herself. The cards slid down her lap and splayed across the floor like a fan as Liam walked in the door.

It wasn't Josie's habit to use swear words when she was shocked. But when she saw her young brother had his hair permed, she closed her back teeth tight and whispered, 'Jesus Christ.' She ran her eyes over his hair as if she was counting, and measuring the length of every curl on the top of his head.

Liam winked at Donal.

He didn't know what else to do so Donal shrugged his shoulders, shoved his hands into the pockets of his trousers, looked down at the floor, and rocked lightly on the balls of his feet.

'A bit early fer confetti,' Liam said, nodding his head down at the carpet of envelopes. He noticed one of the envelopes had the address typed. 'That one is fer you,' he said to his brother picking up the slender white envelope. 'A bit mean of yeh te stick yer bills in with teh cards fer Joan and Tony te pay.'

'How do you know it's a bill?' Josie asked.

Nature failed to grant Liam the spurt of longitudinal growth she often bestows on many of her young men after they had passed their sixteenth year. A little over five feet three he could look Josie in the mouth. This morning his eyes were level with her nose because he was wearing boots with two inch high heels. 'Personal letters are always handwritten,' he returned, raising his head to look Josie in her eyes. He winked, then gave her a hug.

Cathy smiled at the pair of them, as much delighted with watching Josie return Liam's hug as she was with his blue corduroy jacket, red polo-necked shirt, and faded jeans.

Liam glanced down at his mammy and said, 'I see yer restin' yerself until all teh excitement starts with everyone getting ready at teh same time.'

Sheila Malone looked up at her youngest son and smiled.

Donal knew his mammy rested all day and that Liam was being sarcastic. He also guessed that his mammy knew that Liam was being smart. He was relieved when his mammy smiled. If he had known his mammy smiled because Liam had given her a brilliant idea about what she should do with the letter in her handbag, he would have been concerned. At the moment he was more concerned about the phone calls his young brother had made before they had left his flat.

Chapter Twenty-eight

Friday evenings are busy in Irish pubs, so by the time Tony and Donal had encouraged the last drinker out of the Beggars Lodge, locked the doors and tidied up, it was nearly one o'clock. Tony went home to his grandmother and Liam and Donal retired to Donal's flat above the pub.

The two brothers found a lot to laugh about while they sat in easy chairs in front of an electric fire and talked about the other family weddings. Except for when Maurice and Maeve were married, Donal and Liam were only children when their older sisters were married.

Like Josie, Donal didn't think back to his younger days. But Liam was like Una and he could, and often did think back to when he was a very young boy. Right now he could feel the memory of Pauline's wedding buzzing in his ears as if it was only last year. He walked over to the window and drew back the drapes so he could look up the road towards the church.

The church is as old as Liam. He knew every alcove and corner of the big building because he used to play around the grounds from when he was seven until he left school. There were four of them and they were known to hide in the church from the priests. Thinking back now, he wondered if his friend Brian still went to mass every day. From where he was standing, he could just about see the front pillars that held the heavy gates of the church but he smiled and recalled getting out of the car and walking up the steps while Brian Farley and his friends cheered and clapped.

Liam was to be the last to get into the car and while his brothers waved to the neighbours that stood around the gate of the house he got into the black car that was to take Pauline and his daddy. He then got out the other side, skipping around in time to join his brothers. Tonight as he looked up the road he imagined he could hear the cheers from his friends and neighbours.

Liam was only eight at the time and he didn't know his mammy well, but he would have given her away that day if he could have stayed in the big black shiny car. With the memory of the smell of the polish, the feel of the soft velvet brushing his arms and face as he crept along the seats of the car, his mind as fresh as the day he entertained his friends, he turned round from the window and asked his brother, 'Is there a party or anythin' fer the children?'

Donal glanced at his watch and sat forward in his Parker Knoll chair. It was twenty minutes past two and he wanted to go to bed. He put his mug on the small table in front of him and said, 'I haven't heard ev anythin'.'

Liam continued to look out the window. He thought of his friend Brian when he noticed the shops on the far side of the road hadn't been pulled down to accommodate a new road to Belfast. He wondered if his friend Brian was still struggling with his conscience, or had joined the Communist Party.

Brian Farley has been Liam's best friend since they had started school, and they both joined the English Air Force when they were sixteen. They followed different career paths, Brian in engineering and Liam in accounts. A big black car cruising down the road into town brought his thoughts back to the children that wouldn't be going to Joan's wedding. He turned away from the window to his brother and said, 'Do yeh know what I enjoyed most about the other weddin's?'

'Te tell yeh the truth, Liam, I don't,' Donal replied, yawned and looked at his watch again. He wondered where Liam got all his energy. He leaned forward to get out of his chair with the intention of leaving the room if his brother started telling him what he should be remembering because he knew that he would forget it straightaway.

'It was the cars,' Liam said, raising his shoulders like he was standing to attention for a general. 'The black shiny cars.' He laughed loudly and waved his head. 'Come on, Donal, didn't yeh think it was great when all the neighbours called out te yeh when yeh were walkin' down teh garden path in yer blue cotton shorts when yeh were leavin' teh house fer Pauline's weddin'.'

'I don't remember,' Donal lied, recalling he was embarrassed at the time and he would have preferred to have been one of the boys that were doing the clapping and cheering.

'And there was a nice black shiny car waitin' at teh gate fer yeh,' Liam said returning to his chair.

Donal finished his tea in one gulp and stood: 'I'm goin' te bed,' he said. He expected his brother was going to plan a party for the children and he was too tired to remember what he would be agreeing to. He was at the door of his bedroom when he said, 'Turn teh lights off before yeh go te bed.'

Normally Donal never had any trouble going to sleep, but he lay awake for ten minutes trying to remember the black shiny cars his brother had talked about. He had turned on his side for the third time when he recalled he had only been to two weddings when he had worn short trousers – Pauline's and Una's – and each time his Uncle Fred drove them down to the church in a small blue Hillman Imp.

While the memory of Liam making his phone calls was flashing through Donal's mind, Joan was moving the bundle of cards about. 'There's more of them down in Bella's,' he said, smiling at Josie. He wondered if he should go down to the Ballyglass village and bring them back for her. He thought if his two sisters had a bundle of cards each there would be no need for the two of them to argue.

'We can open them when we get to the hotel,' Joan said, sorting the cards so that the large ones were at the back. The bundle made a one-inch pile after she bounced the bottoms of them on the table and shoved the sides in so that the bundle was no bigger than the largest card. She raised her head to Josie smiled and said, 'We won't have time to read them all out at the reception anyhow.'

'I take it that everyone's accounted fer, Josie? Liam said. He sniffed a couple of times to stop from laughing and continued. 'Now before yeh tell me that me perm wasn't worth teh fifty quid that I paid fer, Josie, yeh have te take account ev teh fact that I had te have it done skorepitucsley.' He sniffed again when he saw Josie open her eyes, pull in her chin and look down at her mammy.

'What on earth is skoripitous?' Cathy hollered.

'He means surreptitiously,' Joan said, laughing. She was as stunned as Josie at her young brother's curly hair but she wasn't surprised because he had told her he was going to have his hair permed.

'And what does that mean?' Cathy asked, nudging Josie with her elbow. 'Is it another one ev them fancy hairdressin' places that charge yeh fer hangin' up yer coat?'

'He means that he had to sneak into the hairdressers.' Joan returned Eileen's giggle wondering if the little girl knew what she was laughing about.

'Yeh mean sly like, like yeh were hidin' yerself because yeh didn't want anyone te see yeh?' Cathy asked, lowering her head down to her niece and added, 'That's a terrible way te have yer hair done.'

Josie wanted to cry. She bowed her head towards her brother and said, 'It's a very good perm, Liam, but the next time you want it done come up to me and I'll do it for you.'

During Josie's ten years in school she was kept back to re-peat a year twice because she had been absent so many days. The humiliation from being kept back at all was mild com-pared to having to try to reduce the length of her body. She was always tall and the younger girls used to make her feel twice her height. There was a slight quiver in her voice when she ordered, 'Any time you want your hair permed, Liam, you come up to me. Any time at all.' She imagined she could see her brother shrinking his body to make himself invisible while he sneaked into the hairdressing salon, and she wanted to cry for him.

Jesus, Josie, Liam thought, while he sniffed and rubbed his chin to stop from laughing. He was surprised she had taken him so seriously. 'I was hopin' te hear yeh say that, Josie,' he said, winking at Rory, who was sitting on a stool in the far cor-ner of the room as if he was guarding the ironing basket. He wanted to tell the young boy to go out and play with the other children on the road. He thought that Josie's children would look healthier if they had some dirt on their faces.

'I would be delighted to do it for you,' Josie said, bowing her head like she was giving an order and expected to be obeyed.

Liam ran his eyes over all the combs, clips, brushes, setting lotions and hairnets spread over the table. 'I'd love te say that yez all look lovely,' he said, 'but I can't. Except fer teh children yez are remindin' me of somethin' from outer space with yer rollers and yer coloured hairnets pulled across yer foreheads. But just teh same I see that yez have all been behavin' yer-self fer Josie or yer heads wouldn't be strung up like chickens waitin' fer te be put inte teh oven.'

'We'll all be gargeouss in a couple ev hours,' Cathy sang, 'thanks te Josie here. And we didn't have te go off sneakin' anywhere either.'

The cards felt cold and hard when Joan put them under her arm. She felt small and mean after listening to Cathy and

Liam praising Josie. Recalling how patient Cathy had been all morning with her and their mammy, she was tempted to give the cards to her.

'I would expect no less,' Liam said, smiling at his mammy.

Sheila Malone smiled weakly at her youngest son.

As well as being sorry she had snapped at Josie, Joan felt she had also been unfair to Cathy. She placed the bundle of cards on the table and called out, 'We certainly will, and it will be all thanks to Josie.'

'We have all been busy,' Josie said, turning round to her youngest sister. 'Haven't we, Cathy?' It was the first time she could remember her family praising her so much, and she was embarrassed.

'Indeed we have, Josie,' Cathy returned, wrapping her arm around her young niece's shoulder and continued: 'Eileen here has been on her feet all mornin makin' sure that yeh have everythin yeh need. She's goin te make a great hairdresser some day.'

For the third time in less than five minutes, Joan felt ashamed of her behaviour over the cards.

Two hours earlier when she was walking across the hall to tell her mammy her bath was ready, Joan heard Josie speaking very loudly. Expecting to see her two sisters fighting when she went into the room she found Josie standing in front of her mammy and calling out instructions to Cathy who was sitting at the table writing down every word Josie was shouting at her. Josie was plucking her mammy's eyebrows.

While she was trying to think of something nice to say to Josie, Joan smiled over at Eileen and Rory. The children were sitting on the edge of their seats with their arms on the table watching Liam. They hadn't seen him since the previous summer. He always made a fuss over them and they loved him for it. She was still smiling when she looked down at her mammy.

Sheila Malone smiled back at Joan as though her daughter had given her a present.

Until last summer Liam had no pleasant memories of his eldest sister. When he was growing up he hated her bullying as much as he resented the way she spoilt their mammy. He deliberately timed his holidays home when Josie wouldn't be there. Then last summer he stayed with her a few weekends when he visited her in Kent to see Joan and he got to know her better. He admired her for the way she managed her business and her home.

Josie forgot about Joan and the cards. She didn't argue with her brother, or protest because she had never been praised by her family before, and she wanted to hold on to the moment so she shouted out, 'Do you boys want a trim while you're here?' Her smile was warm and her eyes were sparkling.

Both brothers rubbed their hand down the back of their neck. Donal was so impressed at how easy it had seemed for Liam to get his eldest sister's face to light up so brightly he felt that he should make some effort. He patted the sides of his hair and said, 'Can yeh do anythin' about thin hair on teh top?' He was absolutely sure that she couldn't, because he had already tried six different barbers, and every potion in every chemist on the north side of the River Liffey.

'I'm glad you asked that,' Josie said, 'what you need with your hair on top is layering.' She kept her eyes on Donal's face while she stretched her hand over to the table to get her scissors and tail comb. She fumbled for her tools but she didn't take her eyes away from her brother's face in case he walked away.

Cathy put the scissors into her hand.

Josie decided that Donal wasn't bald but his hair was thin on the top of his head. She moved her chair back from the table so that he would have enough room for his long legs. 'Come on, sit down over here and I'll do it for you,' she said.

Like a lot of men with the same thin hair, Donal wore it down past the collar of his jacket because he believed he would look less bald if he showed more hair. 'Are yeh sure that yeh have teh time?' he asked throwing his eyes up at the clock.

Liam was sure Donal thought Josie would say no, that she couldn't do anything about baldness. He looked over to Eileen when he heard her cough a hearty low laugh. He thought how shy and undemanding the little girl was and saw her bury her face in her folded arms. He couldn't think of anything that Josie could do for baldness, but he thought he would entertain her children so he winked at Eileen and said, 'It's worth a try.'

While Eileen's head wobbled back a yes to her uncle like she was being shaken, Josie was wiping her comb and scissors with her fingers. She didn't see her daughter slip off her seat from trying to hide her face in her arms because she was stand-ing behind her chair waiting for Donal to sit down.

Cathy gave Eileen a tissue to dry her eyes.

Donal had never fought with any of his siblings. He had never questioned anything Josie had asked, or told him to do. He was trying to find the words to tell her that he didn't want his hair cut when he heard her say, 'Take your jacket off first.'

'There yeh go, Josie; now do a good job, we're all countin' on yeh, so don't let the family down,' Cathy hollered while she wrapped the old curtain Josie was using for a gown.

Donal felt like he was a ten-year old boy again. He cast Liam a scowl that said "do something". He thought that the joke had gone far enough

'Fer God's sake, Donal, she's only goin' te cut yer hair, not yer silly flowery shirt,' Liam laughed, rubbing his hands to-gether. He bowed to his sister and said, 'Go ahead, Josie, and do yer best.'

Chapter Twenty-nine

Josie trained her own staff so she was used to demonstrating how to cut hair. She stood behind the low-backed, low-armed chair that her daddy had made for her to cut her siblings' hair when she was an apprentice and smiled at her small audience.

Although this demonstration was different from training her apprentices, Josie set about her task with her usual professional skills. She combed Donal's hair up and over his forehead, sideways, and back over his collar again. She picked up tufts of hair and examined them as if she was looking for gold or other precious metals. While she was designing and doing all the things she usually did before she made up her mind where to cut, Donal was thinking back to when he was five-years old. Nearly all his hair had been clipped off. Then he was eight, and almost bald because Josie used to cut his hair so short.

Every time Josie lifted up a bunch of his hair, Donal imagined he could feel the awful winter cold on his head. He was ten when Josie went to England, and that was the last of the regular monthly haircuts for them all. Sean and Maurice were allowed longer hair with side burns. They paid for them themselves. He and Liam had the regular cut, but not so often, because the barber had to be paid.

'Give Donal that mirror,' Josie said, pointing over to the table. She knew why her brother had taken so long, and why he had been so reluctant to sit in her chair. She had grown used to listening to her younger brothers and sisters when they joked and laughed about the haircuts she used to give them when they were children.

While Joan stretched over to take the hand mirror off the table, Josie placed her hands on the sides of Donal's face, raised his head and said, 'Don't worry, Donal. I won't cut if you don't want me to. I'll just show you what I can do and how it will work.'

'All right, Josie,' Donal kept repeating, even though he didn't understand a word of what she was talking about when she explained the weight of his hair was holding it flat against his head. He looked in the mirror and nodded his head as she held up lumps of his hair, twisted them and then let them fall again. He just wanted to get his hair done and over with. When he saw that Joan was nodding her head in agreement he relaxed.

Only five cheered every time Donal said, 'All right, Josie,' but it sounded like ten. Donal didn't see Cathy nudge Josie on her arm but he heard her call out, 'Like fer teh rest of us, Donal, it'll soon grow again.'

Josie could have cut her brother's hair in less than ten minutes. But she wanted her moment of attention to last so she wiped her scissors on the curtain twice. She swapped her comb, and rearranged the curtain around Donal's shoulders four times.

'Are yeh changin' yer mind?' Cathy roared when Josie glanced up at the clock for the third time.

The Malone children loved to have fun with each other. And they always enjoyed being the centre of the banter because it made them appear clever. Josie had rarely been the centre of attention when her siblings were enjoying their bantering because her pensive nature seldom allowed her to admit to doing anything silly or funny. For the fifteen minutes she was cutting and styling Donal's hair she kept stopping, and calling out, 'Will you all mind your own business,' or, 'Who is the hairdresser here?' Her family laughed more at her than they did at Donal. But just the same for half an hour she was the centre of attention, and she loved every minute of it.

Cathy gave Eileen another tissue to dry her eyes again.

Short of getting out of the chair, there was nothing Donal could do about having his hair cut so he kept whispering into his chest, 'It will grow again. It will grow again.' All he could see in the mirror Joan was holding in front of his face was the reflection of the photographs that were on the wall behind Josie's head. Instead of asking Joan to hold the mirror steady he smiled back at her. It was so good to see her laughing that he was ready to sit in the chair for another hour.

'That'll teach yeh not te trust yer sister,' Liam said, clapping when Donal gave Josie a hug. The children, Joan and Cathy also clapped.

The clapping stopped as though a radio had been turned off during a football match when Josie shouted, 'He-llo,' then slapped her hand over her mouth as if she was stopping a scream from escaping.

When Liam turned and followed Josie's broad smile, he saw his Uncle Fred standing in the doorway.

'I've come fer teh weddin,' Fred said to Cathy who was wide-eyed with surprise as though she had never seen him before. He bowed his head to Sheila then walked over to Josie. 'I brought your husband,' he said when Josie released him from a long tight hug.

'So I see,' Josie said, blinking to clear the water from her eyes while at the same time she ran her hand across the top of his hair as if she was testing to feel if it was real. The last time Josie had seen her Uncle Fred she thought the silver strands in his dark thick wavy hair were so attractive that she had tried to copy them on a customer who was complaining because her hair wasn't going grey. She looked over to the door and watched Mike bend down to help Eileen climb up his body and put her arms around her daddy's neck.

Fred had stopped coming up to Plunkett Road a few weeks after Sue had died but he had kept in touch with Sheila's children. He sent them all birthday cards and he called into the Beggars Lodge every month to see Donal. Although he didn't want to be in the same room as Sheila he would have slept in the same bed today to be at Joan's wedding and enjoy the day with Sheila's children.

Chapter Thirty

The sun was shining and the mountains were clear of mist when Donal moved out on to the path in the front garden and followed Liam's gaze down the road. When he saw that Una, Maurice, Maeve and the children waving up at them he went back into the house. He needed to talk to Mike about the black mini cabs.

Over the last five years since he had moved out of his family home Liam had never missed his mammy but he had often thought about her. He felt sorry for her when Josie was cutting Donal's hair. She just sat in her chair and smiled as though she was a stranger and not part of the family at all. As though he could walk away from the image of his sad mammy, he walked down the path and worried about Cathy living on her own with her after today.

Liam wasn't the only boy in school with a sister old enough to be his mother, but Liam never knew any of them to have three, and they had also been like a mother to Cathy when they lived at home. He prayed Josie and Una would come home to see that Cathy was managing. He opened the gate and smiled at Una and Maeve. They looked more like people from outer space than Cathy, Joan, and his mammy did. They had bright-coloured scarves tied around their huge heads of rollers.

When Una walked into his outstretched arms, he wondered what their mammy would be like now if all her children were like his second eldest sister. All the selfish woman had needed was her family to have stood up to her, and that included his daddy. 'In yeh go, girls,' he said, 'Josie is in great form and workin' wonders with her scissors and combs.' He winked at Maurice's head of curly hair and added, 'I keep askin' her te find a way te give me half ev yers.'

Maurice snorted a giggle then lowered his head to the bags he was carrying. He frowned at the window, and the sound of loud voices.

'If yeh give yer big sister one ev yer big smiles she'll manage te squeeze yeh in fer a shampoo and set,' Liam said, walking past his sourly brother and started walking across the road to Angie Dolan's house.

Maurice seldom smiled; he left the gate open and was making his way up the path when Eileen came out the door.

'Hello Maurice,' she said in her usual sweet voice that was loud enough for him to hear without bending down. She beamed such a bright smile that he wondered for a second if she was the same little girl and said, 'My daddy is here.'

Maurice had to fight a sudden feeling of jealousy on seeing the delight in the little girls' eyes. He couldn't remember ever feeling pleased to see his daddy. 'We are all here then,' he said, glancing over his shoulder where Una and, Maeve and his daughters were at the gate.

Eileen turned back into the house. She met Joan at the bottom of the stairs: 'Una and Maeve are coming in the door,' she panted, then ran into the living room, and ducked under the table so she could stand beside Cathy again.

Josie started to sort through the rollers, lacquers and other things she was using all morning.

'I'll do that,' Cathy said, slapping Josie on the back of her hand. 'You've done enough, sit down fer a while and admire Donal.'

'I only want to clear away the rest of the rollers,' Josie said.

'I know, I know, teh brushes, teh combs and teh lacquer,'
Cathy interrupted, waving Josie's hand away. 'I have a box here
and I'll put them all in that, and teh rest'll go inte yer bags and
I'll put them upstairs in teh big room.' She pulled a brush out
of Josie's hand and pushed her away.

Chapter Thirty-one

For a few seconds after he had walked into the crowded room after Eileen, Maurice thought he was in another house. There were two chairs where the table used to be. He gritted his teeth and squinted his eyes against the shrieks and laughs of his sisters. He nodded his head at Fred, and Mike. He could only see his mammy's feet because Mike was standing in front of her.

The low armless easy chair that Maurice hated was moved beside the chair his mammy was sitting in. He expected that Mike would sit down in it so he sat on one of the chairs that were against the wall. He was looking around the room for the table when he saw Donal squeeze his way past Una and go over to Mike.

When Mike turned round to talk to Donal, Maurice saw his mammy was searching through her handbag. There was nobody he wanted to talk to so he lit a cigarette and watched her reading the front of a white envelope she had pulled out of her bag. Before he finished smoking his cigarette Donal and Mike left the room. He moved over beside his mammy, tapped her gently on her arm and asked her, 'Can I get yeh anythin'?'

Sheila Malone shoved the envelope back into her handbag, raised her head and looked at her daughters as though one of them had said something to her.

As usual Maurice endured his feeling of hurt when his mammy ignores him, but just in case she hadn't heard him over the voices of his sisters talking at the same time he repeated, 'Are yeh sure I can't get yeh anythin', Mammy?'

The clap Sheila Malone made when she walloped the arms on her chair with her hands was loud enough for Fred to hear in the far corner where he was standing beside Rory. He watched her walk over to the door and pull it open. He was moving over towards Maurice when the door slammed shut.

This wasn't the first time Fred had watched his sister-in-law storm out of a room. It used to bother him because it always upset Sue. He didn't care what Sheila was upset about but he was concerned when he saw Maurice rubbing the side of his face.

Stupid child, Fred thought, while he moved away from the corner of the room where he had allowed the women to box him in because he didn't want to be near Sheila.

Eight pregnancies and seven babies were all that Fred could remember because Pauline was a few days old when Sue first brought him to Arbour Hill to meet her older sister Sheila. He was married to Sue when Sean was born, and he joined in the celebrations of the birth of Terry Malone's first son. It could have been because the baby was another girl that there was little celebration when Maura was born three years after Sean. But Fred knew otherwise. There was no ado at all when Maurice was born ten months later, and then Donal was just another baby when he arrived ten months after Maurice.

'Yer probably right there,' Fred had lied when he had agreed with his wife the evening they were driving home after Sue had told Maurice that Joan was pregnant.

Sue had said that if Maurice received half of the attention from the family that had been showered on Maura when he was a baby then he would be more caring about his sisters and brothers now.

But Fred always believed Maurice was like his mammy and that he only ever thought about himself. It was true that Maura was spoilt. He also knew none of Sheila's other children had received any more attention than Maurice from the selfish woman unless they bought it. Fred knew that Maurice was as mean as his mammy and he never bought anything for anybody in the family.

Reflecting on the furious face of Sheila before she dashed out of the room, Fred was reminded of the last time he had seen her so angry and he thought again that if temper encouraged a person to catch fire then Sheila would have been burnt to a cinder the day he had left her in the hospital grounds.

Chapter Thirty-two

Two days before Sue had died, Fred brought Sheila into the hospital to see her sister. Just as they were going in the door Sheila complained of feeling dizzy. He brought her into a pub across the road from the hospital. He ordered two large whiskies placed them in front of her and told her the number of the ward Sue was in and said she could follow him when she felt better.

He had no intention of having a bath, but Fred welcomed the water that had poured from the sky while he made his way back to the hospital. His clothes were soaked through before he completed his stroll around the hospital grounds. But he felt he had washed away the years of bullying that Sue had suffered from her sister all her life. He knew Sue would not come out of the coma, and she would never know that her sister hadn't come to the hospital to see her. He held her hand for a couple of hours and told her he would miss her, and that he would look out for Sheila's children.

It was getting on for nine when Fred had left the hospital. To his astonishment Sheila was standing in the hall foyer. He surmised she was waiting for him to take her home. He told her that Sue was asleep and settled down for the night then walked away. Ten minutes later when he was driving past the front of the hospital, she was walking down the steps dragging on a cigarette so furiously that he thought she was on fire.

Chapter Thirty-three

The loud buzzing echo of so many voices speaking at the same time sounded to Liam like they were all in a small busy pub. He hooshed his shoulders to gain some height then called out, 'I don't know how you girls can enjoy yer chattin' while yez are neglectin' yer children?'

'What are yeh talking about?' Maeve shouted.

'They're all out playing on the road where they should be on a fine day,' Una said as she sat down in her sister's chair and started to remove the scarf that was around her head.

'Except fer Eileen here,' Cathy cut in.

When Una moved her head to whip off her scarf she saw Maurice was sneering at Josie. 'I am speaking for all your sisters, Liam, and I can safely tell you that none of us have ever neglected a child in our life,' she shouted.

'Jesus Christ,' Fred whispered. He prayed Una would remember her sister was getting married in a few hours before she started a fight with her brother. He always thought her temper was every bit as bad as her mother's.

'Now Una, don't get on your high horse,' Josie admonished. She wasn't going to allow her sister to spoil her new friendship with her young brother. 'Liam wasn't being serious.'

Fred didn't know if he wanted to strangle Liam or Una.

'Just the same,' Una retorted, 'child neglect is a very serious offence these days.' She glared at Maurice and added, 'We could all be sent to jail.'

'Thank you, Josie,' Liam said, drinking in his eldest sister's smile. He moved back a couple of steps away from Una. 'I wasn't meanin' that yez don't care fer yer children.'

'Then what are yeh goin' on about?' Maeve asked.

'Well yez are not bringin' them te teh weddin',' Liam said, moving back another step from the table. The silence was sharper than the hiss that came from the chorus of female gasps.

'I take it,' Una panted as she moved her eyes between her two brothers and continued, 'that you are not suggesting that we belt into town now and buy them all new clothes.'

'I don't have teh money,' Maeve said. Her large, dangling earrings hit her neck when she turned her head sharply to her husband She expected him to agree with her but he had his head bowed to the floor.

Maurice stood as Liam moved another step away from his sisters. When Liam heard his big brother inhale he was sure Maurice was going to punch him so he moved back towards his sisters. He mustered the biggest smile his small mouth could manage and said, 'I was only thinkin' that yez could keep teh children here until yez are all leavin'?'

'Do yeh mean fer teh leave them here all on their own,' Cathy shouted, putting her arm around Eileen's shoulders and whined, 'fer teh whole day?'

'No he doesn't,' Josie said, refusing to consider that her brother would think of any such thing. 'Don't be ridiculous, Cathy.'

'Is this all your idea, Fred?' Cathy shouted across the room to her uncle who was standing in the doorway pulling at his tie. She had noticed him staring angrily at door after her mammy had stormed out of the room. Although she didn't know about the evening Fred had left her mammy to make her way home in the bus a couple of days before Sue had died, she suspected something must have happened between them because it was one of the few times she had known her mammy to come home in the bus.

'It has nothin' at all te do with Fred,' Liam called out, lifting his shoulders and resting his hands on his waist as though daring Cathy to contradict him.

'I was just wonderin',' Cathy said, returning Fred's smile. She had also noticed him staring out the front window as if he was in a dream. She suspected he might be missing Sue. This would be the first family party since her aunt had died. She hoped that involving him in a little banter would bring a smile to his face and let him see that they were all delighted he was here.

'We're still listening, Liam,' Una called out.

'All teh excitement is goin' on in here,' Liam said, wanting to thump Una, but he saw that Josie was smiling at him so he continued, 'it always is at teh girl's house fer weddin's.'

True: Una recalled the morning of Maurice's wedding, looking up at her brother and nodding her head. They were all so bored they had played cards for three hours before they left for the church. 'Liam is right,' she said, pulling the last roller from her hair. She was sure there was nothing they could do about it now but she said, 'Anyway not many families have the privilege and benefit of one of the best hairdressers in Dublin.' She turned round to Josie winked and asked, 'Do you think we could squeeze them into the cars that are taking us down to the church?'

'Eileen can come with me,' Cathy said.

Relieved that Una hadn't objected, Liam raised his hand as though to stop his sisters arguing, or taking control of his plan and said, 'No she won't, Cathy. There'll be no need fer squeezin' anyone in anywhere.'

'They could always walk,' Joan said, winking at Josie.

'Not on their own,' Josie wanted to cry.

'Go on, Liam,' Joan encouraged.

'We're all listening,' Una said.

'Yeh'ed better get a move on, Liam,' Fred said, turning round from the window. He saw Sheila move her feet about on the floor as if she was going to get out of her chair and storm out of the room again. As he was near the door he thought it would be easy for him to stick his foot out and trip her up. For a brief second he wondered if he would if it wasn't Joan's wedding day. He buried the though and said, 'Flo and Sean are here.'

Although delighted to see Josie enjoying herself, and being friendly with her siblings, Fred worried about what Sheila would do to get her eldest daughter's attention. He had watched her play with her children's emotions so often he knew how she worked. He also knew that if she ever failed to control Josie, then she would never get any of her other children to pamper her. At the same time he feared that Josie would ignore her mammy so much and give in.

'We are expectin' them,' Cathy said, handing Eileen a hairbrush to give to Josie. 'Will yeh tell us what yer thinkin' about, Liam or none ev us'll get te teh weddin' at all.'

Josie shoved Una's head down and began to brush her hair. 'He's going to tell us now,' she said to Cathy and began to brush Una's hair. She didn't care what her young brother was scheming because she was still enjoying the fuss he had made of her.

Liam still couldn't see anything wrong with his plan to give the children a treat. 'There's no need fer anybody to run around doin' anythin special,' he said. He heard his mammy sniff. He expected she was reminding him that she was also in the room so he lowered his head and said, 'And that goes fer you too, Mammy. So don't start runnin' about now.'

For the first time since Liam had walked into the room Josie smiled down at her mammy. 'Ah Liam,' she said, 'Mammy never runs around.'

A bouquet of scents tickled Liam's nostrils when he sniffed a couple of times to stop from laughing with Una and Joan. He wondered if the lacquer Josie had been inhaling all morning contained alcohol when he said, 'I have arranged fer black mini cabs to be here te take them down to teh church.'

'Sounds perfectly all right to me,' Josie said, smiling down at her mammy again as if her mammy would be delighted. She was still so intoxicated with the attention from her young brother that she didn't notice the scowl on her mammy's face. She turned round quickly to put the hairbrush on the table.

Eileen took the brush out of her mammy's hand and held out the long tube of lacquer.

'How long have you been standing there?' Josie shouted.

'All the time,' Eileen said, her voice barely audible.

'Are you afraid you'll miss something?' Josie asked, shaking the long tube of hair lacquer vigorously like it was a tube of retardant she was going to use to douse a fire.

'She's been helpin' yeh all morning,' Cathy cut in, putting her arm round Eileen's plump little shoulders and hugging her. 'Like yerself Josie she's a great little worker. Teh only reason why Liam didn't include her in his grand speech is because he didn't see teh sweat pourin' down her face when she was antici-patin' yer needs. She's going te make a great hairdresser one day.'

'We'll see about that,' Josie said, raising her head and pulling in her chin. She smiled at her daughter while her heart was saying you will never have to stand all day to earn your living.

Maurice wasn't concerned who was going to mind either of his sisters', or Sean's children. Or who was going to take them to the church. He was annoyed with Josie for neglecting their mammy. His eyes were piercing her face when he asked gruffly, 'What's all settled?'

Josie smiled into Maurice's frown while she sprayed lacquer on Una's hair and said, 'The children will stay here until we are all leaving, and Liam will send mini cabs up for them.'

'Nice black shiny ones,' Liam cut in, smiling gratefully at Josie.

'I don't think teh children will care what colour they are,' Maeve said.

Determined to get his sisters to give some attention to their mammy, Maurice asked, 'Is Mammy's car black?'

'Mammy is not a child,' Cathy retorted, equally determined that their mammy could sniff and scowl all day. 'It's teh children we fergot about,' she said, glaring at Maurice and added, 'I don't think anyone will object if yeh take her down yerself in a black mini cab.'

Oblivious to her mammy's sniffing and panting, Josie waved her hairbrush up and down as if she was thinking about hitting someone with it and said, 'I thought that Mammy was coming with me and Mike?'

'We can let Mammy choose between teh two ev yez,' Liam said. He had never liked Maurice. He knew his brother wasn't the least bit worried about how his mammy would get to the church. He also knew that Maurice was drawing their attention to their mammy because he was finding it difficult to tolerate her sour face.

'Of course she can,' Josie sang, glancing down at the easy chair to smile at her mammy again.

Sheila was fumbling around her feet like she was searching for something.

Fred didn't see Sheila find her handbag because his attention was drawn to the door. Flo and Sean had walked in.

'W–we know all about it,' Sean said, when Josie started to tell him about the mini cabs.

'We're just waiting for Mammy to decide if she wants to go to the church with Maurice, or Mike and myself,' Josie informed her brother in the tone she usually uses when she is in charge.

Sheila Malone pulled a pair of gloves, some letters, her

purse, and her keys, from her handbag before and said, 'Would somebody get me a glass of water?'

'Certainly,' Maurice said. His long legs made it to the door in three strides as if a tiger was chasing him.

'Do you have enough to give me a couple?' Una asked her mammy when she saw her opening a packet of Anadin tablets.

'There's no need to change any of the arrangements for me,' Sheila Malone said, keeping her eyes on her packet of headache tablets. She smiled sadly at Josie and handed her two of her tablets to pass over to Una and added, 'None at all.'

Chapter Thirty-four

All the children were down at the gate when the two new Ford Escort cars pulled away from of the house. Josie and Flo were at the hall door, and with the exception of Mammy who remained sitting in her easy chair the others watched from the window.

When all the comments and arguments about the new cars, Liam's clothes and Fred's white hair died down, Flo and Una began collecting the empty coffee mugs and Josie started brushing out Maeve's hair.

'More tea, Mammy?' Flo asked, leaning over to pick a couple of mugs off the mantelpiece.

'I'll wait until I have something to eat,' Sheila Malone replied, sighed, then pressed her head into the back of her chair, and smiled smugly.

Flo closed her eyes on her mother-in-law's smug face. 'I think that we have fergotten somethin',' she said.

'Like what?' Josie asked joyfully. She had already estimated the time she had left, and what she would need to finish brushing out all the hairs she had to do. She smiled at her daughter who was standing in front of Maeve holding the tube of hair lacquer waiting for her mammy to need it.

'The children will have to be fed,' Flo said, glancing up at the clock, 'teh reason why they were all goin' to teh grannies so early in teh first place was so that we wouldn't have te feed them.'

'What are we having?' Josie asked. She stopped brushing Maeve's hair. Her smile was warm and friendly because she was imagining she could see her young brother when she looked around the room. She waved her hairbrush as though she was going to throw it into the fire while she waited for someone to reply.

'There's sandwiches and coleslaw in the fridge. I made them myself, while Josie, Cathy and Mammy were having their bath,' Joan giggled and added, 'It's just like Liam.'

'He meant well,' Josie said, continuing to swing her hairbrush like it was a baby's rattle. She could feel Liam squeezing her shoulders. She pointed her hairbrush at Una as if she was daring her sister to argue and said, 'And he's right, my two are having a great time.'

For a second Una wondered if her sister had been drinking her hair lacquer. She had never seen Josie looking so happy. Or Josie had sneaked round to Maeve's and had a few sips of her cognac. 'I agree with you, Josie,' she said, 'that Liam always means well, but he is not always right.'

'He's right this time though,' Cathy said, pulling the stool out from under the table and sitting down. She had seen her mammy's smile. She removed her hairnet and added, 'And the cars should be black.'

'Absolutely,' Josie agreed, taking the lacquer off her daughter and said, 'Stand back, everyone.'

While Josie was spraying lacquer over Maeve's hair Flo said, 'I suppose we could get them a bag of chips?'

'My two would love that,' Una said, 'and they could eat them sitting on the stairs. God knows we have done that before now. And it will save on the washing up.'

'I'll have mine on a plate,' Sheila said, picking her handbag up off the floor.

'That settles it,' Josie said. She raised her head from brushing Maeve's hair, nodded at Una, then watched her mammy walking out of the room.

Maeve sat like a cold statue staring at the wall in front of her while Josie stood behind her and pinned up her hair. She was afraid to blink her eyes in case Josie would shout at her, or hit her with the hairbrush if she moved her head. 'We can go one better,' she said, 'they can eat them over in me ma's.'

'Cover your eyes, Maeve,' Josie called out, then sprayed hair lacquer over her head.

Mist from the hairspray was drifting towards the open window when Josie glanced up at the clock and called out, 'Do you want to be done now or after we have eaten, Mammy?' She then lowered her head to her hands and started to rub one of her fingernails while she waited for mammy to answer.

'Granny's gone upstairs,' Eileen said, pressing the top back onto the tube of hair lacquer.

'She might be gone upstairs te lie down fer a while?' Flo suggested.

'Not with all them rollers in her hair,' Cathy said, holding the mirror for Maeve. 'Josie yer getting better at yer trade every minute,' she said and prayed that Josie wouldn't spoil all the fun they were having and go running after their mammy.

'I suppose we can always hope that she's gone up to make the beds,' Una said.

'Thanks Josie it's lovely, really lovely,' Maeve said, and handed the mirror to Eileen.

'You have lovely hair,' Josie said.

'Even so Josie, it's lovely,' Maeve said, pulling at her short skirt. 'Send out fer the chips while I go over and tell me ma,' she said to Flo.

Chapter Thirty-five

Cathy moved Josie's box with her combs, brushes and lacquer to the shelf, then spread a cloth on the table. Una went upstairs to get her mammy so that Josie could brush her hair before they had lunch. Dear God, don't let me find her in bed, she prayed when she walked out the door. On reaching the landing, her mammy walked out of the small front bedroom. Una didn't know how the bedrooms were arranged so she assumed that her mammy had been in her own room. Relieved her mammy hadn't gone to bed like she regularly did when she wanted to be fussed over, she said, 'Josie is ready to do your hair now.'

Sheila moved her handbag to her other hand and walked down the stairs.

That bloody handbag, Una thought, wiping her face with her hands to clear away the memory of how irritated she gets when her mammy is fumbling in her handbag when she avoids answering a direct question. She smiled at the small bags that Maurice stacked against the wall in the hall before she went into the kitchen.

'Where are your glasses?' Una asked Joan, swallowing to hold back the tears that were gushing up the back of her throat.

'They're on the draining board,' Joan replied. 'I had to take them off because of the onions when I opened the container of coleslaw I prepared earlier.' While she tried to think of something to say about not going to see Una in London, she brought one of her hands up to her hair and started twisting a roller over her ear.

'If you mess them rollers up you won't get your glasses back on at all, because Josie will tear your eyes out.'

Joan reduced her height by an inch when she shrank her head into her neck, dropped her arm, and giggled. 'I'm sorry, Una,' she said, her eyes filling up with tears.

Jesus Christ, Una thought, what on earth for? The cast in Joan's left eye encouraged her to see her young sister as a child that was always losing her glasses. She also thought that she must have seemed like a bully to her when she used to nag her all the time about wearing the awful wiry things. She draped her arms around her young sister's shoulder and said, 'Joan, I would like you to believe me when I tell you that Jack would have made you welcome if he had known.'

For a brief moment Joan though the worst was over with meeting Una. But it passed away quickly because she knew it was a small relief compared to talking to her siblings and telling them about the real motives behind her Aunt Sue's reasons for not telling Una. But that would have to wait. By way of a compromise she said, 'I think I allowed Sue to do too much.'

'No you didn't,' Una said, removing her sister's hand from the roller she was tightening and continued, 'If Jack wants the family to see the best side of him then he is going to have to make a better effort to show it.' She smiled with tears in her eyes when she asked, 'What on earth has been going on with Josie before I came in?'

'Liam,' Joan said wiping her nose with the back of her hand. 'He made a fuss of her when he came in.'

Una nodded her head and said, 'About time too.' She hugged Joan and went back into the dining room to get the table ready for their lunch.

Una found her mammy staring out of the front window

as though she was spellbound by something going on in the house across the road. She ignored what might be going on out on the road and walked over to the table. 'What are you laughing at?' she called over to Eileen.

'She's laughin' at me bang,' Flo shouted over the buzz of Josie's dryer.

'That's not a bang,' Una shot back, 'it's a beetle fringe. A bang is a bit of hair that hangs down over one eye.' She moved a chair and said, 'Mammy used to have a bang years ago.'

'Well she won't be having one today,' Josie said. She turned off the hairdryer.

'Sit here, Mammy and I'll take your rollers out,' Una said. Josie is ready and we want to have our lunch.'

Sheila continued to stare out of the window.

'Come on, Mammy,' Josie said firmly, as if she was talking to Cathy, 'I'm starving.'

For as long as she could remember Una had wanted to hear Josie tell her mammy what to do. While she waited for her mammy to make her way over to her, she worried about what her mammy would do now to get back at Josie.

Maeve moved away from the table. She didn't want her mother-in-law to grab her arm. She hated the way her husband's mother pretended that she couldn't walk when she wanted attention. 'I'll go over to me ma now and tell her te children will be comin' over.'

Una also ignored her mammy holding her hand out as if she was having difficulty walking. She moved back towards the door to let Maeve pass and said, 'Maeve, I'm sure you mean that you will ask your ma if the children can sit in her house to eat their chips.'

'It's teh same thing,' Maeve said.

'No it's not. It's not the same thing at all,' Una returned, nodding her head at her mammy who had made it to the table.

Sheila Malone lowered her eyes to the chair Una wanted her to sit in, then dropped her small body into it as though it she had been standing for an hour and needed the rest.

Una didn't doubt that Angie would have the children. She knew that two or three of the neighbours would gladly allow the children sit around their kitchen table to eat their chips. She also knew that her mammy wouldn't have allowed any of the neighbours' children to stand in the hall out of the rain. She unwound the hairnet from around her mammy's head dropped the net into her mammy's lap and said, 'Put the rollers into that when I pass them over to you.'

Sheila moved her arse in her chair and farted.

Una removed all the hairpins from her mammy's rollers and said to Maeve, 'Don't forget to tell your ma to turf them all out again when they are finished.'

'Ah sure, they'll be no trouble,' Maeve said, smiling at Una. She pulled her short skirt down again. 'I think me ma'll be glad ev teh company.'

'Even so, it's very good of her just the same,' Josie said exchanging the hair dryer for the lacquer with Eileen and smiling over at Maeve. 'There's eight of them,' she said, 'will she have enough chairs?'

Probably not, Una thought. Angie has six chairs. Three for sitting at the table when her small family used to be at home for their meals, and three easy chairs for when they used to sit watching the television. She also knew that Josie had never been in Angie's house, and with the mood that Josie was in now she dreaded her sister suggesting that they all start walking across the road with some chairs so she added, 'Angie will manage.'

Sheila farted again.

'I'll come over with yeh,' Cathy said moving behind Josie. 'If someone will give me teh money I'll go on up fer teh chips.'

'Will an Irish tenner be enough?' Una asked, walking over to the back of her mammy's easy chair to get her handbag.

'I'll have a bag of chips,' Sheila said.

'Anyone else want chips,' Una said, opening her purse.

'I'll have some,' Cathy said, 'and yes a tenner will be enough.'

'Keep the change then,' Una said, smiling as she gave Cathy the money.

With Cathy and Maeve gone, the living room seemed to Una to become quieter and cooler. She could hear her mammy breathing and sniffing. She patted her mammy's hair and pulled at a couple of the curls to check that it was dry. 'Do you still have your headache, Mammy?' she asked. Her mammy's head felt as hard as lump of concrete.

'Not to worry,' Josie said as if her mammy having a headache was as simple as her having a pimple on her hand. She picked her brush up of the table and continued as though she was talking about one of her customers. 'I can give her something for it when she has eaten.' She pulled her stool out from the table so that her mammy would have enough space for her legs and said, 'Over here, Mammy and I'll get you done now.'

Chapter Thirty-six

Una stood at the hall door with Flo and watched Maeve run across the road. 'She's a replica for her mother,' she said.

Flo glanced up the road: 'A bit taller though. Angie is only five feet three, but Maeve's bum sticks out the same way.'

'And the freckles,' Una added, surveying the children running in and out of the garden.

Flo moved back into the hall: 'Will yeh stay here, Una, and get teh children into Angie's when yeh see Cathy comin'?' she asked. 'Then give me a shout and I'll do 'er coffee?'

'What do I do if Angie says no?' Una called over her shoulder as she walked down the garden path.

'She won't,' Flo put the catch on lock. 'Angie'll do anythin' fer Joan.' And don't ferget te get yer mammy's and Eileen's chips.'

Seventeen hours Una counted while she walked down the front garden path, recalling when she had walked around to Maeve's house. The grass on the long gardens was greener than the mountains when she raised her eyes over the roofs of the house on the bottom of the road. But the mountains were clear so she thought that the rain would wait for a few hours. She was reliving the laughs that her family had enjoyed with Liam and the taxis when she thought it was a pity that neither of her sisters Pauline nor Maura were here for Joan's wedding. She didn't consider Carl or Harry but she was sure if Jack had known about Joan he would have come with her.

'It's that awful father of his,' Una whispered to the grass, picturing Jim Byrne walking up the driveway of his house swinging his arms like he was a soldier after checking the gates were closed when the postman had turned into the house next door.

'There yeh are, Una,' a voice called over from across the road. It belonged to a tall grey-haired woman about the same age as her mammy. The woman changed her shopping bag to her other hand, then opened the gate on her garden. 'Home fer yer sister's weddin'?' she called out.

Una held out her hand as she crossed the road. 'It looks like the rain is going to hold off.' She couldn't remember if the woman's name was Mary or Brigid, but she recalled that her two eldest sons went to England at the same time as Josie. 'I suppose all yours are married now.'

'All except teh youngest,' Brigid returned, dropping her bag on the ground and folding her arms.

Una nodded though she couldn't remember if Brigid's youngest was a boy or a girl.

Brigid continued, 'Did yeh know that Patrick came back last year?'

'I didn't,' Una said, swinging her head to look up to the top of the road again, remembering that like all the neighbours Brigid would relate all the information she had on her children that had immigrated and she didn't have the time to listen. She also knew that Brigid would want to hear about herself and her sisters, and probably why Joan had come back from England. She looked up the roan again and said, 'I'm waiting for Cathy to come with the chips for our lunch.'

'The year before last,' Brigid continued as though her listener had commented on the weather, 'he was home in teh summer with his wife and two children and he got a job on teh buildin'. She went back and packed everythin' up. They're buyin' their own house now, and they're doin' grand.' She picked up her bag, hooshed it up her arm and closed the gate as she said, 'I'm goin' down fer teh bring teh children up te see Joan when she is settin' off fer teh church.'

'I won't keep you then,' Una said, turning to go back across the road. Even though she had never seen her mammy have any jaunt in her step when she was walking, her neighbour reminded her of her mammy as she watched the woman swing her handbag while she walked briskly down the road,

Una recalled Brigid's son Patrick was tall and skinny like Jack's da. Her mind went on to wonder what Jim Byrne and her mammy would be like now if they had married each other. She had them separated about six times, and for six different reasons by the time she saw Cathy at the top of the road with a large white parcel under her arm.

Cathy was at Angie's gate when Una concluded that if her mammy had married Jack's father then she wouldn't have married Jack because he would have been her brother. Also when she was calling the children, she saw that she wouldn't have her two sons either. In her imagination she was already missing them when she realised that she wouldn't have all her sisters and brothers. 'I'm better off as I am,' she whispered to the birds, darting across the road while waving to Rory to go up to Angie's house.

Chapter Thirty-seven

As she sauntered up the garden path behind Cathy, Una wondered if Jack would want to come home for good. Then when she walked into the living room and saw the sour face of her mammy, she wondered if she would want to herself. 'The place smells like a chemist shop,' she said, walking over to the back of the room and opening the top window wider. 'Sweet as the smell is it doesn't go with freshly made coleslaw.'

'Absolutely,' Josie said, turning to look at the clock. When she saw her daughter smiling broadly at her she opened her mouth wide like she was going to scream.

Please Josie, please don't be angry, Una prayed when she saw that her niece's hair was sticking out on the sides, and the top of her head. The child looked like a scarecrow.

'Cathy,' Josie murmured, smiling at her daughter.

Eileen smiled back at her mammy and said, 'She was copying you when you were doing Maeve's hair.

Josie held her back teeth together to stop from laughing at the style Cathy had created on her daughter's hair and said, 'I will do your hair like Maeve's when you are older.'

'And longer,' Una said, relieved that Josie didn't call Cathy and tell her off. Una said, 'I think that Cathy is treating Eileen like a young sister. After all they are nearer to each other's age than Cathy is to ours.'

'You know, I remember Liam saying that to me the first

time I brought Eileen home,' Josie said smiling at her daughter. 'You were only a little over a year old.'

'Cathy was twelve then,' Eileen said.

Una felt shivers run up the sides of her mouth at the memory of the first time Josie brought Eileen home. It was the weekend of Maura's birthday, and the last time the family were all home together. But it wasn't the memory of the party, or the memory of the family that was causing her mouth to feel like it was being rubbed with sandpaper. It was her mammy's behaviour during that special weekend. She had never talked to Josie about the weekend when Liam had told her that Eileen was more like a sister than a niece to Cathy.

With the shivers in her mouth calming, and not for the first time Una wondered if Josie knew why their mammy's behaviour had been so dreadful. At the time Una had believed that her mammy hadn't wanted the party. That was probably true, but her real reason had been more sinister. The shivers returned to her mouth again while she wondered what her mammy was scheming at now. She didn't doubt her mammy was unhappy because Joan was getting married. Her mammy was unhappy when they all got married.

Sheila Malone farted.

Eileen laughed loudly.

Josie looked from Cathy to Una as if she expected one of them to say something to their mammy about her health, or tell Eileen off for laughing.

Una returned Cathy's wink with a smile and called out, 'Is that a new shade in your hair rinse, Mammy?' There was no difference in the colour of her mammy's hair, but she hoped that for Josie's sake her mammy would respond to some silly praise and smile.

Sheila picked her handbag off the floor and began removing the contents.

'It is a little,' Josie lied, 'there's so many shades to choose from these days that I have tried a couple of new ones.'

'Yeh can get hundreds ev different colours fer changing yer hair in teh supermarkets now,' Flo said, coming into the room with a plate of sandwiches. She waited while Eileen finished putting her mammy's brushes and combs into the box and Una spread a clean cloth on the table and continued, 'Some girls change teh colour ev their hair as often as they change their clothes.'

'Still,' Josie smiled, 'it's good for business.'

Joan came in with an armful of plates and a dish of coleslaw. 'You sit in beside Eileen, Josie,' she said, 'and you're not even to get up to get your cigarettes.' She smiled at Eileen's hair, 'Cathy's here with your chips.' She counted the chairs, then called over to her mammy, 'I take it you'll have yours on your knee in your chair.'

'No,' Sheila replied; returning her junk to her handbag, she rose from her chair, walked over to the table and sat down in the chair that was nearest to her.

'Not there,' Joan said as though she was talking to a child. She pointed to the chairs on the other side of the table and added, 'Just move around or the rest of us will have to climb over your shoulders.'

Sheila moved to the first chair on the other side of the table. During the seventeen years since the family had moved into the house, Sheila Malone had sat at the table she was sitting at now. She had enjoyed a variety of meals and company, but none of her children had ever told her where to sit.

'All the way,' Josie ordered when her mammy moved one seat.

Like all bullies when they are bullied back they do as they are told. Sheila moved another two seats, then rested her elbows on the table.

Cathy handed her mammy and Eileen their white bags of

chips. 'Piping hot,' she said, then sat down beside Eileen, and left her mammy to spill the chips onto her plate.

'I think we should have pulled out one of the leaves,' Flo said, shoving her chair back from the table so that Una could stretch her hand in for the coleslaw.

Una didn't want to upset Josie, or Joan, so she didn't say that if her mammy removed her elbows from the table then they would all have enough room.

'Actually, I think there is somebody here that should be over in Angie's with the rest of the children,' Josie said, smiling proudly at her daughter, then bit into her sandwich.

Cathy wrapped her arm around her niece's shoulders and said, 'Eileen has every right to be here.'

Joan bowed her head to Josie and said, 'Her name might be Cullen but she is still a Malone so that entitles her to be a member of the union.'

'Fully fledged an all,' Cathy cut in.

Josie moved her head about like a mother hen: 'Don't be ridiculous,' she said, 'Eileen's too young to be in a union.' She picked up another sandwich.

'Not this one,' Joan said, winking at Cathy.

Josie had never been asked to join a union, and she had never sought to join one on her own. Mike handled all the accounts for her business and that included paying her staff, and she had no idea if any of them were in a union. She linked all demonstrations to unions. She lost business because of the miners' strike, and the power cuts, and she blamed the unions. She was terrified of any sort of demonstration and she blamed the unions on those too.

For a brief second Josie could see her young daughter walking along the street carrying a banner bigger than she was, as she had seen on the television. She didn't know what the demonstrations were about but images of women with children in pushchairs walking along the street carrying banners flashed across her mind. She inhaled deeply and glared over at Una.

'It's got nothin' te do with yer English, always striking lot,' Cathy bellowed.

'There's nothing wrong with unions,' Una joined in, opening her sandwich to add some coleslaw. 'If it wasn't for the unions getting the rest of us better wages you wouldn't be enjoying the profits you are making from colouring hair because we wouldn't be able to afford them.'

'And our fridges, and carpets,' Cathy said, bowing her head at Joan.

'Don't forget motor cars,' Joan said, winking back at Cathy. Eileen laughed.

'Motor cars are only important fer those like Josie here who can do the drivin',' Cathy cut in. 'If yeh must know she's a member of the very exclusive, BMWHF.'

'Never heard of it,' Una said, then bit into her sandwich. She chewed for a couple of seconds. She needed some time to decide if Josie was so drunk on whatever it was that brought about such a change in her temper that she thought they were serious about the union before she said, 'It must be Irish so Eileen couldn't join it anyhow.'

Josie smiled gratefully at Una.

'It's the Ballyglass Malone Women's Hardworkin' Federation,' Cathy returned.

'You can't blame me this time, Josie,' Una said, picking up her mug of coffee. She waved it at Cathy and added, 'I can drive as well, but I don't have my own car like Josie has.'

Cathy bowed her head in sympathy. 'Don't worry, yeh'll have it soon enough as long as yer husband continues with his union activities.'

'I'm a patient woman, Cathy,' Una returned, 'but I'm concerned about all the slaving that was going on here before I came in.'

'I'm a witness te that,' Joan cut in.

'I heard about Donal's hair,' Una said smiling at Joan, 'but if I had been here I might have protested against hairdressers stealing barbers' jobs.' She sniffed, 'but child labour? Now that is something I would have had to get in touch with Jack about.'

Enjoying herself now, Josie said, 'If barbers can't keep up with the changes in men's hairstyles then they don't deserve to keep their customers.'

'I totally agree with you, Josie,' Una returned, 'but I'm not so sure that Jack would.'

'Even so,' Josie said, sitting up straight.

Cathy tapped the table: '' Er union states that hairdresser are te get proper restin' times. So you are excused from doin' any washin' or tidyin' up fer teh rest ev the day.'

'Yeh might like te lie down fer a while, Josie?' Flo suggested.

Horrified at the suggestion that she was tired, Josie whipped her elbows off the table looked at Flo and demanded, 'Do I look tired?' She was enjoying herself so much that she didn't even want to leave the room to get dressed.

'No you don't Josie,' Una said quickly. She thought that Flo was going to cry. 'But then you never do,' she added, then looked at her mammy and asked, 'What about you, Mammy? Would you like to lie down while we are tidying up and getting dressed?' She was terrified the woman would start walking around and banging the doors just to get their attention. She knew there was a chance that her mammy would sleep so soundly that they would have difficulty waking her. Still Una thought they could have the wedding without her. She was sure her mammy would rally round in time to get to the hotel for the reception meal. She had done that before.

As if she was aware of what her daughter was thinking about, Sheila fixed her thin lips in a smile and said, 'I had an excellent sleep last night.'

'We must have a ghost then,' Cathy said.

'Don't be ridiculous, Cathy,' Josie said.

'I heard it too, Mammy,' Eileen said.

'Heard what?' Maeve asked.

'Footsteps on the stairs, and lights going on.' Eileen said.

'Well I never did and I'm a light sleeper,' Josie lied. She knew it was her mammy walking around the house because Cathy bounced or ran down the stairs and Joan was always very quiet when she went downstairs to the toilet during the night. Still she was relieved that her mammy didn't want to go to bed now. Her memory of the evening when her mammy lay down in the afternoon to rest was as sharp as Una's. She was about ten at the time. The funeral had two parts: one in the evening where the person who had died was taken to the church and after prayers were said they stayed in the church all night. There was a mass the next morning before the body was taken to the graveyard and buried.

Josie had liked her daddy's brother. The smell of his pipe used to stay in the house for hours after he had left. He always had a bar of chocolate in the pocket of his jacket and he would give them all two squares each. He died on a Saturday so it was Sunday afternoon when her mammy lay down and she didn't leave her bed until the Wednesday.

Chapter Thirty-eight

Cathy inhaled the scents from the assortment of cosmetics that were spread over the table. 'We wouldn't all have fitted into teh bathroom anyway,' she said.

'We'll manage,' Josie said, removing the towel from round her mammy's shoulders. 'I'll take your chair now.'

'Yer the first teh come off te conveyor belt, Mammy,' Cathy said. She didn't expect her mammy to laugh but she was surprised when Josie turned her head around to see if her mammy had fallen over. She winked at Maeve and continued, 'It has been like a factory here since ten o'clock with getting 'er hair done, and havin' 'er bath, havin' 'er lunch, and now getting dressed and putting on 'er make-up.'

'People don't come off conveyor belts,' Josie said, dipping her finger into a small jar of face cream. 'You're thinking of cigarettes and motor cars.'

Patience, Cathy told herself. Just because Josie has learned to laugh it doesn't mean she will grow brains. 'I was meanin teh principle ev movin' along and not wastin' time waitin' about,' she explained. 'Like fer instance with Eileen, Maeve and meself tidyin' up in here, while yerself and Mammy were gettin' dressed, and while Una and Flo were doin' the washin' up.

'And then us all changin' about, with Una and Flo gettin' dressed now, and they doin' their make up before us,' Maeve said.

'Exactly,' Cathy said, packing away her make-up, 'and we haven't even had te queue fer teh toilet.'

'I still don't see where the conveyor belt comes in,' Josie said, holding her hand out to Eileen for the mirror.

'She's talking about division of labour,' Sheila Malone said, in the clear and sharp voice she usually uses when she is losing her temper.

Josie continued to apply her make-up. 'Even so,' she said.

Tempted to ask her mammy what she knew about sharing and work, but at the same time she knew she wouldn't get an answer so Cathy smiled at her make-up bag and said, 'We've all done very well. Any anyhow anythin' to do with labour is union business and we don't want te be talking about that when Una comes down. Yeh know how she can go on fer hours. And I never understand half ev what she's talkin' about half ev teh time.'

'Absolutely,' Josie agreed. She was never able to understand any of Una's lectures on the unions either. 'What's in that little box?' she asked Cathy.

'False eyelashes,' Cathy said, opening the little pearly box and asked, 'Do yeh want te borrow them?'

'I tried them a few times,' Maeve said, then patted her lips in a tissue. 'I could never stick them on properly. So one evenin' Maurice pulled one of them out of his bag of chips.'

The four girls were huddled over the table laughing so loudly that they didn't hear the door bang. And they didn't miss their mammy when Joan walked in to have her face made up and her hair brushed and styled. While Josie was trying to please Cathy and Maeve with styling Joan's hair, Flo and Una went upstairs to get Joan's clothes into the big bedroom.

Chapter Thirty-nine

Upstairs the three bedrooms were cooler. The small front one that was Joan's, and now would be Cathy's was the warmest because the chimney breast from the fire in the living room downstairs, also went through the room so it was always warm.

However, it was a small room so Joan was going to get dressed in the large room that ran over the kitchen and the bathroom.

'If these rooms could talk they would tell a lot of stories about all our weddings and parties,' Una said as she passed Flo on the landing for the third time.

'Well it's a good job that they can't,' Flo returned, although she couldn't think of any reason why bedrooms should be able to talk.

'Will you ever forget Maurice and Maeve's wedding? I still can't make up my mind who was worse, Josie or Mammy.' Una chuckled, looking up from dusting a white satin shoe with a tissue. 'Today is the first time I've seen Josie be anyway friendly with Maeve since she married Maurice.'

Indeed I do; Flo thought, but she didn't say that because she also thought that although they enjoyed fun when they were having their lunch they used up too much time. She thought that they could talk about the dramatic change in Josie later. She picked up the box that held Joan's veil. 'I must say I haven't seen them together much.'

'And all because Maeve got her own hairdresser to do her hair for her wedding,' Una said, looking around the floor for a bin to put the tissue paper in. 'God, we really are a stupid lot the way we fight over silly things. I don't know why you put up with us, Flo. I really don't.' She couldn't find a bin or a box for the tissues so she left them on the bed.

Flo gazed at the white crumpled tissue for a few seconds. She wanted to tell Una that she didn't really have a family of her own. She hadn't seen or heard from her sister or her brother since her daddy had died. She was about to say that silly fights are a lot better than hard-hitting and beating ones when she noticed the bundle of envelopes on the end of Joan's bed so she asked, 'What are they doin' there?'

'Bring them into the room with you,' Una said, glancing at her watch. The sounds of the children laughing and calling out in the front garden reminded her of the time. 'Joan brought them up. She wants to open them herself first. I think she's expecting something special from Pauline or Maura.'

When Flo was walking across the landing after Una with the cards tucked under her arm, the hall door burst open and an unwelcome breeze fluttered into the hall followed by all the children.

Josie said, 'We mustn't forget to take that key out of the hall door before we go.' She held her hand out to Eileen for the hair lacquer. 'Cover your face, Joan,' she shouted, then sprayed so much lacquer over Joan's hair that all the children started coughing.

'How're yez all doin?' a soft nervous voice said from the doorway.

Josie stopped flapping her hand in front of her face to disperse the mist from the hair lacquer from her eyes when she saw the pink plastic spectacles resting on the bottom of a small nose that was stuck to the small face peering around the door. When the short, wiry body followed the grey hair with the ponytail into room, Josie recognized Maeve's mother.

The table was still over beside the back window, and Sheila Malone was still sitting in her easy chair at an angle to the door. When she heard Angie Dolan's voice she leaned her body towards the fireplace, picked up her handbag and began searching through it.

Because she was sitting down, and her head was lowered for Josie to spray her hair with the lacquer all Joan could see was tatty slippers on small feet, and the narrow bottoms of her friend's trousers. 'Come in,' she said.

'I thought that yez all might need somethin' te settle yer nerves, so I brought yez this,' Angie said, placing a long brown paper bag on the table. She peeked over the top of her glasses at Josie, then turned back to the easy chair and said, 'Yeh look very smart, Mrs Malone.'

Sheila raised her head from her handbag, fixed her skinny lips in a smile and nodded her head to the side of her son's mother-in-law's face.

Angie knew her daughter's mother-in-law well enough not to wait for a reply.

Harvey's Bristol Cream, Cathy read the label on the bottle of sherry when she removed the paper bag. She didn't like sherry but she liked Maeve's ma so she said, 'It's just what we need right now, Angie.' She nudged Josie in her arm. 'And nobody deserves it more than Josie because she's been slavin' all mornin.'

Dear God, Joan began her prayer when she saw Josie staring at the royal blue bottle. Please God, don't let a bottle of sherry spoil the last hour of my time before I leave the house. She doubted her younger sister knew that Josie didn't drink alcohol. 'Cathy's right, Josie,' she said, and you certainly do deserve a treat for all your hard work, but I wouldn't be a bit surprised if you would prefer a nice cup of tea.'

'Not in the least,' Josie replied quickly. She was determined to remain one of the girls. 'What about us all going to Holy Communion?' she asked.

'And what do yeh think is in teh Holy Communion but bread and wine?' Cathy said. 'If we have a little drop now then all we're doin' is havin' an early start.' She bowed to Josie, 'And anyone who wants te can pray while they're drinkin'.'

'I didn't know it was that kind of wine they used,' Josie said, smiling at the bottle of sherry as though she was being friendly with it before she drank it.

'It's not,' Cathy replied peeling the wrapping from around the neck of the bottle. 'At least I hope they don't put as much vinegar in this one. If teh Catholic Church used this stuff fer teh Holy Communion they'd charge us fer teh walk in teh door.' She pulled at the cork on the top of the bottle for a few seconds then held it out to Josie and said, 'here your hands are stronger than mine. Get the plug out of that while Angie and meslf get us some glasses.'

Angie trotted out of the room after Cathy. 'Take yer time,' she called out when Cathy was walking into the kitchen. 'Yeh don't need te get yer dress spilt on with anythin'.'

'I'm only gettin' a few glasses,' Cathy replied.

'Even so,' Angie replied, 'them little puff sleeves weren't made fer stretchen yer arms so tell me where teh glasses are and I'll get them.'

'We only have ordinary water drinkin' glasses,' Cathy said, pointing to the lowest shelf in the new cupboard over the small table in the kitchen. 'It will be safer fer me te get them,' she added, stretching out her right hand and taking one of them out.

'Safer?' Angie shouted, lifting her spectacles up on her nose.

'Yes safer,' Cathy replied, taking another two glasses out of the cupboard. She placed them on the table, nodded her head down to the small women and said, 'I'm delighted that yeh came over, and I admire yeh fer bein' in teh same room as me muther wearin' them slippers, but yer not getting on a stool teh reach teh glasses wearin' them.' She moved some cups about, looked over to the draining board pointed to a couple of glasses and added, 'Yer tatty slippers won't stop yeh from dryin' up them two.'

Chapter Forty

Joan was climbing the stairs when she saw Una standing on the landing pointing to her watch, so she picked up the bottom of her dressing gown and took the steps two at a time.

'We have everything I can think of in there,' Una said stretching out her arms so she could direct her sister into the big bedroom.

'There's something I still want to do.' Joan said pointing a finger towards her own bedroom.

'If you mean your cards I brought them in as well. Let's get you into your dress first and you can sort them while I'm stitching you into it.

Flo sat on a low stool under the window to the back of the house slitting the tops of the envelopes with a nail file and handing the cards to Joan. 'There must be over sixty here,' she said passing the third card over to Joan. She opened the last card she had placed on the bed asked, 'Is there something to write with here?'

'What do you want something to write with for?' Una asked.

'I could write the names of teh bundles on these and leave them on teh bed,' Flo said, holing up two envelopes. 'I can't remember where I am puttin' te ones from the family, teh neighbours, and teh Beggars Lodge.'

Though barely audible, a young clear voice said from the doorway, 'I could take them out of the envelopes.'

Una stopped stitching and with Flo and Joan she watched in silence as the door slowly opened and Eileen poked her head around it. 'You could use three different coloured envelopes for the different piles if you want to,' Eileen said. She looked over at Joan, then Flo, then up at Una, as though she needed permission from all three of them to come into the room.

'Now why didn't I think of that?' Flo said, taking Eileen's arm and steering her over to the stool. 'You sit here, and you can take teh cards out of teh envelopes and hand them te Joan. I'll go over to teh other side and when Joan passes them te me I'll put them inte their different piles, and I'll use teh coloured envelopes.'

After fifteen minutes Una had tacked the dress on Joan. Eileen opened the last envelope and handed a white sheet of paper to Flo.

Flo wasn't a fast reader but she could distinguish the difference between the alphabet and numbers. She read the first sentence and the numbers before she looked at whom the letter was for because she knew it couldn't be for Joan. She could only imagine how the letter had found its way into Joan's bundle of cards. She decided there was no need to tell Joan so she shoved the letter under her bum.

With her little lap empty of greeting cards, Eileen jumped up from her seat and left the room when she heard a loud cheer downstairs.

Una secured a single string of pearls around Joan's neck, then stepped back as far from Joan as she could with the bed in her way and said, 'Well Flo what do you think? Will she do?'

Pearls for tears, Flo thought, nodding her head in approval at Joan in her wedding dress. It would be another twenty-six hours before tears would flow, but it wouldn't be Flo or Joan that would cry. 'Yeh look lovely?' she said. She didn't want to get off the bed because she was sitting on the letter, and she didn't want Joan to know about it now so she said, 'You two go down while I tidy up teh bed.'

Una could hear the children in the hall waiting for Joan to come down and she also knew they wouldn't want to see her so she held her hand out and said, 'Age before beauty, Joan.'

As Joan was walking out the bedroom door, Flo caught Una's hand and said, 'I think you need to see this.' She retrieved the letter and handed it to Una. 'It was in Joan's bundle of cards.'

Una had seen other letters like it before and she remembered how her mammy had behaved when they had arrived. 'I'll keep this,' she said, holding her hand out for the envelope. 'Was it opened before Eileen took the letter out?' she asked, examining the back of the envelope for signs that her mammy had opened it then stuck it back again.

'I can't be sure if it was,' Flo said.

'There's no need to say anything to the rest of the family, and there's nothing we can do today,' Una said, recalling her mammy coming out of the front bedroom after lunch, swinging her handbag. She guessed her mammy had deliberately put the letter into Joan's bundle of cards so that she would find it. She pictured her mammy's face when her mammy learned that it was her difficult daughter who had found the letter. She smiled at Flo and said, 'I will deal with it later but for now let's gather the cards and go down and join the party.'

Together they opened up one of each coloured envelope and wrapped them around the different bundles of cards. Flo wrote the names of the groups so that Joan would know them, and Una wrapped some thread around each bundle to keep them together.

'What about teh rest of teh envelopes?' Flo asked, gathering them into one pile.

'I suppose they can go on the fire,' Una said, 'but Joan might want to keep them so bring them down as well and she can decide.'

Chapter Forty-one

When Una and Flo walked into the living room, Josie was arranging Joan's hair.

'I left your cards on the hall table Joan,' Una said, stealing a glance at her mammy who was staring out the back window as though she was admiring the birds. 'I also left the envelopes in case you wanted to keep them.'

'Can I have teh stamps off them, Joan?' Eileen asked.

'Of course you can,' Joan said, 'take them now before we put them on the fire. I will only need to keep the cards.'

'I'll take them off for you,' Sheila Malone said, getting out of her chair.

'I'll bring them in for you,' Una said, 'you can do them sitting where you are then put the envelopes on the fire.'

Sheila tossed her head back and said, 'I'll do them out in the kitchen,' then walked out of the room and left the door open.

Like Una, Flo suspected her mother-in-law was going to search through the envelopes for the letter they had found. She worried that her mother-in-law would find an excuse for not going to the wedding if she didn't get some attention so she called out loud enough to be heard in the hall, 'Don't ferget that yer mammy has te have her hat put on, Josie.'

Right now Josie didn't care if her mammy never wore a hat. And she didn't want to see the one she had bought her. 'We're all right at the moment,' she said, holding the veil up in the air to fix it on Joan's head. When Joan stood up and turned around to her she inhaled deeply as if she was going to scream.

Joan put her arms around her sister's neck and said, 'Thanks Josie. Thanks for everything.'

Watching his two nieces embrace, Fred felt lonely for Sue. He thought how pleased his wife would be if she saw them. He recalled the time they had taken Josie and Eileen to the airport on the Friday evening after Maura's birthday party four years ago and Sue had said that Josie should give less attention to her selfish mother and more to her sisters. He though how pleased she would be to see her now. He was smiling at the warm expression on Josie's face when he saw her staring at Joan's neck.

Fred didn't know anything about pearls or any other precious stones. Sue had told him the pearls were worth a lot of money. She couldn't make up her mind which of Sheila's girls to leave them to so she left them to Eileen. She had said the pearls had belonged to her Granny Duffy's mammy and that they were even older than that.

Fred knew his wife was dying when she told him she had never worn the pearls when she was with Sheila because she was afraid to remind her sister that their mother had given them to her even though she wasn't the eldest daughter. She also told him if she left the pearls to any of Sheila's children that Sheila would find a way to get them. Sue also believed that her sister would sell them, and she was confident that Mike would never allow that to happen if they were Eileen's.

'They were Sue's pearls,' Una said.

'I know,' Josie said, 'she left them to Eileen.'

'We only have to make sure she has something blue now,' Una said. 'The pearls are old and borrowed.'

'Give her a good dollop of blue eye shadow.' Cathy said, nudging Josie in her arm.

'I'll do no such thing,' Josie retorted, turning round to Cathy and slapping her back on her hand.

'We could give her a couple of bruises?' Una suggested, winking at Fred.

'Put a blue envelope in her shoe,' Eileen said.

'I'll get one,' Una said, jumping at the idea of going out to the kitchen to see what her mammy was doing with the envelopes. She found her mammy sitting on a stool with her back to the door, tearing the stamps off the pink envelopes when she walked into the kitchen. 'I want one of the blue envelopes,' she said, noticing all the white ones were in a sloppy pile. 'We want to put some of it in Joan's shoe.'

Sheila Malone picked up another pink envelope, looked inside it, then tore the stamp off the corner and placed it on top of the sloppy pile of white ones.

Stupid woman, Una thought, suspecting her mammy would think she would put the letter into one of the other envelopes. She was tempted to ask her mammy if she was looking for something, but she was afraid her mammy would tell her. She didn't want to give it back to her until she had shown it to the rest of the family. She was determined to get her siblings to work with her to stop any more of the same letters coming in through the letterbox. They would have to for Cathy's sake who would now be living on her own with her. They had to. She picked up one of the blue envelopes, tore the stamp off the corner, placed the stamp in the pile her mammy had made with the others, then threw the envelope into the pile and left the kitchen.

Chapter Forty-two

With his emotions dancing around in his chest, Fred stayed standing beside the ironing basket, watching and listening to Sheila's daughters argue about something blue for Joan. All his anxieties about coming up to the house and seeing Sheila melted, and he was glad to be here.

Two weeks after Sue had died, Fred stopped coming up to Plunkett Road to see Sheila's children. They were the only family he had known since he had married Sue. He still wanted to stamp on Sheila's foot every time he remembered how she used to walk around the house when he came in. He missed Sheila's children.

Although Sue was gone nearly five months now, Fred was still learning he had lived a very selfish married life. His cooking was dreadful but he had lost his appetite and he didn't care what he ate. It had taken him six weeks to discover that carpets needed to be hoovered at least once a month, and that the vacuum cleaner had its own space under the stairs.

Christmas was the hardest time for Fred when the cards started to drop through the letterbox. He had drunk half a bottle of whiskey before he had admitted he was every bit as selfish as Sheila. Sue always did everything. She had even told him when the grass needed to be cut.

While Fred was missing his wife, Joan thought if it was all right for Josie to have a couple of sherries before she went to holy communion then it must be all right for her to laugh when she says a prayer. She laughed at Una cutting the blue envelope into a shape to fit into a shoe and thanked God for her family.

Sheila Malone came back into the room, sat down in her easy chair and farted.

Anxious about the time when Joan reached the door on her short journey to show her family how she looked now that she was ready to leave for the church, Flo called out, 'It's your turn now, Mammy.'

Josie pulled her chair back from the table and said, 'Would you hand me over the bag that's on the basket behind you, Maeve?'

Sheila Malone farted again as she was getting out of her easy chair and walked slowly over to Josie.

Una didn't wear hats but she knew her fashions. The upside-down, white, net-covered, paper basket that Josie was securing on Mammy's head was over ten years out of date.

'That's grand, Josie,' Flo lied.

'Just the job to give her some height,' Una said, wondering how Josie had allowed her mammy to buy it.

Josie looked at Una and her eyes said; "you were not in the shop with me when Mammy had insisted on having it."

Una had no idea what Josie was thinking, but she understood the sad expression in her sister's eyes, so she smiled as if she knew and said, 'Now that we are all ready I suppose we could sing a song while we're waiting.'

'You go ahead if yeh want te, Una,' Cathy said, 'but I'm savin' me voice fer teh church.'

'I agree with Cathy,' Josie said. She was too embarrassed over her mammy's hat to sing.

When Cathy turned round to put Josie's brushes on the bookshelf, her eyes fell on the family photographs spread over the wall. They reminded her that Joan would not be coming home to stay after she left the house and her other sisters would be going back to England when all the fun was over. They always did. She closed her eyes tight and willed herself not to think about it.

Growing up in a large family had been easier for Cathy than it had been for her older sisters. She had never had to care for, or worry about younger siblings. She had enjoyed freedom from housework and played out on the streets as much as her sisters would have done if they had been given the same opportunities. But she had the same mother, and as her sisters and brothers left home and her mammy was out most of the time there were times when she was very lonely.

Josie closed her eyes at her mammy's hat and called out, 'Well, we're all ready in time.' She cast her eyes around the room and smiled at all the new clothes and lovely hairstyles and said, 'I must say that we all look very smart.'

'Indeed we do,' Una agreed. She thought Josie looked like a young girl, and Cathy looked lovely with the flowers in her hair. 'But right now I could mess up Josie's hair.'

They're still the bloody same, Fred whispered into his neck. He wanted to slap Una while he watched her move about the room.

'What fer?' Cathy bellowed.

'Her trouser suit,' Una said, calmly brushing the long skirt of her petrol blue polyester suit, and then patted her size sixteen hips. 'I'd give my eye teeth to be slim enough to get into one and look that good.'

'Yer too old te have any eye teeth,' Cathy said.

'She doesn't have any teeth,' Josie said, laughing so heartily and for so long that Cathy had to hold her arm.

'Jeasus,' Fred whispered again while he watched Josie try to stand up on her own for the third time.

Cathy was also laughing when she shouted out, 'Josie, yeh should laugh more often. Yer very good at it and it really suits yeh.'

Mortified, and with tears in her eyes, from laughing, and from shame at what she had just said, Josie pleaded, 'I'm sorry, Una,' she inhaled deeply to suppress her laugh, 'I don't know what made me say that.'

'I can't argue,' Una said, smiling, while she thought of saying; it is the sherry, Josie. She had always been ashamed of her teeth. She was the only one in her family that should have had dental care when she was child. By the time she could afford to go to a dentist, her teeth needed so many repeated fillings that she eventually had to have them all extracted.

During their years growing up, the two sisters had always fought, but Josie had never said anything offensive to Una before. 'Cathy is absolutely right,' she said, 'and so are you, Josie, about the teeth, and so am I about the suit. You look terrific.'

Watching and listening to the girls bantering, Fred felt angry with his God. He doubted that all the gaiety would last because he had watched them fool and laugh about before, and the laughing usually ended in tears. But just the same he thought that God could have allowed Sue another six months.

Sitting in her easy chair by the side of the fireplace, holding her handbag in her lap, Sheila Malone raised her face from the floor to her laughing daughters a few times as though she was looking at strangers.

Watching Sheila, Fred wondered if at last she had pushed them all away from her, and they didn't care about her any more. Even Josie appeared to have forgotten her mammy was in the room. Shuffling his way out of the corner towards the door, he touched Una on her waist. When he tried to move, he felt her catch hold of one of his hands. 'The cars are here,' he said, pointing to the door with his free hand. As she was standing in front of the fireplace, she was just in front of her mother and he didn't want talk to Sheila.

'You look smashing,' Una said, turning round and placing her hands on her uncle's shoulder, and kissing him on the side of his face. 'Sue would be right proud of you,' she continued, struggling to hold back her tears when she saw the sadness in his moist eyes.

'I know Una, I know,' Fred whispered in her ear. His sadness eased and he laughed lightly. He should have known that Una would be the first one to say something about Sue. He was sorry he had wanted to slap her because he knew that she was right. Sue would be delighted with them all and Una was right to say so. He felt like his heart was going to break when he smiled at the glistening eyes of Sue's nieces and said, 'I know she is very proud of the whole lot of us.' He hugged Una, then straightened his tie and walked over to the door to join Mike, Donal and Liam in the hall.

Chapter Forty-three

Mike Cullen never shouted, but his voice always carried to his intended listeners. As if something had tapped all the girls on their shoulder at the same time, they turned round to the door where Mike was standing after they heard him say, 'Everybody ready to go?' He rubbed his hands together with enough energy to set his fingers alight.

Like all the men, Mike wore a black morning suit, white shirt and bow tie. He nodded to his mother-in-law and said, 'Mammy,' then to Josie and said, 'My dear, then to Una, then Flo, then Maeve, and Cathy. He walked over to Joan and he was about to take her hands when she put her arms around his neck. He closed his eyes and held her for a few seconds and whispered, 'God bless you, dear.'

'I think he has already,' Joan whispered back to him.

'I see we're all here anyway,' Mike said, rubbing his hands together again when he had stepped back from embracing Joan. He was always rubbing, wringing or squashing his fingers or his hands.

Liam said that Mike was practising for the day when he would have the courage to strangle Josie.

Apart for Una, Mike never really knew his wife's family until Joan came to stay with them. He had stayed in Plunkett Road with Josie after they were married, but few of the family had been there at the same time. Una and Jack came for tea in Kent and Mike and Josie went to Dagenham for tea but he had never been excited by, or about any of these visits. They always had a lovely meal, admired a newly decorated room, or newly acquired piece of furniture, and listened to Jack prognosticate about the unions and the labour party.

It was no surprise to any of the family when Josie married a man that was ten years older than her. Or that he was quiet. He suited Josie because she was also boring. Mike was five-feet seven, slim but not skinny. He wore his hair combed back from his forehead in the manner of George Raft. He showed more energy today with rubbing his hands than at any other time he was with the family.

Una didn't know whether she did or she didn't like Mike. There were times when she thought he agreed with her when she argued with Josie but he had never taken her side. He had never taken Josie's side either, and although he never argued with Jack against the Labour Party he never agreed with him either. 'I'll get the children's bags,' she said. Mike reminded her that Jack should be here with her.

Maeve followed Una: 'Yer man'll rub his hands away if he keeps on like that,' Maeve said.

'I think we frighten him a bit when we're all together,' Una returned.

'Yez frighten us all when yez are all tegether,' Maeve giggled, 'I think yez even frighten each other sometimes.'

Una thought of her husband again and she wondered if her family frightened him as well.

The hall door wasn't caught on the latch and it began to slowly open so Maeve walked back over to close it again. On hearing a group of children laughing, she looked out into the garden. 'Would yeh take a look at that,' she called and opened the door wider instead of closing it.

'Now what's the matter?' Una asked, coming out of the kitchen with her cigarettes. She walked over to see what Maeve was staring at.

'This is me ma's idea,' Maeve said, opening the door all the way to reveal about twenty laughing and smiling children lined up along both sides of the garden path. They had little plastic bags with coloured bits of paper in them. The voices of everyone talking at the same time drowned out the chatter of the children when the door to the living room opened and Donal came out followed by Mike and Josie.

'Have yez got all teh children's bags ready?' Donal asked, then, without waiting for an answer, he stepped out on to garden path and looked up and down the road and said, 'They're all here.'

'Who's all here?' Josie asked, following her brother's gaze down the road. She didn't know any of the children, and all she could see on the road were parked cars.

'You go ahead, Mike,' Donal said. 'You two get ready as well,' he said to Una and Maeve. 'All the mini cabs are here.'

'Get Mammy, Josie, we three are on our way,' Mike said, moving back into the hall so that his wife could go into the living room for her mammy. When Josie hesitated, he snapped, 'It's time we moved.'

Josie didn't want to go. 'Why us?' she asked.

Mike pushed in the door to the living room, and waved his hand at his wife to get her mother.

Surprised that Mike had spoken so sharply to Josie, Donal said, 'We have te move, Josie.'

Josie didn't want to go with her mammy so she continued to hesitate.

'Don't worry, Josie,' Donal said, 'we'll see to teh children.' He waited until she had gone back into the house, then turned to the small crowd of children and nodded his smile to the ones he knew.

Chapter Forty-four

Mike put his hand on his mother-in-law's arm and steered her over to the door like he was going to throw her out of the house. He knew by the expression on her face that she didn't want to go with him, but he tucked her hand under his elbow. He had promised Liam he would bring her out of the house first, and if he had to drag her down the road, then that was what he was going to do.

With her mouth closed tight, Sheila Malone smiled at Donal before she walked down the garden path on Mike's arm. She lowered her face to the ground when the children started to cheer.

'What car are we in?' Josie asked, bringing her hand up to her head in case the slight breeze would blow her hat off, or Donal would take it off her. Her brother had never spoken so rudely to her before and for a few seconds she was afraid of him.

'Teh blue one,' Donal said, pointing down the road, 'it's teh last one on this side. Tell Mike te take it easy because we want te get all teh children off before we go.'

'The Escort estate?' Josie exclaimed, although she had no idea if the car was any good – but it was new. She smiled at her brother, then followed her mammy down the path. Because her mammy was walking slowly, Josie caught up with her. Sheila Malone always walked slowly when she was worried. When she was worried and angry she walked very slowly.

Before Mike had left his home in Kent for the airport he had already counted the years since when his sister used to be happy. While he waited for his mother-in-law to make up her mind about moving one of her feet another inch, he said a prayer for his sister Theresa. He calculated that she was a lively ten-year and two-month-old little girl when she used to play her dolly steps games. He didn't know how Theresa and her friends measured the winners and losers of the games but Theresa never won any of them because her feet were big.

When he felt Josie's mother pulling on his arm like she was wanting him to slow down, Mike wondered if his mother-in-law wanted to go to the wedding at all. They were near the car so he unhooked his arm from her tight grip and walked round to the other side of the car.

While she was taking her time to get into car, Mike smiled at the memory of Liam when his young brother-in-law went over all his plans for the day before they left Bella's house. Liam had been adamant that his mammy was to be out of the house before Joan. 'Take your time, Mammy,' he said and continued to think about his youngest brother-in-law and wondered how long it was since Liam had taken his mammy for a walk.

But just the same a flaw is a flaw, Mike told himself when he felt his mother-in-law pull on his arm again as he was helping her to get into the car. He made a mental note to tell Liam he would probably need an ambulance for his mammy if she wanted to go to the next family wedding.

It was when two black mini cabs pulled into the kerb in front of Tony's car that Mike agreed with Liam about why the car that he was driving needed to be parked so far away from the house. He smiled again when he thought that he should have put his mammy into one of the mini cabs to take her down to this one.

Seated behind her husband in the car, Josie said, 'We have a radio?' She beamed at the small rectangle box that was on the dashboard of Tony's car.

'It doesn't work until I turn on the engine,' Mike said. He was about to close the door of the car when music from the strumming of a couple of guitars was nearly drowned because the children starting to sing, 'You must have been a beautiful baby.'

Busy examining the inside of the car, Josie didn't see Joan and Fred when they came out of the house. She inhaled the scent of the new plastic and polish then asked, 'Is this Tony's car? She hoped that her mammy wouldn't light a cigarette.

'We have it for the week,' Mike said. He moved the mirror over the dashboard to try and catch Josie's reaction, but all he saw was her head moving about because she was still examining the inside of the car is if she was a detective looking for clues in a murder enquiry.

'Of course, I forgot,' Josie said, bowing her head in approval. 'They are going away tomorrow.'

Mike started the engine so he could turn on the radio for Josie. He needed to do everything he could to please her until he told her he was going down to Limerick on Monday. There was nothing he could do about it now but he thought Josie should be back in the house having fun with her sisters. God knows she needs all the fun she could get before he told her about his father.

After Donal closed the doors of the bridal car and the neighbours were running around the road, Mike rolled the window back up again.

'Is the cigarette lighter working?' Josie asked when she saw her mammy with a cigarette in her mouth fumbling in her bag. She still didn't want her mammy to smoke but she also knew that her mammy wouldn't stop panting down her nose until her cigarette was lit.

'Tony removed it,' Mike said, and continued to watch the

neighbours rush about to the few cars that were still on the road. He was anxious to get Josie and her mammy down to the church, but he didn't want to knock anyone down before he had left the road. He wondered if Liam remembered how many neighbours the family had when he said, 'Tony doesn't approve of smoking.'

Josie had only met Tony a couple of times and she had found him to be very pleasant and polite. When she saw her mammy drop her cigarette into her handbag, she wondered if her mammy was afraid of him rather than believing that her mammy didn't like him. Her mind went back a few days to when her mammy had gone into town on the day that Tony was coming up for dinner.

Mike watched five adults and a child work their bodies into a mini, then eased the car away from the kerb. Ten minutes later, a sharp light breeze tossed his hair when he opened the door of the car outside the church. He prayed Josie's mammy would feel chilly because it might make her walk a bit faster. Unfortunately for Mike's tired legs, Sheila Malone showed no more enthusiasm for attending her daughter's wedding service than she did when she was walking down Plunkett Road to his car.

People were taking their seat in the church while he worried about Una with every step he took. He had left her sitting behind the steering wheel of Tony's new car. He prayed that she wouldn't have to drive it away. The calves of his legs were exhausted when his prayers were answered. He forgave Liam for the flaw in his plans when he saw him making his way up the aisle of the church towards him.

After Liam took charge of Josie and her mammy, Mike ran back out of the church. He found Una sitting in Tony's car with the engine running. He opened the door for her to get out so he could get behind the wheel.

Una wanted to laugh at the serious expression on Mike's

face. 'Just giving myself a driving lesson,' she said, turning off the engine and checking to see the hand break was on.

Mike ran both of his hands across the crown of his head then said, 'I thought you'd passed your test.'

'I have,' she replied, sliding her legs out the door. 'I now have to learn to drive.'

Mike nodded his head in approval, then got into the car and drove it to the car park in the nearby supermarket and was back at the kerb to help Donal when the children arrived.

Chapter Forty-five

The buzz of murmuring voices ceased as if they had been startled by a loud shout when Mike took his seat in the first pew beside his mother-in-law. Josie sat on the other side of her mammy. Una sat beside Josie.

Una nodded her head over to Tony and Liam. She then cast her eyes over the flowers around the paintings and statues. Although she wasn't very religious she liked churches. She always saw them as palaces that belonged to everyone who wanted to sit in the seats and pray. She nudged Josie and said, 'They look nervous.'

Josie thought about Tony and her mammy again. She remembered that her mammy didn't like Una's husband Jack either but she couldn't say that to Una so she said, 'All the boys look great.'

'Including Mike,' Una lied. She had never seen her sister's husband untidy, and even when he wasn't wearing a tie he appeared as if he had only just dressed. So it wasn't unusual for her see him looking smart. But she thought he looked tired, and his face was paler than usual.

When the organ started to play for Joan coming down the aisle, Josie smiled approvingly while she watched her husband take hold of her mammy's elbow, and assist her mammy to stand up – as if her mammy was incapable of standing on her own. She was still a little worried because he had spoken harshly to her about getting her mammy before they had left the house, and not allowing her mammy to smoke in the car.

She turned to Una and whispered, 'I don't know what has got into Mike.'

Una hadn't heard Mike when he had ordered Josie to get their mammy, but she wondered if Josie also noticed her husband looked tired and pale. She thought she was cheering her sister up when she suggested, 'Perhaps he had a pint with the boys before he came up to the house.'

Josie delivered Una a hard stare as though her sister had told her that Mike was guilty of a serious crime. 'Certainly not,' she snapped. 'Mike won't even eat trifle if it has port wine in it.' She closed her eyes at Una as if to tell her sister she should be ashamed of herself.

Fred drank in and returned the smiles from all the neighbours and Joan's friends, while he walked slowly down the aisle with his young niece on his arm. When he saw the frown on Una's face he followed her gaze down to his feet. For a brief second he wondered if he hadn't tied his shoelaces, or if he was still wearing his slippers. When he raised his head Una had her back to him.

All the family knew that Mike didn't drink. And like others of his generation he had taken the pledge when he had made his confirmation. And like a few from generations before him he never broke it. Una knew that none of the family ever thought any the less of Mike because he didn't drink. But just the same she wondered why Josie had been upset about suggesting that Mike had had a pint.

The organ was droning to a stop when Una decided that she didn't have enough room in her head right now to worry about Mike Cullen's diet or drinking habits. She stood for the start of the mass, and she responded automatically to the service. Her mind was on weddings, marriage and partnerships. She stood, knelt, and sat at all the appropriate times. She said, 'Amen' and 'And also with you' along with everyone else like she was joining in the chorus of a song. The quietness and calmness of the church cleared her head of all the excitements that had been swimming in it since she had left Heathrow Airport less than twenty-four hours earlier.

'Ting-a-ling, Ting-a-ling.' The soft sweet sounds from the small gold bells the altar boy was swinging interrupted Josie's thoughts. It was some years since the mass was being read in English, but it had never made any difference to Josie because she never understood what was going on in the service. The responses like standing and kneeling were all still the same, but she liked to go to mass because she always felt refreshed, and living in England she felt close to her family and her home country.

The church that Josie was praying in now was bigger and brighter than the old one she usually went to in Kent. She could hear more whispering, and the ceiling was so high she felt her thoughts were flying away as soon as they came into her head. But she was able to relive all the fun she had enjoyed when she was standing behind her special chair. When she lifted her head up to the altar again she wondered briefly how her two youngest sisters became young women so quickly.

Una wondered how she had looked to the rest of her family, and her friends when she was kneeling just outside the same altar more than ten years earlier. 'God almighty,' she whispered in her throat as if she was praying, 'where has all the time gone?' She remembered she was very happy on her wedding day, and she was looking forward to starting a new life in a new country with new people. Jack was already working and living in London. His wages were nearly twice what he had been earning in Dublin. She was also expecting to get a good job in London. There was a shortage of trained and experienced dressmakers in the West End. She wasn't afraid of anything.

There was a long and slow procession for Holy Communion because all the neighbours especially the children from

Ballyglass slowed down at the altar gates and smiled at Joan and Cathy.

It was customary for the family that were sitting in the front rows to receive Holy Communion after the bridal group. So this gave Una and Josie some time with nothing to do but study the altar, or watch the other communicants as they knelt in front of the priest. Or study the bridal group, or pray. At first there was a quiet, though clearly audible scraping noise from the sound of feet shuffling down the centre aisle. This grew to a buzzing sound when the communicants returned to their seats and started whispering after they had prayed for their special intentions.

Una's communion prayers were short. She asked her daddy and Sue to look after Joan and see that she was happy in her new life. She didn't know what else to pray for so she sat up on her seat and stared at the green moulding around the wall. She thought how much nicer her sister's ceremony was compared to her own wedding.

Today everything was so much brighter. Joan and Tony were sitting inside the altar at an angle towards their family and friends. Una felt it helped them all to be included in the service. When Jack and she were married they had their backs to everybody all the time.

When Josie sat up after brushing the knees of her suit, Una nudged her gently in her elbow and said, 'She looks happy, doesn't she?'

'She looks lovely,' Josie returned as though Una has spoken about the weather. Her thoughts were on her prayers. She had prayed that her new house would be finished soon. She thought that Cathy might like to come over to stay with her for a couple of weeks. She could work in her salon for a few days to see if she would like to be a hairdresser.

Unlike Una, Josie never nursed memories of her young siblings. There were so many of them, and she always had her mammy to worry about. She had enjoyed the bantering from

Liam and Cathy so much during the morning that it was the first time she saw them as individuals instead of the children that had surrounded her all her life when she had been living at home. While Josie was enjoying the memory of her morning, Mike stared at the wide alcove that housed the altar as though he was thinking of redecorating it when he noticed a small statue that reminded him of his sister Theresa.

The figurine of Saint Jude, the patron saint of lost causes, stood about eighteen inches tall and it rested on a corner shelf between two doors that led into the side of the church and the back of the altar. It was taller than the ones Theresa kept on the windowsills in his family home in Limerick.

Josie had only been to Limerick once, and when they were on the road to Cork city to catch the ferry back to England she never wanted to set foot in the place again. They had stayed with Mike's sister Theresa in his daddy's house. Everything about the big house on the old street had reminded her of a large house in Arbour Hill with front gardens. The rooms were dark and they were all painted brown. She hadn't minded when Theresa had said that her daddy wasn't well enough for extra visitors. She had seen the hospital from the distance and it resembled a prison. She always thought about Limerick at the end of April because she knew she had become pregnant with Rory when she had been there.

Looking lovely, and looking happy were not the same thing at all to Una. While Mike was wondering about the lost cause his sister Theresa prayed about all day, Una thought about a woman she knew in London who always looked lovely. But the girl wasn't happy. Her husband was constantly hitting her. She wasn't going to say this to Josie so she joined her sister in smiling over at the four young people sitting inside the altar. She suspected when the priest smiled down at the half-filled large church he was asking if everyone that had wanted to had received communion. He smiled approvingly at her mammy before he turned and went back to the little gold house at the back of the altar and locked up his gold chalice again.

'I can't get over how pretty Cathy is,' Josie whispered to Una.

Not for the first time Una wondered what Josie saw when she came home. Cathy had been pretty all her life. She remembered her promise to Sean, not to argue with her but she thought she would take advantage of her sister's good humour and tell her about her worry over Cathy so she said, 'I'm a little concerned with her being on her own now that Joan is married though.'

'She won't be on her own,' Josie returned, 'Mammy will still be there.'

God almighty, Una thought, will Josie ever open her eyes to how useless their mammy was and still is to them all. 'That's right,' she returned, then closed her eyes and said a prayer for Cathy. She then thought about the letter in her handbag and said a prayer for her mammy.

Chapter Forty-six

Walking out of the church with her mammy holding on to her arm, Josie assured herself that if her mammy raised her head to respond to her comments about the mass, then her hat would roll down her back. She was also sure her mammy would agree with everything she had said about the wedding ceremony. So she had chatted away to her mammy's hat for the five minutes it took them to walk up the aisle of the church.

Josie's height allowed her to see over the heads of all the bodies that were pressing against, and jostling with each other to get out of the church. Although the centre of the church was darker than at the top where the altar was, or the door where some light came in, Josie was able to sort through all the people and identify her family and friends. None of the neighbours wore a hat.

Sheila Malone lowered her head to her feet again when she saw Josie's husband was standing in the bright sunshine just outside the porch of the church. Mike moved his eyes from the top of his lovely wife's face to his mother-in-law's hat while he contemplated asking her if she wanted a wheelchair.

By the time Sheila Malone took two more steps towards him, the top of Mike's body leaned forward as though he had been hit in the back. He nodded a laugh at Josie while he slapped his hands together so that he could wipe a sudden thought from his mind. He didn't know what he would do if his mother-in-law had said, 'Yes Mike, a wheelchair would be nice,' if he asked her.

Enjoying a feeling that he had told a joke, Mike smiled brightly. He knew that his mother-in-law didn't need a wheelchair. 'All the family are around in the grotto,' he said as he held his hands out like he was going to sing a song.

'For the photographs, I suppose?' Josie said.

Mike thought Josie would be able to join her family if she could get away from her mammy. He also knew Josie wouldn't get a chance to talk to anyone with her mammy hanging on to her. 'Mammy looks tired,' he said. 'When we are done with the photographs I'll bring her over to the coach.'

Josie's mammy let go of her arm and walked sprightlily over to her friend Ena.

'I never noticed how long that church aisle was before,' Josie said.

Neither had Mike. He recalled that he thought he would never reach the front seat when he was walking his mother-in-law up the aisle until Liam came up and took his mammy. 'A distance always seems long when you are walking slowly,' he said, taking her arm and steering her over towards Una.

By the time the last photograph was taken, the light breeze had grown to a soft wind. Everyone who was going to the reception meal were making their way over to the church gates to get on the coach that was to take them to the hotel. There were two black cars inside the gate. One had white ribbons on the bonnet. This was to take Joan and Tony. The other one was to take Cathy, Donal and Liam.

While everyone was talking about how nice Joan looked and admiring each other's outfits and hats, Mike was staring at his mother-in-law's backside sticking out of a black car so he didn't see the white hat roll away into the bush. He didn't see Josie run after her mammy's hat because he was watching Donal make his way over to the car his mammy was getting into.

He had forgotten about her since she had joined her friend; he had assumed that she would spend the rest of the day with Ena.

'Leave her,' Donal said, catching Mike's arm and pulling him away from the car.

'I never thought that she would be able to walk off like that on her own,' Mike said.

Neither did Donal. He couldn't remember seeing her walk anywhere. He watched Maurice run after his mammy's hat while he wondered how he would get her out of the bridal car.

Maurice retrieved his mammy's hat from under a bush gave it to Josie and hurried after everyone to get on the coach to get away from having to be involved with getting his mammy out of the car she was sitting in.

'Your mammy can come out with me,' Mike said, pointing to a flag flapping in the breeze from the top of the supermarket at the back of the church where he had left Tony's car. 'It won't take me a minute to get the car and bring it round.'

From where he was standing Donal could see the grotto. He saw Liam posing for photographs with Angie and some of the other neighbours. He had no idea how he was going to get his mammy out of the bridal car. 'We'll sort somethin' out Mike, when Liam comes over.' He knew that whatever car his mammy went out to the hotel in it wasn't going to be the one she was sitting in now.

The white hat flapped in another light wind when Josie was walking towards Donal and Mike. 'It's fine,' she said, holding her mammy's hat out to Donal.

'Good,' Donal said, smiling at the hat his sister was holding out to him. He had no intention of arriving at the hotel with his mammy's hat so he said, 'You look after it for her.'

Josie looked at the hat, then at Donal, then into the car, then back to her brother and using her mammy's hat to point to the car her mammy was sitting in bellowed, 'She can't go in that.'

Sheila Malone pulled the door shut with a slam so loud that Josie jumped.

'We'll take care of everything,' Donal said, putting his arm around Josie's shoulders and steering her away from the bridal car. He rescued his mammy's hat from her hands, turned to Mike and added, 'You go ahead too. We need yeh te be at teh hotel before any of teh cars get there.'

Chapter Forty-seven

From where she was sitting in the coach, Josie could see Joan, Tony, Cathy and Liam walking over to the big black cars. She suspected when she saw Liam talking to Donal they were discussing her mammy. Instead of worrying about her mammy like she normally would, she closed her eyes to shut and thought about the fuss her youngest brother had made of her when he had come into the house. She was smiling when people started getting on the coach.

'Yer hat's garges, Josie.'

Josie raised her head from her lap.

'Wasn't yer sister lovely, Josie?'

Josie pulled in her chin while she said, 'Yes she was.'

'Did yer mammy get her hat back all right, Josie?'

The three young girls moved up to the back of the coach before Josie decided that she had no idea who they were. But she noticed that they were all young, so they were probably Joan's friends. She was flattered that they knew who she was, and their happy faces reminded her of Cathy.

By the time the family were making their way over to the coach they had all heard about their mammy getting into the bridal car. The story was told around the white hat, and they found it so funny that nobody thought of asking how the seating was going to be rearranged between the two cars.

'Will yez all take yer seats down there in teh back,' Sean called out from the front of the coach where he was standing beside the driver. 'Bella,' he mumbled, then looked down the coach.

Una knew her brother was referring to Tony's gran. She turned round and looked down the coach. She saw a small woman wearing a pink hat move her head out into the aisle and wave up at Sean. Sean counted heads again, then said to the driver, 'We are all here.'

While the coach driver waited for a break in the traffic so he could pull out into the main road Josie saw four young girls all dressed the same. They were wearing their school uniform. She turned sharply round to Sean and asked, 'Why didn't Joan have the reception in the school hall?'

'It's not teh d-done thing over here,' Sean returned and stared at his sister for a few seconds like he was checking his memory to make sure that he had heard her right. 'Nearly all w-weddins are in hotels these d-days.'

'I just wondered,' Josie said, recalling she had hired the school hall for her wedding reception. The school had been so near the church that everyone had walked to it.

'It's money, Josie,' Sean said. 'In our day weddin's were much smaller and teh breakfast was at home because not many people could afford teh hotel.'

'And certainly not if they wanted te get married when they were young,' Flo added.

'Also,' Una continued, 'we never used church halls here for weddings like they do in England.' She also recalled they were just as much work as having a wedding at home. And that was with or without a marquee like she had had. She remembered going round to the church hall in Kent to help clean up after Josie's wedding.

'We all have m-more money these d-days,' Sean bellowed.

'Thanks to the unions,' Una added.

'Probably,' Josie said. She had no idea how the unions had given people more money for weddings. But she enjoyed the memory of laughing with her sisters when they had joked about Eileen being in a union. Reliving the memory helped to dampen some of the hurt that kept jumping into her mind over her mammy slamming the car door in her face.

Money, bloody money, Una tossed the word around in her head. She squeezed her handbag as if she could make sure the letter wouldn't jump out and fall into Josie's lap. She was determined that this time Josie wouldn't see the letters before her brothers. She decided it was about time they learned about their mammy's spending habits. She closed her eyes so she could think about what she should do and when.

'Wow,' the passengers in the back of the coach sang together when the wheels on one side of the coach went over the pavement as the driver eased out of the church grounds. To keep from dozing off as the long heavy vehicle rocked out on to the road, Una counted the hours since she had left her house in Dagenham. For a few seconds she hungered for the routine of her life in London – with her two children, her house, her part-time job in a boutique, and her evening classes.

It was ten o'clock when the children had stirred Una from her slumber that morning. She was still tired but she hadn't wanted to go back to sleep. She needed to come to terms with the shock and anger over what had happened to Joan before she would be able to lay her head on a pillow again.

Physical activity was always Una's therapy for coping with her temper. So after she had washed and set her hair, then pressed her suit, she ironed all the clothes in Maeve's basket. When she brought the freshly ironed clothes up to the bedroom she was tempted to lie down on the bed and sleep. But she knew if she did her mind would only go over the events of last night again. While that coach cruised along the main road into town she tried to imagine what her mammy would have spent all the money on in one store.

Chapter Forty-eight

Yeh d-don't have te come down t–this way any more,'
Sean said, leaning forward so that the coach driver
would hear him.

'Just givin' yez a jant,' the driver said, depressing the brake
pedal. 'Me orders are te take me time so that teh other cars can
be there before us.'

Sean nodded his head, smiled, then joined everyone else on
the coach and looked out of the window.

The old high stone wall, and the railings of Glassnevin
Cemetery brought Una's thoughts to when she used to see it
twice a day on her way to and from work when she was living
at home. She sometimes travelled on the crowded bus with
Josie. Josie never had anything to talk about so she was poor
company. She found other people to chat to on the half-hour
journey into town. A burst of laughing from the back of the
coach broke into her thoughts and encouraged her to recall
how heartily Josie had laughed when they were all waiting to
leave for the church.

As if Josie had been reading Una's thoughts, she turned her
head away from the window and smiled. It was the warmest
smile Una had ever seen on her sister's face. Josie wasn't thinking about when she used to travel on the bus to work because
she never allowed her mind to think back. She was recalling
her morning still with her family and all the people Liam and
Cathy had introduced her to while the photographs were be-

ing taken. She smiled at the memory of a small lady Liam had brought her over to meet and said to Una, 'I am surprised at how small Tony's grandmother is.'

'When did you meet Bella?' Una asked.

Surprised at Una's question, Sean turned round and frowned at her.

'I have never met her,' Una said to her brother.

'I'll go down and bring her up,' Sean said, nodding his head at the empty seat beside Una. The coach was swaying so Sean stayed behind Bella when he was bringing her down to meet his sister.

'Sorry,' Bella repeated as she passed down the aisle of the coach when her handbag bashed on every head, or shoulder from her handbag swinging on her arm.

As Bella settled in her seat, Una recalled her mammy's wedding photographs. Her Granny Duffy had worn a hat much the same as Bella was wearing now except that her Granny Duffy's had probably been made from real straw. The wide brim made Bella's small face look tiny. She also saw that when Bella moved her head her hat stayed in the same place because it was too big for her. Bella patted her hat on her head, then Sean knocked it off again as he passed her to get to his own seat.

Una suggested Bella remove her hat and give it to Josie to keep with her own. She took the small hand from Bella's lap and said, 'I am really pleased to meet you.

'And I am delighted to meet you at last,' Bella returned, placing her other hand on top of Una's.

'I think I have been a bit rude in not talking to you sooner, but I was caught up with my boys,' Una said, feeling Bella's small hand soft and warm. 'They don't know whether they are coming or going with all the excitement that has been going on since we arrived last night.'

'Don't give it another thought. I understand,' Bella said, nudging Una with her elbow. She tilted her body sideways into the aisle of the coach and moved her head between Josie and Una and said, 'It must be great when yer all together.'

'It has its ups and downs,' Una said before Josie had time to think of a reply and prayed that her sister agreed with her.

'I'll bet there are more ups than downs,' Bella said.

'Yes, there are,' Una replied, nodding her head and raising her eyes over to Josie who was now examining Bella's hat like she was thinking of either ripping it up or buying it.

The two hats Josie was pressing into each other were refusing to stay together while she tried to recall 'ups' and 'downs' in the family. She always avoided thinking back on her childhood but now she imagined she could hear the cheers from her family when she was cutting Donal's hair. 'Una's right,' she said.

Pleased Josie hadn't argued, Una said, 'We've never had a fight yet when someone didn't win, and we have had hundreds of laughs.' She smiled into Bella's small bright blue eyes and added, 'I only hope that Tony knows what he has let himself in for.'

Josie wouldn't have said hundreds of laughs, but she recalled the awful pain in her side when she couldn't stop laughing over Una's teeth. She smiled at the memory when she raised her head from torturing the hats.

Bella knew that Josie had her own hairdressing salon in a posh part of Kent. She assumed when Joan's lovely sister was looking at her head that Josie was inspecting her hair. Convinced that her hair was all messed up because of her hat, she raised her arms and started to pat both sides of her head.

Bubble cut; Josie thought watching Bella pull at her almost snow-white, neatly curled short hair. 'I wouldn't worry about it,' she ordered, 'the hat will only flatten it again.'

Taking Josie's comment to be official, Bella dropped her hands into her lap. From what Joan had told her about her sisters, she had deduced Josie bullied them all and that she was snob. She hoped she was saying the right thing to the lovely elegant girl when she said, 'Your husband Mike is a real gentle-man.'

Josie bowed her head as though she was accepting applause for a speech or singing a song.

Bella continued, 'He kept calling me Mrs Murphy until Liam told him that if he didn't stop and start calling me Bella like everyone else he would take him back to the airport.' She then shrank her head into the neck of her pink crimplene coat and tugged on Una's hand and laughed.

Una returned the tug on Bella's hand said, 'I think Mike is really enjoying himself today.' She smiled at Josie and said, 'I wish he was able to give Jack some of his patience.'

Josie couldn't think of anything nice to say about her sister's husband so she said, 'It's a pity that Jack's not here.'

Sean frowned, he couldn't think of anything to pity Jack for. He worried that his two sisters would argue over their husbands.

'Jack's my husband,' Una said, closing her eyes at Sean's frown. She tried to think of a lie to explain why he wasn't with her. She hated telling lies; one lie always led to another, then another. She also believed that not telling about something was the same as telling a lie. Right now her heart was telling her that Jack would have been here if had known what had happened to Joan.

'I know,' Bella replied, 'I know his sister Freda.'

Una didn't want to talk about any of Jack's family. She squeezed Bella's hand again and said, 'Tony has two more sisters to meet yet.'

'He'll b-be blessed among w-women like teh rest ev us boys,' Sean cut in, laughing loudly at his joke. He hoped that Una wouldn't want to talk about their sisters in Canada.

'He'll get used to us all in time,' Josie said, thinking back to when Joan had stayed with them in Kent and how good Mike had been to her. She recalled her mammy went out when Tony was coming up to dinner but the memory passed and was replaced with her siblings. She nodded her head to Una and said, 'Jack and Mike haven't had any problems.'

Una nodded agreement and went on to recall that both Mike and Jack already had a sister. She had met Mike's sister once when she came over to Kent for his wedding. She found the girl as snobbish as Josie. She was tall and had a long face. At forty she was four years older than Mike but Una thought she looked nearly fifty.

'Ah s-sure all families are d-different,' Sean said, recalling that Tony didn't have a mother or father. He also felt sorry for Flo when neither her sister, nor her brother came home from England when she was married. To move the conversation away from their own family he said, 'I w-worked with a f-fella years ago that n-never came on teh site on a M-Monday because he used te h-have te go around D-Dublin lookin' fer his m-mammy.'

'Every Monday?' Josie said sounding appalled.

'She u–used te set off fer teh pub on a F-Friday evening after Fergus c-came home with his w-wages.'

'That's a whole weekend,' Una gasped. 'If he knew what she was going to do then why did he give her the money?'

'S-she was his m-mother,' Sean said, smiling. He was delighted he had moved his sisters away from their own families. 'All teh other fella's use te a-ask him that and he always said t-that she w-was also a great c-cook.'

'God almighty,' Una gasped again, 'he must have known that he was helping her to kill herself.'

'I d-don't know about that,' Sean giggled, 'but teh two ev them were happy enough.'

Bella had never been in Plunkett Road but she knew all the family as if she was a neighbour. She had known the Malone boys since Tony was about eight, and he used to bring Donal, and sometimes Maurice home after football matches for something to eat. She was as happy as Tony was when he told her he was going to marry Joan. She loved her grandson, and she believed he was happy, but she was sure if he hadn't had Donal's friendship he would have been very lonely.

'Tony is delighted to be getting five sisters today,' Bella said, smiling at Josie.

'And that's the way it should be,' Flo cut in. 'Anyway Tony has known yez all fer years.'

So did Jack before he married me, Una thought. She smiled down at the smooth pink of Bella's forehead and asked, 'How do you know Freda?'

'She works in Frank's,' Bella said raising her head to Una.

'In the factory?' Josie asked, sounding shocked. She remembered Jack's sister had gone to The Holy Faith Convent School. She was surprised that anyone who went to a convent school would be working in a factory.

'She works in accounts and sales,' Bella told Josie.

Una was used to her older sister looking down her nose at factory workers. Before she left for England nearly everyone in Dublin did. There weren't many factories, and they mostly employed girls and women. Girls like her and Josie whose parents couldn't afford to send them to secondary school.

Luck had been responsible for the jobs that many girls like Una and Josie had been able to get in the 1950s. Josie was available for work the same week the local hairdresser needed an apprentice. Una wanted to learn dressmaking. Two weeks after she sat for her primary certificate a friend of her aunt Sue's knew of a small factory that was looking for a girl so Una got the job.

Like her sister, Una loved her job, and although she had earned a very low wage when she started at fourteen, she had worked hard and learned her trade. She had her sisters to practise making clothes for and by the time she was sixteen she was making for her sisters' friends.

'I have never been in a factory,' Josie confessed, then sidled back to the seat near the window.

Sean was surprised to learn that the Freda Byrne he knew from the Beggars Lodge was Jack's sister. He knew she had gone to school with his younger sisters and that she worked with Bella and Cathy.

'We should have brought er togs with us,' one of Joan's friends shouted out while the coach was rolling along the Malahide road.

Surprised they were so near the hotel, Sean went up the driver so he could see out of the large front window. He noticed the sea was like a sheet of glass with tiny white waves breaking on surface near the sand. He turned and called down the coach,'Yer welcome to a swim in that, girls, but it would be too cold fer me.'

'Go way with yerself, Sean, yer too old,' the girls chorused back.

He waved to the girls then bent down to Bella and said, 'Well Bella, d-do yeh still t-think yeh will be able te c-cope with us all?'

'I'll manage, Sean,' Bella returned, shrinking her head into her shoulders.

Chapter Forty-nine

The aroma of coffee, Guinness, and whiskey hit Una's nostrils when she walked into the warm foyer of the hotel in front of her sister. 'Yes please,' she said to Mike, 'I would love a cup of coffee.'

'Me to,' Josie agreed, raising her eyebrows at the framed pictures hanging on the wall behind the long table that was full of white cups and saucers. She didn't try to make any sense of the overlapping squares and circles of the paintings while she waited with Una to congratulate Joan and Tony.

'It feels most peculiar to be standing in a queue to kiss your sister,' Una said, nodding her head over to Tony and Joan who were standing at the bottom of a staircase that was the width of four ordinary doors.

Mike spilled coffee into the two saucers when he was walking across the foyer into the bar behind his wife and her sister. He was surprised and pleased that his wife was laughing. He expected her to be brooding over her mammy not going in the coach. He prayed the good humour between the sisters would last because he was sure that Josie was going to need Una's friendship when he told her why he was going to Limerick on Monday.

All the tables in the small lounge were occupied with at least two people sitting at them. 'I hope we aren't intruding,' Una said when she pulled out a small stool at the table her mammy and Bella were sitting at. She wasn't surprised to see

Bella's face brighten. She could just about see the bright smile behind a pint of Guinness. She noticed that her mammy had nearly finished her glass of scotch and thought she must have tossed it back in one go because they couldn't have been there more than five minutes.

'Now what would you two ladies like from the bar?' Mike asked, placing the two coffees on the small round table and rubbing his hands together like he was getting fit to fight his way to the bar.

'I would love a dry sherry,' Una said, winking at Bella who had been staring at Mike's hands.

'And you, my dear?' Mike asked his wife.

'The same,' Josie said, remembering the sweet and fruity scent that burst out of the bottle that Angie brought over to the house when she was setting Joan's hair.

'Two dry sherries then,' Mile sang and bowed like a waiter before he walked away.

'What is the difference between a dry sherry and a sherry?' Josie asked, as she moved her eyes from the half-full pint glass of Guinness to the smaller clear glass that was in front of her mammy.

'I have no idea Josie,' Una said, 'I just thought I'd try to impress Mike because he's working so hard.'

'Does Cathy drink sherry all the time?' Josie asked.

'Cathy doesn't like sherry all that much,' Una said, smiling at Bella. 'I don't think anyone does really except the upper and middle classes. They always have a sherry before dinner.'

'Angie isn't middle, or upper class,' Josie cut in, 'she's just like us.'

Yes Josie, just like us, Una thought, smiling in agreement. 'Angie knows what they're like because she has spent most of her life working for them,' she said, opening her handbag to get her cigarettes. 'You should sit and talk with her sometime. She has some great memories of the lengths they go to, and the things they do to avoid paying their bills.'

'A dry sherry is not sweet,' Sheila Malone said. She drank the last of her scotch and added, 'I prefer a dry one myself.'

Josie pointed to her mammy's empty glass and asked, 'Do you want one now?'

'I would prefer a scotch.'

'And you, Bella?' Josie asked, moving to get up off her chair.

'No thank you, Josie,' Bella said, putting her hand on the top of her large glass as if Josie was going to take it away. 'One is enough fer me fer a couple of hours.'

Josie didn't agree. She thought that a glass of alcohol that size should be enough for a woman as small as Bella for a couple of days. 'Dry or sweet?' she asked her mammy.'

'Teachers,' Sheila Malone said, smiling sadly at her eldest daughter as she added, 'it's the name of a scotch whisky.'

'A double dry Teacher's,' Josie recited before she drank some of her coffee then went after her husband.

I like Bella; Una thought of Barbie dolls, and she was sure that if she ever saw a granny doll it would look just like Bella. Soft grey curly hair, pink skin, bright blue eyes, and a small mouth with pearly teeth. They would be dressed in blue or pink. Her mammy looked smart in navy and white, but as a granny she didn't have the softness of Bella.

When Josie came back to the table, Flo was sitting in her chair and Tony was kissing Bella. There was less space and more bodies around all the tables. All the guests had arrived and they were waiting to be called in for the meal. Sean found a stool for Joan and Josie.

'Some small quiet wedding,' Josie said. She could never tolerate a lull in a conversation, and she usually said something related to what was on her mind. Some of Joan's friends were in the bar drinking with Cathy, and Cathy had called her over and introduced her to them all. She was now intoxicated on a cocktail of praise from Cathy and her friends over all the hairstyles, and a glass of sherry. It encouraged her see the wedding was much bigger than what it was because she had spoken to more people than she knew.

She means well, Sean thought, stretching his arm out between Una and Flo to take his pint off the table. He also thought Josie was right; the wedding was much bigger than Joan had wanted. The only thing small about it was the short time it had taken to arrange everything.

'We only have sixty sitting down,' Tony said, moving back from the table a couple of steps and extending both of his arms like he was going to give them all a blessing and smiled broadly at Josie.

'Really,' Josie said, holding out her glass like she was going to throw the contents over her shoulder and announced, 'I had that many, but it only seemed half the size.'

The family smiled and watched her drink half of the sherry in the glass.

Tony stared into his mother-in-law's cold face like he was telling her he knew Donal had taken the white ribbons off the car she had been sitting in before he told the driver to take her out to the hotel on her own.

From as far back as Tony could remember he was able to feel people looking at him. When he started school and he mixed with many other children he knew the stares were because of his brown skin and tight curly hair. By the time he was sixteen he could read people's thoughts by the expressions in their eyes. Watching his mother-in-law puff on her cigarette like she always did when she was angry, he hoped she would read his eyes now that he was telling her he would never allow her to bully Joan again.

'Well here's to teh both of yeh,' Flo said, holding out her glass, 'and yeh'ed better make a good job of yer lives tegether or teh neighbours'll be wantin' their singin' back.'

'I'll drink to that.' Una held her glass up to Mike who was standing behind Bella with his hands on the back of her chair as if he was protecting her from an imagined onslaught of something.

Mike released his hands from Bella's chair. 'What will you have to drink?' he called over to Tony.

'No, no,' Tony said, bringing his hand up to his face like he was fending off a blow. 'I'll get the first drinks.'

'Yer a b–bit late fer that,' Sean said, moving back from the crowded small table so he could survey the happy faces and enjoy the peel of laughing he was getting for his joke.

'Can we have thirds?' Flo asked, hoping that Tony would know she was joking because she thought if Josie had another drink she would start singing.

'Thirds?' Sean smiled over at Bella. 'Are we all o–on er t–thirds already?' He waited a couple of seconds because he was expecting a clap for his second joke. He enjoyed the laughing for a few more seconds before he winked at his young sister as he said, 'Joan yed b–better smarten that man ev yers I–if he's te s–stay in teh c–clan. It's time he l–learned how te count.' He raised his glass to Bella.

If Tony hadn't been half black African his face would have turned red. But he enjoyed listening to, and watching his gran join the rest of his new family applauding Sean.

Chapter Fifty

Joan, Donal and Bella stood at the door into the restaurant and watched some of her relations and friends scurry around and between the tables picking up and putting down the little white cards,

'What are they all doing?' Joan asked.

'It looks like they're changing the cards around,' Bella laughed.

Tony wanted to have a balance of relations and friends sitting at all the tables. Two weeks earlier Bella had spent an evening around her kitchen table with Joan shuffling cards with names on them between seven bundles so that they would mix and match all the guests.

It was usual for the guests that were invited to the reception meal to, enjoy coffee or, a drink from the hotel bar while they waited to be called into the dining room. As Joan was the third Malone to be married in Dublin, few of the family and their friends were strangers to each other. During the hour when they were in the bar everyone moved about and mixed while they exchanged news and gossip. They refreshed their friendships and some of them wanted to sit together.

Donal couldn't see what difference it made so he said, 'There's nothing we can do about it now.' He was also hungry.

'At least I tried,' Joan said, laughing with Bella. She was so happy with her day so far that she didn't care where anyone sat. She also prayed that her mammy had done her worst with refusing to come out to the hotel in the coach.

Half an hour later the wedding party were seated and had been served their starter.

'This is just like teh old days of Henry teh eight,' Cathy said to Liam, inserting her spoon into her watermelon.

'And how do yeh make that out?' Liam asked, raising his head from his food. He ran his eyes over the people that were sitting at the seven round tables in the centre of the large room for a clue as to why Cathy was thinking about any royal family.

'Well,' Cathy said, nodding her head out into the large room, 'if we had a gun we could shoot them all.'

'They didn't have guns at teh time of Henry the eight,' Liam said passing his cherry over into his sister's dish. 'But, who would yeh shoot first then, that is, if yeh had a gun?'

'I don't want te shoot anyone,' Cathy whined, 'I was just sayin' that we could, from here, if we wanted te.'

'I see, well is there anyone that yeh would like te throw teh cherry that I've just given yeh at, from here, because yeh could, if yeh wanted te?' Liam asked.

'Not now,' Cathy said, softly raising her head to the tables. 'But yesterday I think I would have liked te have thrown two cherries and an apple at Josie, that's fer sure.'

'When I was your age I would have thrown four cherries and four apples at Josie from here, if I could, and I wanted te,' Liam replied, looking out at the tables to see where his eldest sister was sitting.

Cathy broke her bread roll open while she glanced out at the tables again and wondered what Josie could have done to upset her brother four years ago. Especially since he had praised her so much this morning.

'Don't look out like that,' Liam said, leaning over and whispering, 'she'll know we're talkin' about her.'

'So what!' Cathy returned, spotting Josie was chatting away

to her mammy's best friend, Ena. 'Everyone keeps looking up here, so that means they're probably all talkin' about us.'

Liam sat back in his chair and fiddled with his bow tie. 'I suppose yer right there, and I'm sure they're talkin' a lot about you.'

'I don't see why. I've been very good,' Cathy pouted. She always knew when she had been difficult, and she had always had her reasons. She smiled at her favourite brother and said, 'It's been a great day so far.'

'Yes Cathy it has,' Liam returned. 'It's been a great day.'

When the plates were being cleared after the main course, Cathy wiped her mouth with her napkin and said, 'I don't know how we get er food down, we do so much talkin' while we're eatin'.' She waved down to Josie's table and continued, 'Anyway it was a lovely dinner.'

'Are yeh wavin' at Jose or Ena?' Liam asked, nodding his head down to the table where Josie and his mammy's friend were waving up to him.

'The two ev them,' Cathy said. 'Yeh don't like Ena, do yeh?'

'I don't mind her,' Liam lied, 'but why do you like her?' He couldn't think of any reason why any of his siblings would like the tall woman who spoke loudly and wore her long grey hair in a plait down her back.

'I don't know her all that well, but I'll never ferget her fer me brown gloves,' Cathy said, sitting back in her chair to enjoy the memory of when Ena had bought her gloves when she was ten.

'And when did yeh get yer brown gloves?'

'Fer me confirmation,' Cathy said, and sat back in her chair to enjoy a brief memory of her brown gloves. 'I was in Cleary's with mammy fer te get me shoes and we met Ena when we were lookin' at teh gloves. I knew that mammy was goin' teh buy teh yelleha knitted ones even though she made me try on all teh other lovely ones she had asked teh girl te show her.'

'So Ena bought yeh teh gloves,' Liam said, recalling when his mammy used to buy his shoes. He hated having to try on every shoe in the shop that would fit him. He came near do doing his wee in his trousers the time when she had asked him to try the heavy boots on for the second time.

'She did,' Cathy said, recalling the feel of the gloves when she had tried them on, 'but I didn't know that at teh time because I was plannin' te steal them.' She moved the fingers on her hands like they were swaying to music: 'God, Liam when I felt them soft gloves on me hand I thought there was magic in them because they felt so light. I was cryin' when I had to take them off.'

'Were they light or dark brown?' Liam asked. All he could remember about when Cathy made her confirmation was that his daddy had died a couple of months earlier.

'Dark chocolate brown, and I knew that Mammy wasn't goin' te buy them,' Cathy continued, 'so te hide me face I said that I had a pain in me belly and I went off to teh toilet.'

Liam wanted to hug her. He had never missed his daddy, and on the day after his daddy's funeral when his two older sisters returned to England he believed that his two younger sisters were better off without him. He had a long memory and all he ever saw his daddy do for his sisters was to encourage them to please his mammy. 'Tell me what yeh were plannin' te do.'

'Well, when I was in teh toilet I checked over me knickers te make sure that teh elastic was tight everywhere. I was goin te go back te teh girl and have her show me all teh gloves again, then when she wasn't lookin' I was goin te put teh magic ones up leg ev me knickers.'

'But yeh didn't,' Liam said, easing his arm around the back of her chair.

'I didn't even get teh chance te try them on again,' Cathy as though she was going to cry, 'because teh pair ev'em were waitin' fer me at teh bottom of teh stairs.'

'De yeh think that Ena knew what yeh were up te?'

Cathy continued as though she hadn't heard her brother: 'I could hardly see teh lovely wooden door when I was leavin' teh shop because me eyes were all full ev me tears again. I only knew I had me bus fare because I could feel teh coins in me hand. I never said goodbye or anthin when Mammy put teh bag with me shoes, and teh yelleh knitted gloves inte me hand. I was cryin' really bad when Ena put her big hand on me shoulder and gave me another bag. I thought that it was a pair ev socks so I didn't say thank you, or open teh bag until I was on the bus.'

'And yeh found yer gloves,' Liam said, pulling her head over to the side of his face and asked, 'What did yeh do with teh yelleh knitted ones?'

'I sold them to a girl in school.'

'Is she comin' this evenin?' Liam asked.

'Te tell yeh truth, Liam, I can't remember,' Cathy said, looking along teh table to where her new brother-in-law was sitting, 'I asked Tony how many I could have and he said as many as I like.'

'So how many is that,' Liam asked

'I made a list of thirty, but right now I can't remember who was on it,' Cathy said and laughed.

Liam laughed with her.

Cathy knew her brother wanted to find out about one particular friend. She had spread the rumour herself a few weeks ago. Right now she thought she would tease him so she continued, 'I think I added one or two back again, but I don't remember who they were.'

'Are they all boys?' Liam asked. He didn't like what he had heard about a lad called Donald that Cathy had been seen with. And neither Donal nor Tony could find out anything about him. Liam didn't know Ballyglass any more.

'I can't remember,' Cathy lied.

It is six years since Liam had worried that his friend Brian was going to stay in Ballyglass to save the village instead of joining the English Air Force with him. Brian wanted to prevent the Dublin Corporation from building a new road through the village to Belfast. The village wasn't destroyed but the housing estate had more than doubled. There was now an east, a west and a north Ballyglass. Liam didn't meet anyone he knew on the bus when he went into town the last time he was home.

Still, Liam thought while he contemplated asking his young sister about her boyfriends, at least more people have better homes now that the tenements were nearly all torn down. 'I hope yer not two-timin' any ev teh poor young lads in teh football club,' he said.

Cathy moved her head so that the waitress could place her dessert on the table as she said, 'There's nothin' poor about any ev teh lads in teh football club.'

Liam liked a black forest gateau, and Josie made the best he had ever tasted. He felt a stab of shame because he had never thanked her for all the meals she had cooked for the family when she had been living at home. It was for Joan's sake that he had made a fuss of her when he had come up to the house. He wondered if he really knew her at all. He always believed she lived in a world of her own where she only saw what she wanted to see. He was thinking out loud when he said, 'People can be surprisin', sometimes.'

'Are yeh thinkin' ev anyone in particular?' Cathy asked dipping her spoon into her brother's dish to take some of his cream.

'Do yeh still have yer gloves?' Liam asked, tapping Cathy's spoon.

'I kept teh tips ev teh fingers fer a few years.'

'The tips ev teh fingers?'

'I had teh cut them out when me hands started teh grow so that I could move me fingers.'

Liam smiled.

'Yeh can't do anythin with gloves on yer hands if they don't come all teh way down,' Cathy said pressing the fingers on one of her hands down into the skin between the fingers on her other one to show her brother what she meant. 'Why de yeh want te know about me gloves? It was years ago now.'

Liam didn't really want to know about the gloves; it was something to talk about because he didn't want to talk about Josie so he said, 'I just thought that yeh might still have them because they made yeh so happy.'

'I was only ten at teh time,' Cathy said, and I really loved them gloves and I'll always be grateful te Ena fer buyin' them fer me.' She waved down to her mammy's friend again.

Ena's heart was heavy with jealousy when she waved back to Cathy. This wasn't the first time she had felt jealous of her friend Sheila but it was hurting much deeper than ever before this time. She had never envied Sheila when her friend had told her she was pregnant again, and again. Like Fred she could count eleven pregnancies, but unlike Fred she could remember them all.

The large room buzzed with everyone talking when they were drinking coffee. Champagne and orange juice were served and a small bell rang to silence the room for the speeches. Fred toasted the bride and groom. He also toasted Cathy and the rest of the family.

Tony's speech was also short; he thanked everyone for coming to his wedding, and he hoped they would all have a good day. He also thanked Fred for the reception. He left the jokes to Liam and when Liam sat down everyone forgot about Tony's weak performance.

Donal delivered a short speech for the Murphys. He promised his siblings that Tony and Joan would add a few little lodgers but no beggars to the family.

Chapter Fifty-one

I t must've cost hundreds,' Cathy said to her brother. She thought that Tony was paying for the wedding.

'It did,' Liam replied.

'Did yeh know?' she asked. 'I mean about Fred payin' before now?'

'Yes.'

'Did Mammy?' she pressed.

'I doubt if she knew,' Liam said and for the first time he thought about Cathy living on her own with their mammy now that Joan was married and he wondered how she would manage. He felt a little guilty because he knew that he would never go back to Plunkett Road to live. When he stole a glance at her face and saw her moving her eyes about the room as though she was trying to find somebody in particular he said quickly, 'It was just Joan, Tony, Donal and meself that knew.'

'She'll be livid fer weeks,' Cathy said, folding her arms, and continued to search the room.

'I don't see why,' Liam said, leaning back and putting his arm around the back of her chair. 'Fred has saved her some money.'

'No he hasn't,' Cathy retorted, slapping her hand on the table. She remembered Joan buying all the paint and wallpaper when the house was decorated. And she knew that her mammy bought new curtains, and bedclothes in Barents on the weekly. She also knew that her mammy was expecting Joan and herself to pay the instalments. 'Yeh know as well as I do that Mammy wouldn't have paid fer anythin'.'

Liam nodded his head in agreement.

'Why was it kept a secret anyway?' Cathy asked. 'It's not like it is anythin bad. In fact it's great, and very good of him.'

Liam gave her a light hug and said, 'There'll be a reason. It was Fred who wanted it this way, and I'm sure we'll all find out in good time.'

In good time could be years away and right now Cathy knew her mammy will be furious over Fred paying for Joan's wedding. The whole family knew that Tony could afford to pay for it. She also knew that Josie, Una and Pauline had paid for their own weddings. She leaned her head towards her favourite brother's shoulder and asked, 'When are yeh comin' home fer good, Liam?'

'Soon Cathy, soon,' Liam lied, squeezing her shoulders again.

Chapter Fifty-two

Screeches and screams sounding like a pack of cats and dogs fighting, poured out from two large speakers on each side of a small platform where a small musical group were tuning their instruments while the tables were being cleared and moved back from the centre of the room.

'We're all over in the corner,' Cathy said pointing over to a table at the far side of the band and said to her friend, 'Donal and Liam are gettin us more chairs.'

The bright glow on Doreen's round face faded when her eyes followed the direction her best friend was pointing to. 'Is yer brothers goin' te be sittin' with us?' she asked. She liked Cathy's brothers, but they were old. The youngest one Liam was twenty-two, and Donal was bald on the top of his head.

'Not that I'm expectin', but I'm sure that they'll do their duty well enough all evenin',' Cathy said, moving back from the door to let two of her aunts come in.

Doreen didn't notice the trace of sarcasm in Cathy's tone, then she never did. Cathy is the best and only friend Doreen has ever had. She sniffed and asked, 'Will we come in now?'

'The sooner teh better, so that we can keep all er chairs,' Cathy said, waving over to Donal. She patted Doreen on her back and pushed her friend into the room while she said, 'You go over and mind teh table.'

'Yer not goin' te change, are yeh?' Doreen asked, feeling her skirt on her ankles again. 'We're all wearin' long skirts,' she said.

It was the first time she had worn a long skirt and she loved the feel of it around her legs. She was delighted when Cathy had asked her to come out for the evening party because she wanted to wear a long skirt.

Neither Doreen nor Cathy had ever heard of Mutt and Jeff so they weren't upset when they heard that was what their friends called them. Although Cathy wasn't thin like the character in the cartoon that used to be in one of the evening newspapers. She was tall. Doreen was Mutt because she was short.

Doreen always seemed like she was looking up to Cathy because her nose tilted towards her forehead and her upper lip curled upwards towards her nose like she had been pressing her face on a sheet of glass. She started school with Cathy. She made her communion, and her confirmation with Cathy, and they started work together. Doreen would have walked over hot coals for her friend because Cathy never made her feel stupid. 'I think yeh look lovely,' she said, dreading the thought that Cathy was going to change, and the other girls would be wearing trousers.

Doreen had memories of the girls saying they would be wearing trousers when they had planned to go out to a gig to-gether, and then they all turned up wearing mini skirts. Doreen knew she wasn't pretty like them and she believed she blended in with them if they were all wearing the same clothes.

'I want te get rid of teh flowers in me hair,' Cathy said as four more of her friends walked over towards them. 'In yeh all go now and mind teh table,' she said and left.

'Yez can all have whatever yez want te drink,' Donal said to the group of young people when they sat down around the table Cathy had directed them to. He didn't like one of the boys, but he smiled at him before he turned his attention to the eight girls and asked, 'Will yez want any more chairs?' He wondered where he was going to get another five chairs if there were another seven boys still to come.

'Yeh will have te ask Cathy when she comes back,' Doreen said.

'Will the barman remember us all?' the boy that Donal didn't like asked and stood up quickly in case Donal changed his mind.

Whining from guitars being tuned, and the ear-piercing screams from the microphones encouraged Donal to turn away from the arrogant, sneering little pup that was standing in front of him. 'He'll come out every half hour,' he said and pretended to be interested in watching the small band set their gear up until he saw Cathy coming back in.

'God, tenite,' Cathy whined, 'I wish I was a fella.' She laughed into her brother's face and continued, 'The queue fer teh ladies,' she explained. 'I don't know why these places don't bring a few of them movin' toilets inte that big hall out there fer times like this.'

'De yeh have many more ev yer friends te come, Cathy?' Donal asked. He thought his sister was right, about some extra toilets. He didn't ask her why she would like to be a fella because he was afraid that she would give him a demonstration. He noticed she had taken the flowers out of her hair.

Cathy moved and counted heads over at her tabled and said, 'Two more.'

Relieved, Donal said, 'Yez should have enough chairs then.' He put his hand up to his tie like he expected Cathy to pull it off him when he added, 'So all teh girls don't have a fella each then?'

'We have enough between us and we could do without them,' Cathy said, throwing her head back. 'I don't know where yeh go fer yer dancing, Donal, but I thought that yeh'ed have noticed by now that girls don't need fellas te dance with any more. We manage better on er own.'

Donal had never learned to dance. He was delighted there would be no more teenage boys drinking themselves stupid because the beer was free. 'Sorry Cathy,' he said, 'I'll send yer barman over te yez right away.'

Cathy smiled at her brother and said, 'There's no need te be sorry about anythin', Donal. I expect there will be enough fellas from teh football team if we get tired ev each other.' She smiled at him and added, 'And there's always yerself and Liam te chase after if teh fancy takes us.'

Shocked at the prospect of any the young girls wanting to chase him Donal turned and looked at the table in the corner.

'Don't get yer hopes up, Donal,' Cathy said, 'we are all very fussy about who we chase after,' then walked over to her friends satisfied he would leave them alone for the evening.

Chapter Fifty-three

Leg weary, and happy, Tony sat down beside his new wife. 'Two fellahs between eleven girls,' he told his gran.

'Were any of them able to do a waltz?' Una asked.

'I never knew that "The old bog road" lasted ten minutes,' Tony said. He knew he couldn't waltz properly but he had some pride.

'I think the band only knew how to play one waltzing tune,' Josie cut in.

'I think they were practising,' Joan said, patting her husband's hand, 'the girls enjoyed themselves, and Cathy is delighted with you for asking them all to dance.'

Tony took Joan's hand and said, 'I don't know if you were lucky, or have been sold short with only two boys to dance with.'

It was getting on for ten and time for the band to take a break and it was usual at this time for anyone or everyone at the party to perform their party piece. Joan started the singing with "Hunny Bun" from *South Pacific*. Fred followed by the family's favourite, "King of the Road". Bella made her stage debut when she sang "Frankie and Johnny". She always liked to sing but she had never sung a song in front of people. She had enjoyed watching and listening to the Malones do their party pieces at the football club's annual dinners so much that she was determined she would stand on the stage and do something for the Murphys at Tony's wedding. She had practised with Joan for three weeks.

While everyone was clapping and cheering Bella, Liam helped her down from the stage and led her back to her table. He was walking backwards towards the stage, and looking around the room for someone to call up to sing and he was still clapping Bella when he turned round to the band to take the microphone. It was then he saw his mammy was standing on the stage talking to the lad that was playing a key instrument.

Liam couldn't think of any reason his mammy would be standing on the stage. He swung the cable from the microphone around the floor while he tried to calculate how many scotches she would have drunk. He also recalled that during all the years when his daddy used to encourage them all to sing he had never heard his mammy sing once. He turned back to the stage to ask his mammy what she was going to sing; the lad that was operating the keyboard, and drummer played the last few notes of what sounded something like "Miss Oatis Regrets".

After the microphone was taken from his hand, Liam moved away from the stage and listened to his mammy talk through her song while the guitar and drums strummed softly in the background. Mike enjoyed a hearty bout of laughing when he watched her walk smartly down the length of the room with her face towards the ceiling like a young shy girl. Maurice bought her a double scotch.

Chapter Fifty-four

Apart from the older guests who were making their way to the coaches everyone was sitting at the tables finishing their drinks and singing. Una was sitting at a table with Sean listening to Cathy and her friends singing when Donal walked over to the drummer and handed the man a white envelope.

Una had stopped worrying about the letter in her bag when she had heard that Fred had paid for Joan's reception because she remembered that Sue had been insured with her job and that she would also get a large sum of money when she retired. She expected that Fred had used Sue's insurance money to pay for the reception. She was also hopeful that Sue would have left her mammy enough money to pay the bill she had in her bag. Her mammy never paid any of her bills until the last minute.

'Now the band has been paid,' Sean said, 'we can all get movin'.'

Una opened her bag and withdrew her mammy's letter.

'Yer not goin te p-pay them as well, are y-yeh?' Sean said and laughed.

Una placed the envelope on the table, then folded over the flap on her handbag and returned it to the floor. 'I need your help with this,' she said. While Sean was taking the letter out of the envelope she placed her elbows on the table and rested her chin on her hands and said, 'I don't want Josie to see it before tomorrow. It was mixed in with Joan's cards and we opened it by mistake.' She glanced at the envelope again and wished she hadn't found it.

Sean read the letter, looked at Una, then closed his eyes.

Dear God, Una prayed, don't let this spoil the great day we have enjoyed, before she said, 'One of us, and I don't believe it was me was meant to find it.' She held her brother's stare for a few seconds. 'Mammy has done this before and she will do it again if we don't stop her.' She looked around the room then continued, 'We have to think of Cathy living on her own with Mammy now that Joan is married.'

Sean nodded his head in agreement while he pressed his fingers into the side of his mouth, then rubbed them into his face. His reading ability was poor but he knew numbers and pound signs.

Although she was still hopeful that her mammy had the money Una said, 'It has happened before. And more than once, and Mammy has never had to find the money. We can't do anything right now, but we should all sort this one out together.'

Sean caught her hand to stop her tapping it on the table and said, 'Y-yer right, Una. Yer right about keeping teh l-letter, yer r-right about showin' it te me, a-and yer r-right about C-cathy as w-well.

'We don't have much time,' Una said. 'I go back tomorrow evening.'

Sean stood: 'I'll tell them all te meet out in my place temarra afternoon, and I'll g-get Donal te bring yeh o-out,' he said and went off to find his brothers and Mike.

Chapter Fifty-five

Donal knew he wouldn't get Cathy and her friends on the coach until the band had left the room so he helped the lads to pack up their kit. When he paid the barman he was surprised at how low the bill had been for Cathy's table He was so pleased and proud of his young sister that he wanted to leave her singing with her friends for as long as he could.

'Low lie the fields of Athen-nry where once____' Donal didn't know the verses of the song but he wanted to join in the chorus. He swung his left leg like he was playing with a football. Although his dreams of becoming a good and famous footballer were well behind him he was still proud of his left kick. The wooden area on the floor where his family had been dancing earlier seemed much bigger now that it was almost empty. He could hear the taps of his shoes while he was walking over towards Mike.

'I would like,' Donal said to Mike when he was close, 'te leave Cathy fer a while longer.'

'Not a good idea,' Mike said raising his hand and showing Donal his wrist. When Donal frowned he wondered how his brother-in-law emptied the Beggars Lodge at the weekends. 'I'll get them out,' he said, 'you go up and help your mammy and Bella.'

Mike pulled at the sleeve of his shirt while he waited for Cathy's friends to finish the second verse of the "The Fields

of Attennry." 'If you want the back seats of the coach to your-
selves I can hold it for you for two minutes,' he said to the
group of girls around Cathy's table.

Instead of starting the chorus of the popular football song
all the young people looked at Cathy.

'The first coach is pulling away any minute,' Mike lied, 'because there are so many of you together I'm sure that Liam will
let you all on to the second one if you can get out now.'

'By a lonely harbour wa–all,' Cathy and her friends started
the third verse of their favourite song when they were walking
out the door behind Mike.

When Donal arrived at the table his mammy was sitting
at, Una was talking to Bella, Josie was talking to Ena and his
mammy was searching through her handbag. 'Time we started
moving,' he said.

'It's a pity that we all have to go home,' Josie said, looking
out to the clear floor where she had spent the evening dancing
with her brothers and Cathy's friends.

'Yeh had a good time then, Josie?' Donal asked.

'It was really great,' Josie replied, smiling at the floor, then
raised her head to her brother and said, 'I didn't see you dancing.'

'Dancin' is fer women,' Donal said.

'I think he means that you haven't taught him yet, Josie,'
Una said, 'but I am inclined to agree with him about the dancing. We do get more women than men that like to dance, and
like every other time that we have been at a dance together I
wish that I was married to your husband.'

'That's ridiculus,' Josie panted, turning her head to see if
anyone was listening.

'Why?' Una said, winking at Bella who was laughing.

'For one thing,' Josie said, 'Mike wouldn't live in Dagenham.'

'And for another,' Una continued, 'I could never live in
Kent.'

'Why not?' Donal asked. He had never been to Dagenham, or Kent. The only reason he knew the places were in England was because his sisters lived there. He was very pleased with his haircut and he wanted to support Josie.

'Kent is far too blue for me,' Una said, smiling into Donal's frown.

Donal looked over at Josie as though he had never seen her before.

'Too many Tory voters, and women with blue rinses in their hair,' Una said, coughing a giggle, 'I also have to agree with you about today, Josie. I can't remember having enjoyed myself so much.'

'I don't know where you get some of your ideas from,' Josie said, feeling the warmth in her brother's smile. 'I'll teach you to dance at the next party, Donal,' she said.

'Drink up, Bella,' Una called out. 'I take it you're going back with Mike?' she asked her mammy while she watched her pass one of her arms through the straps of her handbag.

'You go with Mammy,' Donal said, taking Josie's jacket off the back of a chair.

'I would like to go back in the coach if there is enough room,' Sheila Malone said, raising her head from her handbag and smiling at Donal.

'That's fine,' Donal said, holding Josie's jacket.

'I'll take you, Ena and Bella out to the car. Mammy can go with Una.'

Now what is she up to, Una wondered? But right now she didn't care. The wedding was over, and they'd all had a great time. She also felt better about the letter in her bag now that she had told Sean. They would all sort everything out tomorrow.

Chapter Fifty-six

Cool, fresh salty air blew into Una's face when she walked into the foyer of the hotel behind her mammy who was swinging her handbag like she was happy about something. She didn't trust her mammy not to go wandering off just to give them all the trouble of searching for her so she searched the small crowd for someone to take her over to the coach while she went to the toilet. She suspected the reason why her mammy decided to come in the coach was to do something to get some silly attention. She saw Maurice, and waved him towards her. When she turned back again her mammy was walking out the door.

She ran out to the path and caught her mammy's arm. 'Take your time,' she said, 'Maurice will take you on to the coach. I need to go to the loo.'

Sheila Malone changed her handbag to her other hand and said, 'I'll go with you,' and walked back into the hotel.

Una turned round to see where the singing was coming from, and saw the row of lights along the lengths of the two coaches.

Maurice started to walk over towards the lights and the singing.

Una caught his hand and said, 'Stay where you are, and don't take your eyes away from this door in case Mammy comes out on her own. If she does, come over straight away and put her on the coach.'

Maurice coughed a laugh and said, 'Yer not serious?' and made to walk away.

'Maurice,' Una snapped, 'I never joke about Mammy.' She saw her mammy turning the corner at the stairs. She didn't know whether her mammy didn't want to go with Maurice or whether Maurice didn't want to take care of her mammy, and she didn't care. Given a choice she wouldn't want to go with either of them. 'You wait here and if Mammy comes out before me walk her over to the coach and stay with her until I come.

'Mna,' was written in gold paint under a little picture of a woman on the wooden door. It wasn't quite closed when Una pushed it in again. Because she didn't see her mammy on the corridor when she had turned the corner she assumed that she had already gone into the ladies room.

The whiff of stale soap, cosmetics, and perfumes made Una close her eyes to her reflection in the long mirror that greeted her when she walked into the room. The click of a light bolt, and the rattle on one of the six doors told her that her mammy was probably in the first toilet. She didn't call out to her because she was desperate for a pee and she wasn't going to wait for her mammy to answer.

Small puddles of water on the floor along the sinks glistened in the lights so Una kept her head down while she made her way to the last toilet in the row because it was usually the cleanest after a busy evening in every pub and hotel. When she kicked at some crumpled-up tissue paper she uncovered a long white envelope propped up against the wall. She was pulling down the lining on her skirt when the envelope fell over flat on the ground.

The unfamiliar stamp on the envelope caught Una's attention when she stooped lower. It wasn't English, Canadian or Irish. The light was very poor so she picked it up. She didn't usually look at the postmark or date on her letters. But the mark on the letter that was on the floor was clear. The idea came to her to check the post date on her mammy's letter. She counted the four days backwards on her fingers and found that the letter had come on the Tuesday. When she heard a bolt click, she expected it would be her mammy leaving the toilet. She fixed her clothes quickly and left without drying her hands.

Chapter Fifty-seven

Stepping out into the dark evening Una saw Maurice running after their mammy.

'Where is yeh goin', Mammy?' Maurice shouted while he ran across the car park away from where the coaches were. 'Yer on teh first coach,' he shouted. When he caught up with her he looked around for Una.

Una ignored her brother and her mammy, and continued to walk over towards the coach. She could smell the sea, and felt the light mist on her face. She felt as if a tidal wave had gushed over her head and left memories of her childhood like they were shells or stones before the water receded again.

Absolutely sure that her mammy knew the letter had been found, Una now started to wonder why it was inserted into Joan's cards. Her mammy could not be sure that Josie would find it. Why her mammy decided to come on the coach was also bothering Una. Six years, Una counted back to her sister Maura's party. It had been such a busy weekend. Apart from the joy of seeing Pauline again it had been a dreadful weekend. Her mammy had manipulated her sisters to such a degree that Josie had avoided talking about Maura or Pauline ever since.

Maybe Pauline has done the right thing, Una thought, when she heard her brother calling her. She quickened her step towards the coach. 'I couldn't do that,' she whispered into the wind. 'I could never not come home again,' she told the wind. She walked past the coach towards the ocean because she wanted to have an excuse for the tears in her eyes. She thought that the sea breeze would either blow her tears away or make them run down her face. She ignored her brother's second call. She raised her voice above a whisper and said to the waves she could hear bashing against the wall, 'Pauline, Mammy has started her old games again.'

Nobody could hear Una tossing the words out to the Irish Sea to her sister in Canada. She could hear the singing drifting over from the coach. With her memory on a roll-back, and anger in her heart, she thought back to when her daddy used to encourage them to sing. Her fondest memories of her daddy were the winter evenings when she was about ten and he used to get them to sing while he mended their shoes. She smiled at the memory of Pauline. She was the only one that could reach the high notes. This brought another memory about Pauline when they were in their teens. She had said their daddy used to help them to do the housework to keep their mammy happy. All he had wanted their mammy for was sex and that wasn't love.

While Una was walking back to the coach, her mammy's friend Ena was sitting beside Bella in the back of Tony Murphy's car as Mike drove it along the coast road back towards the city. Like her friend's second eldest daughter, Ena was fighting back tears. Also like Una she was angry with Sheila but her tears were anger at herself and regret over her own behaviour.

'I think they were laughing at me all the time,' Josie said to Mike.

'They are always laughing at something or someone,' Mike replied. He patted his wife on her knee and added, 'I am sure they didn't mean any harm.'

'Probably,' Josie said, smiling at the memory of her daughter joining a union.

'It's called having fun,' Mike said.

It's also called survival, Ena wanted to say. She knew every one of her friends' children. She closed her eyes, recalling talking to her son after the evening six years ago when Pauline had stayed the night. She didn't regret the talk with her son or the evening Pauline had stayed the night. They were two of the best events of her life. Her biggest regret was sending her son Dominic down the country to stay with his father's people every summer so that he wouldn't spend any of his time with Josie Malone.

As the coach moved away from the ocean and turned right towards the north of the city the singing got louder as more people joined in the newly formed choir. Una joined in the singing while her mammy stared at her handbag. When the coach started to slow down, the crowd started singing, 'Now it's the hour.' Sean walked up to the driver and guided him to the drop-off points so that everyone on the coach was left as near as possible outside their own house.

Chapter Fifty-eight

Una left her mammy standing on the pavement looking after the coach. She didn't wait for her mammy
to make up her mind if she wanted to stay there or
come into the house. If her mammy wanted to behave like
she was suffering from Alzheimer's, then she will treat like she
had. She didn't know much about the condition except that
patients were not to be pressured into doing anything. She met
Mike in the hall. 'Mammy is admiring the stars,' she said.

Mike frowned and looked out the door.

'Leave her there for a while,' Una said, she had a lot to drink
and smoke so she is probable getting some fresh air into her
lungs.'

Mike closed the door, then walked over to the kitchen.

'Wow what a day,' Una said, while she prised off her shoes.
When she bent down to pick up her shoes she pressed her
bum against the door and closed it.

'You enjoyed yourself then, Una,' Mike called out from the
kitchen.

'I certainly did,' Una returned, 'but my poor feet.'

'Well you ladies will consider fashions instead of your feet
when buying your shoes,' Mike called back. He returned to the
doorway, rubbing his hands together as though he was waiting
for her to move so he could take up the carpet she was standing on.

'It's some sympathy I want right now, Mike, not a sermon,'

Una said, removing her jacket. She thought about her comfortable bed in Dagenham and Jack's warm arms around her. 'It's been a full weekend.'

'It was a great wedding,' Mike said, continuing to rub his hands together.

It was a small navy-coloured hard plastic bag about the size of a reading book and Una searched the hall table for a safe place to put it so she would see it all the time. She propped it against the wall beside the telephone. She caught Mike's hand and said, 'Thanks for everything you did for Joan last year.'

Mike eased his hand free of Una's hold, then placed it palms together with his other hand as if he was going to say prayers. His memory went back to the second he saw Joan dragging her suitcase through the arrivals at Heathrow Airport, and he loved her as passionately as he would if she was his own young sister, or his daughter. His heart was still heavy with memories of her thin body, and lonely eyes but the occasion that had affected him the most was the day he brought her home from the hospital. 'She had a very rough time,' he said with a quiver in his voice.

'I understand the reasons why I wasn't told,' Una lied.

A soft sound came from Mike's hands. He loosened the grip on his fingers and said, 'I didn't agree with Sue that neither you nor Jack should be told, but for Joan's sake I went along with her decision.'

'I don't know the Byrnes,' Mike continued, 'but I'm positive that Jack would have done all he could, and more for Joan.'

'I know he would,' Una said, 'but just the same you looked after her better than my daddy would have done.'

'Most of us do what falls to our lot to do, Una,' Mike said, relaxing his hands. 'I did talk to Sue about you and she said that you had done enough for the family by the time you were Joan's age. She said that you would understand in time.'

'Did Sue know that she was very sick?' Una asked.

Mike still wondered how Sue thought she was going to manage to bring up a child, but he thought that Una should know what her aunt had intended. 'She knew she had cancer.'

Una nodded her head.

Mike glanced at the hall door, saw it was closed tight, then moved so he had his back to it in case his mother-in-law was listening and said, 'Sue intended to adopt Joan's baby.' He opened the hall door and walked into the kitchen.

'God almighty,' Una breathed as her mammy walked into the hall. She followed Mike into the kitchen.

A clicking noise followed by gushing water from the small room down the lobby told Mike that Josie would walk up the lobby any minute so he turned his back to the door and said quietly, 'I'm the only one who knows for sure, and you because I have just told you.'

This time when Josie walked into the living room after Una she noticed the table was back against the wall and all the chairs were back in their usual place. 'Did someone stay behind and tidy up?' she asked her mammy.

'It's not worth lighting the fire now,' Sheila Malone said, lowering her head to the grate where the newspapers were sticking out waiting for a match. She picked her handbag up off the floor and rested it on her lap.

Tidy rooms were cold rooms for Una. She was an excellent housekeeper and her own house was spotless but she always left something on a chair or on the table. It reminded her of her family, and her home in Dublin where there was always something on all the chairs and the table. 'Flo and myself pulled the furniture back before we left, and Angie came in after she got back from the church, tidied up and set the fire.'

'That was very good of her,' Josie said.

'She is a good neighbour and great friend to Joan and Cathy,' Una returned.

Sheila removed the usual small bottles and notebooks from

her handbag left them on her lap and continued to fumble around like she was searching for something.

Expecting her mammy was looking for a lighter for her cigarette Josie said, 'There's a box of matches on the mantelpiece.'

Mike came in with two mugs of tea.

'I won't have tea,' Sheila said. 'It keeps me awake. I'll have a glass of milk.'

'Sorry Mammy,' Mike said. 'There's only enough milk left for one more cup of tea.'

Sheila looked at the clock, then at Josie.

Mike had never told Josie he didn't like her mammy. He had never complained about the demands her mammy had her. He knew by the way his mother-in-law had looked at his wife that she expected Josie to tell him to go out and get some milk. For the first time since he had met the awful woman he was prepared to say no if she asked him to find a van, or one of the small shops in the village that stayed open until two in the morning. He looked at Una with pleading eyes to support him.

Josie also looked at the clock then said, 'That will be enough for Cathy when she comes in.'

Sheila inhaled deeply through her nose.

Una had also assessed her mammy expected Josie to send Mike to the get the milk and she was delighted that her sister was more concerned about Cathy. She winked at Mike and said, 'You two take you tea and go on up to bed. I'll wait up for Cathy. God knows you've both earned a good night's sleep. Cathy could keep us all up for another hour. You know as well as I do what she's like when she's in the humour for talking,'

'Una's right,' Mike said, 'you go on up, Josie, I'll bring up our tea. We'll hear it all again tomorrow anyhow.'

'Probably,' Josie said dreamily, not sure if she was too tired to stay up and enjoy her young sister. She would be able to stay in bed all morning if she wanted to because Eileen and

Rory were sleeping over with her cousin. She raised her head to the front window when a stream of light flashed across the room. Una pulled back the net curtain to confirm it was the headlights of a coach.

'It's them,' she said, knowing the Josie, Mike and her mammy would know that she meant Cathy and her friends. The faint sound of young voices singing drifted out of the coach when the doors opened. 'I hope Cathy doesn't bring her friends in to continue their party,' she said, dropping the curtain and walking out to the hall.

Chapter Fifty-nine

Drowning in a flood of memories swimming around her head in the dark bedroom, Una couldn't close her eyes. She half sat up and searched the bottom of the bed where Cathy or Liam used to sleep. She then patted the other side of the bed that was nearest to the wall.

The bed used to be against the wall when they were all living at home. Una smiled as she recalled that Pauline and Josie used to sleep on the inside so that they wouldn't have to get up in the middle of the night to warm the baby's bottle. When she lay down again she noticed the built-in wardrobe facing her. The door was half open, and there was a dress slung across the top of it.

An edge of the brass knob handle glinted in a sliver of light that came from the window by Cathy's bed. A brown plastic bag was draped around the neck of the handle. Una imagined it was half-full of papers, probably envelopes. She was tempted to get up and go through it. She was sure she would find receipts and bills. Her mammy always put her bills into bags and then hung them on the door handles. She stared at the blank ceiling for a few minutes but she still couldn't clear her mind of the letter from Barents.

Sleep came eventually but footsteps on the stairs awoke her. She assumed that Josie, Mike or her mammy had gone downstairs to the toilet. She wanted to pee herself but she waited a while to allow whoever had gone down to finish with the toilet. The smell of toast grew stronger when she was descending the stairs; she was near the bottom when Josie came out of the kitchen with a small plate of toast and cup of tea. She assumed it was for her mammy so she said, 'Do you want me to take that up for you?'

'Yes please,' Josie replied quickly. She didn't want to see her mammy.

When Una walked into the small bedroom, her mammy killed the smile she had prepared for Josie. Una moved the clock, a small radio, and the ashtray to make room for the plate of toast and the cup of tea. She then left the room without waking her mammy and went into the room she had been sleeping in to get dressed. The light was poor but not as dark as it was when she went to bed. She draped the dressing gown she had borrowed on the bottom of Cathy's bed.

'Yeh needn't creep around, Una,' Cathy said, 'I'm awake.'

'Go back to sleep,' Una whispered. 'It's only nine.'

Cathy threw back the blankets and swung her legs out of the bed. 'I have an appointment in town,' she said, pulling back the curtains and opening the side window.

'What kind of an appointment?' Una asked, zipping up her skirt.

Cathy buttoned the housecoat and was walking out the door as she said, 'I have te do me wee.'

Please God, Una prayed, don't let Cathy start Mammy's habit of not answering questions, or answering them with a statement that had nothing to do with the question that was asked.

The fire was blazing up the chimney, and Cathy was trying to tune in the radio. It was an old, dark brown portable that Josie had bought before she had left home. It looked the worse for wear because it had been moved about the rooms downstairs so much.

When Cathy started to get frustrated with all the cackling

coming from the dirty box, Una said, 'Your own little radio is in Mammy's room. Will I go up and get it for you?'

'No, Mammy uses it in teh mornin's,' Cathy said. She picked the radio up off the bookshelf and brought it over to the window. She was still trying to tune it in when she said, 'This one sounds better.' She fiddled with the dials for another couple of minutes then turned round and displayed a broad smug smile.

The voice of a pleasant young man was clear over the light buzzing on the battered radio. 'Four more birthdays for today.'

'I know him,' Cathy said, bowing to the radio. 'I sent in a best wishes request fer Joan and Tony.'

'The duck?' Mike said and bit on his toast, recalling Liam and Donal telling him they had tried to find a boy called Donald among Cathy's friends at the wedding.

Cathy nodded approvingly at Josie: 'His name is Donald.'

Josie and Una nodded congratulations at Mike.

Mike shook his head quickly from side to side, in a gesture that said 'don't blame me', then took another bite of his toast.

Cathy buttered her toast while they listened to the record that was playing. Then just before she started to eat she straightened her back, turned round to the radio and said, 'He does a programme every Sunday mornin' fer fifteen minutes.'

'We are impressed,' Josie said.

'Is that why mammy wanted a radio?' Una asked.

'I doubt it,' Cathy said and looked at the radio again as if she might see a picture of her friend. 'Mammy can't stand him.'

'What's his second name?' Una asked.

'Gundlesoft,' Cathy lied.

'No wonder Mammy doesn't like him,' Josie said, laughing loudly.

'She's kidding,' Una laughed with Josie.

'Anyhow,' Cathy said, looking at Una, 'how come yeh stayed here last night?'

'Because I wanted to,' Una lied.

'You usually stay with the Byrnes,' Cathy said.

Una closed her eyes at the memory of when she used to stay with Jack's family. 'There was no room here when Jack came with me,' she said, 'and if I remember correctly we were already sleeping two in a bed.'

'All large families did,' Mike said. 'It's a small price to pay for always having friends.'

If Mike had said that two weeks ago Josie would not have agreed with him. But now her memory opened up like a burst balloon and she felt a new fondness towards her siblings. 'Sometimes three in a bed,' she said.

'Is it true that I used to sleep in the laundry basket?' Cathy asked.

'It was a bread basket,' Josie corrected, 'and it was the best baby cradle we ever had.' She smiled at the memory of when they used to carry the baby around in the basket. 'When you became too big for it we used it for the laundry.'

'Was I a good baby?' Cathy asked.

'No,' Una cut in, 'you were a cheeky, stubborn little bitch.' She was used to Josie not wanting to talk about when they were all living at home. She knew they would have to talk about some difficult times later and she didn't want her to be depressed before she showed her the letter from Barents. Recalling Cathy complaining about Josie, and Josie moaning about Cathy, she thought by taking Josie's side now Josie wouldn't argue.

Tightly packed scenes of when Cathy was a baby poured into Josie's memory like sugar would spill from a burst bag. She recalled with shame that she had not welcomed the new baby. She put her knife into the glass dish and scooped out more butter and said, 'We were all cheeky.'

'No we were not,' Una said, 'but I was.' She watched Josie spread the butter on her toast. 'I grew out of it, and I expect Cathy will in time.' She shoved back her chair. 'I had better make a move. I promised Maeve I would be round to unpick Joan's wedding dress.'

'Give Mammy a call,' Josie said. 'I told her we would take her down to Ena before one o'clock. They are going into St. Martins to see Pam.'

Una felt sorry for her mammy's friend but she was pleased that Pam was in St. Martins again because she knew that her mammy would go to see her rather than come over to Sean's.

Chapter Sixty

Had Mike known the trauma Josie was to endure during the afternoon, he might have had different thoughts in his head while he watched his handsome, and well-groomed wife change the station on the radio after Una and Cathy had left the room. The crackling sounds shooting out of the brown box aggravated the tremors of fear that he might lose her. He knew he allowed her to have her way too much, but for all that she had never made any unreasonable demands on him.

Since he had married Josie, Mike enjoyed a more ordered and comfortable life than he had ever dreamed of. Their two children were healthy and smart, and Josie worked as hard as he did to provide them with a sound future. He always derived comfort from knowing that she cared about, and had done so much for her family. It told him that she would always care for her own.

Unlike the thousands of young energetic Irish people who responded to the lure of jobs with high wages in England in the late fifties, Mike was one of the few that left because he wanted to leave his hometown. He had lied to Josie about his family because he had lied to himself. And Josie was easy to lie to because she never questioned him about anything he told her.

Settling for a station with music but no crackling, Josie walked back to her chair. 'That radio should have gone in the bin years ago,' she said, 'the knobs will barely move. I'll buy Cathy a new one when I'm in town during the week.'

Pleased that Josie said Cathy, and not her mammy, Mike said, 'We can buy her one in Limerick.'

Josie moved the small plates about and made more space to rest her elbows. She placed her chin on her knuckles and watched the clouds floating by through the back window. She wasn't going to Limerick.

'Could you get the children ready to go to Limerick to-morrow?' Mike asked, feeling his heart drop a few inches. He knew that Eileen would be ready in a minute because she was always asking him about his hometown. With the neck of his shirt open and both of his arms draped over the back of his chair, he looked casual and relaxed. He stared at the jar of marmalade and said, 'I have to go, and I'll take Eileen with me.'

'For the day?' Josie asked, her chin props collapsing like a ladder when she took her hands away. She folded her arms, then leaned her body over and rested them on the table and waited for Mike to answer her while she thought: what a thing to ask at this time of the day.

'For a few days,' Mike said, 'Limerick is too far a drive for one day.' He kept his eyes on the centre of the table and brought his arms forward like he was doing the butterfly stroke in a swimming pool. He joined his hands like he was going to pray, rested them on the table and said, 'I have to go, and I would like you and the children to come with me.'

Josie had brief visions of Mike being very quiet during the last couple of months after he had been on the phone to Lim-erick but he hadn't said anything. She inhaled deeply as if she was bracing herself for a reply she didn't want to hear and asked, 'Is something wrong?'

It's now or never, Mike thought. 'I'm afraid there is,' he said, and looked up at the ceiling as if he was thinking a prayer and continued, 'There is a lot wrong.'

'It's your daddy, isn't it?' Josie said. She had never met his daddy. He didn't come over to Kent for their wedding, or to see them during the ten years they were married. He was in hospital on the two times she had been to Limerick. She sat up straight and re-folded her arms tightly across her chest and said, 'He's had another stroke.'

Mike raised his head to the muffled noise on the ceiling. Una was walking around upstairs. He moved his mug, and his plate; he then rested his wrists on the edge of the table and said, 'Josie, my daddy has never had a stroke, and he has never been in hospital.' He studied the back of his hand while he listened to the sounds in the ceiling, and the light scraping of Josie's hands as they moved around the tablecloth.

With her thoughts flitting between wanting to know why her husband wanted to go to Limerick, why his father had never been in hospital, where his father had been, why she hadn't met him, and why Mike had lied to her, Josie continued to move her hands around the tablecloth.

'I didn't choose to tell you now, Josie,' Mike said, stealing a glance at her still and frozen face. He counted the pats that Una's feet made on the ceiling while he waited for Josie to ask him where his father had been when she had been in Limerick. After a few seconds of silence he walked over to the door and closed it. He was so nervous that he bumped into a chair when he was walking over to the back window to turn off the radio.

Because he seemed so determined in what he said about going to Limerick, and the briskness of his strides as he moved about the room, for a brief second Josie imagined he was going to want to go to Limerick before she had time to get dressed.

'Like I said, Josie, there is a lot wrong,' Mike said, sitting back down at the table and praying from the soles of his feet that she would understand. He put his hands together, rubbed them once, then entwined his fingers. 'The worst part is that I have lied to you for a long time.' He twisted his hands sharply as if he had been stung before he continued, 'No. That's not true.' He inhaled deeply. 'The worst is that I have lied to myself.'

Ridiculous, Josie thought. Lied about what, she wondered struggling to remember, and deny what her husband had just said to her. Mike was such a good practising catholic that he wasn't capable of telling lies. She was thinking out loud when she asked, 'Why?' She picked up the small bowl of sugar and began smoothing the white shiny grains; 'I mean why tell me now?' She didn't want an answer so she replaced the sugar bowl and smoothed the creases she had made in the tablecloth with her hands while she thought; this is ridiculous. She couldn't think of anything that Mike would possibly lie to her about.

'Because I was ashamed,' Mike said.

Josie couldn't think of what could be so awful that Mike would lie about his daddy's stroke? 'Where was he when we were in Limerick if he wasn't in hospital?' she asked. She didn't want to know what he was ashamed of.

Fear and courage fought for space in Mike's heart as he tried to remember one of a dozen scenarios he had rehearsed in his mind with Josie while he was on his own every night after she had left Kent to come home. As he waited for Josie to recover from the shock of what he had just told her he wondered if she would ever feel any of the warmth for his family that he did for hers.

Impatient now to get conversation over Josie asked, 'Did you know you wanted to go to Limerick before you came home?'

As he struggled to find the words to tell her about his father Mike remembered when Joan had been in England and how the family had clustered around her and he was proud to be part of them. He prayed she would now show some of the warmth for his small family. Although he wanted to shout, he spoke softly when he said, 'I'm sorry to have to tell you, Josie, my daddy is in prison.'

For Josie the silence was almost deafening because the words were loud enough in her head for her to imagine she could feel her ears pop. 'Since when?' she asked, picking Una's mug up off the table, then putting it down beside her own as though she was getting ready sell them. Rapid hot sensations ran up and down the sides of her mouth, her chest was tight and her eyes started to sting.

'There was nothing I could do, Josie, so I kept it to myself,' Mike said, then bowed his head like he used to when he was a boy and he had told his sins to the priest in the confession box.

Josie had never known anyone who had been in prison. 'Why didn't you tell me?' she asked. If she hadn't felt stuck to her chair she would have walked out of the room. 'Why tell me now?' she asked, thinking it would be easier to talk about why Mike hadn't told her than learn about why his daddy was in jail. 'What's so special about now?'

'Because Theresa is dying,' Mike said. He covered his face with his hands for a couple of seconds, then rubbed his eyes before he entwined his fingers again.

'Oh my God,' Josie whined, placing Cathy's empty mug beside Una's. 'I'm sorry,' she said softly, then rested her chin in her entwined knuckles and gazed into the fire. She felt very cold.

'I had a phone call from Patrick the day after you left to come home. He told me she has secondary cancer, and she is not expected to live for more than a couple of weeks,' Mike explained in his usual soft, controlled voice. He needed some comfort so he told himself again that he didn't tell Josie about his father because he hadn't expected him to survive for longer that ten months let alone ten years. He had been a skeletal of a man that was so dependent on alcohol that he hadn't known what was happening to him when he had been taken from the court. The poor still didn't remember he had been in a fight and a man had been killed.

Josie's thoughts and fears were running through her head so fast that she wanted to turn the radio on again so that some music would slow them down.

'I'm going to Limerick tomorrow,' Mike said, smothering the pity he was allowing himself and brought his thoughts back to his sister.

'I did try to get on with her, Mike,' Josie said, closing her eyes but she couldn't bring one pleasant memory of her husband's sister to her mind.

'I know, Josie,' Mike said softly. 'Everyone who met her did,' he added sadly. 'Theresa has been a good sister to me and I have a lot to be grateful to her for. Although she left school at fourteen she fought to get me into good schools until I had done my leaving. She was disappointed that I chose to be an accountant instead of going into the civil service, but she was happy enough when I continued to study and passed more exams.'

'I never knew that,' Josie whispered, moving the jar of marmalade.

'However, she never forgave me for going to work in England.' Mike continued bowing his head as if he was praying for forgiveness because at the time he had wanted to get away from his sister.

'And she blamed me for that,' Josie said, recalling how cold Theresa had been to her the first time when Mike had taken her to Limerick.

'No,' Mike returned, quickly slapping his hand on the edge of the table, 'she blamed you for keeping me there, because she had to blame somebody.' When he saw Josie nodding her head to the three mugs that were lined up in front of her elbows he raised he voice and added. 'Theresa would not accept that I could manage on my own.'

'God,' Josie whispered and covered her face with her hands. She felt guilty because she had never liked Theresa.

'And she was right,' Mike went on, 'I don't think I would still be in England if you hadn't married me. I wouldn't have the two lovely children I have either, or the comfortable home that I will die for, or go to prison to keep.'

Go to prison, were the only words Josie heard.

They both looked up quickly to the cupboard in the corner of the room from where they heard a rumble. 'It's the boiler,' Josie said and from habit she shoved her chair back. 'I'll run Mammy's bath.' She stood to go over to the hot press so she could turn off the immersion heater. With the fire lighting, there would be enough hot water for the rest of the day.

Mike put his hand on her arm and said, 'Go and have a bath yourself. Your mammy can wait. She has plenty of time. I'll go round to Noreen and get the children. We can talk about all this later.' He patted her arm. 'This is a bad time to tell you, but I didn't want to spoil Joan's wedding.' He leaned into the table and picked up the three mugs that Josie was staring at and said, 'Have your bath, Josie.' He felt like he had just climbed a hill and he now wanted to rest for a while. He prayed he had told Josie the worst and he now needed time to think about how he would tell her all the details. He intended to tell her everything.

Towels of every size and colour greeted Josie when she opened the door of the hot press. Although they were wrapped tightly around the large copper tube, she could feel the warmth from the boiler. Yes, she thought, a hot bath. She was so desperate for something pleasant to think about that the clean smell from the towels gave her mind a flashing glimpse of her first bath in a proper bathroom. She stared at the towels and recalled that when she was alone in the tiny room she would forget about her mammy sulking, and shut out the noise of her siblings shouting at each other.

Mike watched her staring at the towels: 'Go on, Josie,' he insisted, 'I'll get the children.' He heard Una on the stairs and for a couple of seconds his courage worked overtime. He walked over to the hot press and pulled out some towels, draped them over Josie's shoulder and closed the door so that she wouldn't put them back in again. 'It won't do your mammy any harm to wait until you're finished for a change.'

Both Josie and Mike were relieved when Una walked in. Josie didn't want to think any more, and Mike knew she wouldn't really hear anything he would say to her for some time. He was determined she would listen when he told her why his father was in jail.

Josie pulled more towels out of the press, then after she had pushed a few of them back around the water tank she walked out of the room with four of them over her shoulder.

Chapter Sixty-one

Ten minutes after Josie closed the door on the bathroom Mike closed the fridge with his knee and said, 'That's the lot.'

'You could go round to Noreen for Eileen and Rory now if you like, Mike,' Una said, 'I'll wait until Josie is out of the bath in case anyone calls, or Mammy comes down.'

This time Mike was cold when he rubbed his hands together. There was no heater in the kitchen and a light breeze waved the net curtain on the open window over the sink. He wondered if Josie would be warm enough in the bathroom. He moved out to the hall and turned his face down the lobby where he could hear the two taps squirting out water.

Una was thinking about them all getting to Sean's and then catching her plane for six. 'It's only a suggestion, Mike, but you know yourself that if Josie goes she'll be there for at least an hour.'

Mike decided not to tell her that Josie was upset. He felt some comfort in knowing that Una would be here until he came back. He had never seen his wife cry, but he knew that her mammy wouldn't be any comfort to her at all. He looked at his watch and asked, 'Are you sure, Una.'

Una turned round from the sink picked up the tea cloth and said, 'The reason why I stayed last night is because Liam and Donal asked me to. They were afraid that Cathy would annoy Josie.'

'Una.' Mike dropped his hands from his face and placed them on his hips. 'One of them is as bad as the other, and the boys were right.' He nodded at the floor and grew a smile before he raised he head and said, 'Don't worry about Cathy; she'll be fine.' He glanced down the lobby again before he left.

Thick white steam filled the bathroom before Josie opened the small window over the sink. She heard the hall door close but she didn't wonder, or care who had come in or gone out. She parted the suds and got into the bath. After a few seconds she wondered where on earth Cathy had got the bubble bath lotion foam.

The bathroom was five feet square, but it had a bath, a hand basin and the door opened all the way into the room. While Josie was trying to get comfortable in the small bath that was too short for her long body she recalled how she used to wash while standing at the kitchen sink when her family had lived in Arbour Hill. She used to smell the soap on herself for hours afterwards because she could never rinse it away properly. The light curtain they had used to separate the living room from the scullery always waved from the draught that came in through the back door. And it never made any difference what time she decided to wash herself. Someone always wanted to get to the toilet in the yard before she was finished.

No bath had ever come close to the comfort of the first one that Josie enjoyed when her family moved from the city to Ballymore. She had been very upset with the move to Bal-lyglass. But even though the bathroom was smaller she could still have her bath in private.

Even on the coldest of winter days when the steam died before it reached the ceiling there was always the smell of soap and shampoo, but there was never any trace of ammonia or perm lotions. But most important of all for Josie the room was too small for her to even imagine other people being with her. She wasn't asked any questions, or told anything unpleasant. Even though she wasn't comfortable now the hot water around her body dissolved the nausea in her stomach.

Three minutes after staring at the wall trying not to think of anything, the tightness in Josie's chest eased, and tears oozed from her eyes. The birds on the wallpaper flying up into the ceiling replaced the image of Mike sweeping his hair back with his hands like he always does when he has finished doing an arduous task. The masses of bubbles made her sneeze and she couldn't find the face cloth in the water because of all the suds. When she sat up and stretched her arm out for the towel to wipe her eyes the light balls of water on her back and shoulders were cold.

After she opened the hot tap again the squirting water made more bubbles. Josie never raised her hand in anger but she ran her arms across the top of the water and wiped all the globules that were on the top of the water on to the floor. By the time she had turned off the hot tap and lay back in the bath again she had stopped crying. Then after five minutes of watching and listening to the tiny clear shiny balls bursting, she decided they would all go to Limerick.

Chapter Sixty-two

Water from her sister's bath was gushing and gurgling into the drain when Una was walking back into the lobby from putting some rubbish in the bin. She didn't want to be on her own with Josie in case her sister wanted to know why they were going to Sean's so she checked that the fire was safe then went upstairs to call her mammy. On entering the room she had slept in she found her mammy searching through the clothes in the built in wardrobe. She left the room and went down stairs to check her handbag.

Five minutes later when her mammy was walking up the lobby from the toilet Una said, 'there's still plenty of hot water in the tank if you want to have a bath.' She didn't offer to run the water.

Sheila Malone tossed her head back and pulled on the collar of her housecoat. She then bowed her head so that she would only see the floor in front of her and walked into the kitchen.

'The fire is lighting inside,' Una said as she walked into the kitchen after her mammy. 'Would you like me to bring you in a cup of tea?' she asked.

'No thank you,' her mammy replied then walked out of the kitchen and went over to the hall door and stood under the concrete shelf.

'Is that Mike back?' Josie shouted from the top of the stairs when she heard the hall door open. She was halfway down the stairs when she said, 'Mammy, you will get your death of cold standing there in your housecoat.'

'I should imagine he will be here any minute,' Una said. She saw Josie was dressed so she said, 'I'll be off round to Maurice's now.'

'Would you give me a hand with a couple of suitcases before you go?' Josie asked, turning to go back up the stairs as she added, 'I don't want to mark the wallpaper.'

The hall door was still wide open when Una climbed the stairs. 'Where do you want to move them to?'

'Into the big room, I'll need more space to pack everything,

'Where are you going?' Una asked, as they dragged the case across the landing.

'To Limerick,' Josie replied, as they hoisted the case on the bed Una had slept in.

'Now?'

'In the morning,' Josie replied. She sat down on the bed and told Una about Mike's sister.

Five minutes later when the sisters were descending the stairs, the hall door and the living-room door were wide open. Their mammy was sitting by the fire in the living room searching through her handbag.

'Leave the hall door open for Mike,' Josie called out when Una had stretched her arm over to close it.

'I'll leave it on the catch,' Una said and closed the door, then followed her sister into the living room. 'If you get on the road by ten you should be well there before it gets dark,' she said, slipping one arm into the sleeve of her jacket.

Josie looked up from rummaging through the ironing basket and said, 'And there are the two of us to drive,. She had pulled out all her children's clothes when Mike walked in behind Eileen and Rory. He nodded his head to his mother-in-law and started to rub his hands together.

'Is it that cold out, Mike?' Sheila Malone asked, raising her head from her handbag and smiling.

'It's not cold at all, Mammy.' Mike bowed his head to Josie and continued to rub his hands.

Josie put her arms out and Rory walked over and stood beside her. She hugged him around his shoulders, then smoothed his hair with her fingers and said, 'Has your daddy told you where we're all going tomorrow?'

'No, not yet,' Mike answered for his children. He swept his tidy hair back with his hand and ran his eyes around the room as if he was trying to decide where to sit.

Josie smiled as though she was supplying the answer to a question her children had asked her a hundred times and said, 'We are all going down to Limerick for a few days.'

'Josie told me about Theresa,' Una said. 'I'm sorry, Mike.' She tried to recall a memory of his sister but all she could remember was Patrick and Jack laughing together. She moved away from the fireplace when she saw her mammy bending her body forward to stand.

Mike opened the door for his wife's mother.

'It's an awful illness,' Josie said speaking to the floor at her husband's feet, her mind full of images of some of her customers that had died from cancer. 'She's not fifty yet,' she added, recalling when she had offered to give her sourly, unfriendly sister-in-law some highlights to brighten her dull, thin greying hair. A pang of guilt hit her stomach because Theresa was now dying but she still couldn't warm to the image of the girl's skinny body.

Eileen came back in with a plastic bag. 'Will you show me how to make the little book before you go?' she asked Una. She emptied the bag of pastel coloured envelopes out on the table.

'How many have you got there?' Josie asked, moving the folded tablecloth back against the wall so her daughter could spread the envelopes.

'Fifty-nine,' Eileen said, smiling triumphantly up at her mammy.

Time was running on, but Una promised her niece she would only have to show her how to do one. 'We will need a pair of scissors.'

Rory moved away from his mammy and said, 'I'll get them. I know where they are.'

The hall door was open when Rory ran out of the room. He found his granny sitting on a stool in the kitchen. 'I need the scissors,' he said, but I know where they are.' He opened the bottom drawer in the sink unit. He searched for the long carving knife, pulled it out and placed it on the draining board like his mammy told him to do before he moved anything about. After he had found the scissors he turned round to his granny and said, 'Una is going to show Eileen how to make a little book from the envelopes of Joan's cards.' He closed the drawer and left the kitchen.

Sheila went over to the sink, picked up the carving knife that Rory had forgotten to put back into the drawer and ran the sharp edge of it along the top of her thumb. Unable to stand the sight of blood she sat back down on the stool and waited until she could feel the warm liquid running into the palm of her hand.

Chapter Sixty-three

Una cut around the edges of one of the envelopes, discarded the small back parts and using only the front folded it in two with the writing on the inside. She then showed Eileen how to make two holes down the side of the edges that didn't have the fold with the points of the scissors so she could use them to pass a string through and hold them together. She then cut up another couple of envelopes and prepared them the same way and put them inside the first one so there was a small booklet with six pages.

Eileen was making another one when Sheila came in holding her bloodstained hand out in front of her.

'What did you do?' Josie shouted.

For a second Una thought twenty years had rolled back and her sister was talking to Maurice when he was a boy. She turned round to the door.

'I cut my hand when I picked up the carving knife,' Sheila returned softly.

'By the blade?' Josie hollered.

Una walked over and looked at her mammy's cut hand. 'We have all done it, Josie,' she said. She turned round to Eileen and asked, 'Will you manage now?'

Eileen nodded her head and said, 'thanks Una.'

Una glanced at the clock and walked her mammy into the bathroom.

Dribbles of moisture were running down the frosted glass

in the window from Josie's bath. Una ran the hot tap into the hand basin and plunged her mammy's bleeding hand into it. The cut was about an inch long, and by the time Una was dabbing it dry with the small towel the bleeding had stopped. 'Hold the towel over it and I will get a plaster dressing,' she said.

How can a right-handed person cut the top of their thumb on their left hand from picking up a carving knife, Una asked herself when she was searching in the drawer for a dressing?

'How is she?' Mike asked from the doorway.

'She won't be doing any washing-up for a day or two,' Una said, smiling. She then whispered, 'I think she cut herself deliberately.'

Mike closed his eyes.

'There is no need to tell Josie,' Una said.

Mike nodded his head in agreement.

Una continued, 'It will be hard for Josie this afternoon in Sean's when she learns why we are all meeting.' She opened the drawer of the sink unit all the way and found a couple plaster dressings, then turned round to Mike and said firmly, 'But it is time Josie started to see that people are the way they are and not the way she wants them to be.' She returned one of the dressings to the back of the door. 'We don't choose our families, Mike, and we don't have to like them, but as you told me last night we do what falls to our lot to do.'

Mike nodded his head again.

'Josie,' Una continued, 'allowed Mammy to bully her. 'She could have done what Jack did with his father bullying him and walked away. But that is not important right now. Mammy will survive even if she loses her finger. My concern with us meeting today is to protect Cathy.' She looked at her watch: 'Time is running on so I'll put a plaster on Mammy's finger and get off to Maurice's.'

Mike took the plaster off Una and said, 'I'll put the plaster on your mammy's finger, you go on around to Maurice.'

Chapter Sixty-four

The Church bells rang out the angelus when Una used the key in the hall door to enter her family home when she returned from her brother's house. She gasped when she saw her mammy walking down the stairs.

'Is it cold out, Una?' Sheila Malone asked, enjoying the shock on her daughter's face; she then lowered her eyes to the floor in the hall slowly and descended the last three steps.

'You will need a coat,' Una said, smiling broadly while she thought that if she ever loved her mammy, it was then and there at that moment. For an instant she felt very sad, and ashamed of her years of impatience but she thought; God almighty, what will Josie do? Her mammy was wearing a purple, flared knee-length polyester crimplene skirt, a multi-coloured knitted tank top over a bright yellow shirt that had long pointed collars. Her knee-length boots matched the shirt, but they looked extravagant with the fishnet tights.

More concerned her sister would want to wait until her mammy changed her clothes than she was about how silly her mammy looked, Una walked into the kitchen. She worried about Josie enduring another shock while she waited.

'Una?' Josie's second call sounded very urgent.

'I'm in the kitchen,' Una sang her reply again. The vision of her mammy dressed in some of Cathy's clothes brought some humour back into her temper. She felt less despondent even though Maurice avoided talking to her when she was unpicking the tucks she had made in Joan's wedding dress.

Josie stood in the kitchen doorway with her hands on her hips, panting.

Una held her chin in her hand to stop herself from laughing at the shock and embarrassment that was lighting up her sister's face. 'They wouldn't have gone with a bright blue rinse would they, Josie?' she said.

'She's going to visit someone in hospital, for god's sake,' Josie said pointing across the hall to the living room to show she was talking about their mammy.

'No she's not,' Una returned, slapping the table sharply. 'Herself and Ena are going to St. Martins to play cards with Pam.'

'St. Martins is a hospital,' Josie panted, and glared at Una as if she was stupid.

'Yes,' Una sighed and nodded her head a few times. 'Yes, It is,' she said, 'and a private one, and Pam is in there again for the second time this year, and for the same reason she was in there five times last year.' She held her sister's stare for a few seconds and added, 'I know, I know.'

Josie moved the four mugs on the draining board.

The milk started to sizzle so Una turned the gas off under the saucepan. She closed over the door before she sat down again and said,

'I'm sorry, Josie, but I thought you knew about Pam.'

'What's there to know about?' Josie said picking up the saucepan and swirling the milk around.

'Pam is drying out,' Una said. She waited a few seconds for her sister to reply then said, 'Again.'

Una concluded by the way Josie was staring at the milk that her sister really didn't know, and she wondered again how Josie was able to ignore so many things that she didn't like.

Josie continued to swirl the milk.

High time she found out, Una thought. 'Sit down Josie,' she said, and moved the other stool with her foot, then curled her hair behind her ears. When Josie was moving towards the small table she said, 'Both Joe and Pam O'Mara are alcoholics. Pam gets a lot better after a week or two in St. Martin's, but she starts drinking again when she comes out.'

'Has Ena been in St. Martins as well?' Josie asked.

'Not that I know about,' Una said, then stood. She didn't have the time to talk about her mammy's friends. 'Anyway Josie,' she said, 'you have enough on your mind without worrying about Pam O'Mara.'

As if her memory was returning, Josie murmured, 'Pam doesn't have any children.' It was everything she knew, and wanted to know about her mammy's wealthy friend. She closed her eyes and her back teeth like she always does when a long buried memory starts to stir.

'That's right,' Una said, 'she used to wear a very soft fur coat and she always smelled like flowers. She gave me my first tin of talcum powder and scented soap.'

'She is very small,' Josie whispered. When in her teens and she learned where babies came from she believed the reason why Pam didn't have any children was because she was so small.

When Una was a child she used to be terrified of her mammy's friend Ena because she was so tall and she shouted all the time. But with all their money, neither Pam nor Joe O'Mara looked down on the family. She felt mean because she thought she was running Pam down so she said, 'The three of them are all old school friends that are standing by each other.'

Josie stared out the window where the end of a cloud was breaking up and fading away. 'I really had no idea about Pam,' she said. 'I can't remember now what she had said, but Sue led me to believe that Pam was in hospital so many times because she was pregnant.'

Una recalled when Pam and Joe O'Mara were so desperate to have a child they were prepared to buy one. She also knew they would probably have to talk about the O'Maras this afternoon. 'Let's face it, Josie,' she said, 'if Mammy's outfit is all right for Ena and Pam then it should be all right for us.'

'I suppose so,' Josie said, turning the gas off under the pot of milk as she said, 'Ena has only one child.'

'And he is still the apple of her eye,' Una said. She poured the milk into the mugs. 'We can talk about the two of them later, it's time you were going.'

'I have so much talking to do later I'll never get to sleep,' Josie said. She waited until Una had poured the milk into the mugs, then stirred the coffee into them. She picked up two of them and walked out the kitchen towards the living room. If she had known what was going to be revealed about Pam O'Mara later in the afternoon she would have dropped the mugs of coffee in the hall.

There was nothing wrong with the curtain in the living room but Una straightened it. She was concerned about the time; she saw it was ten minutes to one. She knew her mammy found things to do when she knew someone wanted her to hurry up so she eased Eileen out of her easy chair, then sat down and lifted the little girl on to her lap. She nodded a smile to her mammy who was sitting facing them in the other easy chair on the opposite side of the fireplace.

'I think we should make a move when we've drunk our coffee, Mammy,' Josie said as she walked around to the other side of the table and sat down. She didn't want to go down to Ena's house because she never wanted to go to Arbour Hill. But she wanted to get out of the house and away from the memory of Mike telling her about his father.

Rory walked away from his daddy and went over to his granny and stood looking at her legs.

Una prayed that Josie wouldn't say anything about her

mammy's clothes. She believed her mammy was wearing the clothes to shock Josie, and she was worried what her mammy might do, or say to prevent Josie going to Limerick.

Rory placed his hand on his granny's legs.

Una thought she should give her mammy's clothes some attention and get it over with so she said, 'How do you manage to keep those boots so clean and shiny?'

Sheila Malone smiled and stretched out her legs.

Rory ran his hand along the yellow shiny plastic. He then rested his hand on one of her knees, hooked a finger round one of the strings of her fishnet tights and gave it a little pull. While his granny was smiling in appreciation of the attention she was getting, Rory looked gravely into her face, then turned round to his daddy and said, 'This is for holding billiard balls.'

'What a clever boy you are,' Una said, bowing a smile over to her sister.

'Absolutely,' Josie said. Her humour was so low that she welcomed any praise about her husband or her children. She passed her sister's smile on to Mike.

Feeling Eileen's body shaking, Una knew her niece was laughing while they all watched in silence as her mammy leaned forward and removed Rory's finger.

'At least they don't ladder,' Una said, hugging Eileen while her mammy picked her handbag up off the floor and stood.

Josie closed her eyes at her mammy's legs and said, 'I have never worn them and I don't intend to either. They remind me of prostitutes.'

Una wanted to clap when her mammy walked out of the room.

Chapter Sixty-five

It was a seven-minute drive to Ballymore and every time Donal had occasion to pass through the area he found it more difficult to see the social and economic seams between the two housing estates. Though they were not all taxed, or insured many families were very proud to have at least one car. With, and without permission from the Dublin Corporation, some of the residents of the Ballyglass Estate knocked out the front garden wall and replaced it with wide double gates, and a wide concrete path for the car.

They arrived at the Byrnes' house, with its wide double gates, well-kept lawn, but no porch or car in the driveway. The gates were wide open, and inviting a very nice car like Donal's to rest for a while. Donal left the car on the road.

Betty Byrne opened the hall door wide when Una and Donal were walking up the driveway. Jim Byrne came trotting down behind her from the kitchen wiping his hands on a small towel. 'Bring the car into the driveway,' he ordered loudly.

Donal stepped back and he was about to tell Una he would wait for her in the car when he saw a familiar face behind the awful tall skinny man with the red face that had shouted at him.

Freda Byrne was less surprised to see Donal standing behind her sister-in-law than Donal was to see her. She had known from the day she had started dating the permanent barman in the Beggars Lodge that one of the owners was her sister-in-law's brother. 'Hello Una,' Freda called out.

Jim Byrne was used to being obeyed in his own house. He pushed past his wife and walked out the hall door.

Una moved back and said, 'I have closed the gates.' She knew how passionate her father-in-law was about the gates being closed all the time.

Donal also moved back to allow the man to walk down the driveway. He had few memories of Jim Byrne when his family used to live in a house up the road so he didn't know that when he was told to bring the car into the driveway, that he was supposed to do just that. Una knew but now wasn't the right time to tell her brother. She waited outside the door until Jim had walked down the path and looked up and down the road. His small eyes disappeared into the lines of flesh from the tight squint he made when he was walking slowly back up the driveway.

'Can we come in? Una had to say something so that Betty would move away from the door.

Betty giggled nervously and waited while Jim stared at his empty driveway for another few seconds, then moved back into the hall.

Una could smell the oil that Betty combed into her hair when she walked behind her towards the kitchen.

The house sounded hollow to Donal after the hall door closed. Three doors into rooms off the hall were closed. The hall brightened when Jim opened the door facing the hall door into the kitchen.

A few memories of his own daddy being angry flashed through Donal's mind when he walked into the kitchen after his sister and saw the small Formica table was covered with bars, screws and other metal bits. He thought that a broken cooker on a Sunday would put anyone in a grumpy humour. 'Having trouble with the cooker?' he asked.

Jim Byrne glared at Donal as if he had said something rude and said, 'There's never been any trouble with this cooker in the twenty years that we've had it.' He then he moved his tall skinny body to the frame of the stove and began wiping over the white enamel surface as if he was polishing a mahogany table. He swung his head back sharply to the door as if to check that someone was still there before he took two steps sideways to the sink. He put his hands into the basin of water and raised his face to the window and stared out at the back garden.

Twenty years, Donal thought and stared in wonder at the cooker pieces. He had no idea how long a cooker should last but twenty years was older than his sister Cathy. He recalled that his family had about three cookers since his youngest sister was born. 'That's great,' he said.

And it will last another twenty before you will admit that the thermostat on the oven is broken, Una wanted to say. She knew what was happening with the cooker and she thought a smile at the bemused face of her brother. She didn't know if Donal remembered her father-in-law from when they used to live around the corner. She also knew that Jim Byrne was furious because Donal hadn't parked his car in the driveway for his neighbours to see. And she knew that her father-in-law's temper would continue to boil for the rest of the day. She tipped her brother on his elbow and moved back towards the hall and said, 'Let's say hello to the boys.'

Betty was standing in the hall waiting for them as though she was a porter doing her job. She touched the door of the front room so that it would open. Una didn't want to go into the cold, tidy, never-used room so she pushed in the door into the back room. She stepped back to let Betty go in first. Donal walked in behind her.

Sun shone on the floor where Shea and Liam were kneeling helping Freda to put the pieces of the vacuum cleaner into polythene bags. They watched Liam struggle with trying to get a small plastic tube into a tattered plastic bag that was too tight.

'Good,' Freda shouted when the bag split. 'I'm delighted

that bag is burst at last.' She fumbled in the cardboard box and pulled out another bag.

'I'll do it,' Liam said, holding the nozzle into his chest when Donal stretched out his hand. When his granny had moaned at Freda because all the attachments were on the floor he said he would put them all back. He had never seen his mammy take the vacuum out of a box before or seen so many small brushes so he examined them all and asked Freda what they were used for. He had also grown very fond of his daddy's sister since she brought him into town after his mammy had gone off in the big coach yesterday. She laughed all the time and she didn't keep telling him to hurry up when he wanted to look at something. She never once asked him why he didn't like football and she put two soft hot water bottles in his bed.

When the nozzle slipped easily into the plastic bag, Liam smiled gratefully at Freda. He then helped her to put all the carefully wrapped attachments into their rightful places in the cardboard box that the vacuum cleaner had arrived in ten years earlier.

'They're all back,' Liam told his granny.

Freda picked up the large box and he followed her out of the room.

While Una was talking to Shea about what he had been doing during the morning, Donal studied the Celtic pattern on the rug under his feet and tried to think of what he should not say to Freda when she would come back into the room. With the door open, he could hear the banging and rattling of the cooker being put back together after its weekly clean.

The room was bright, and the mid-April sun was shining on the modern mahogany-veneered sideboard. The tiled fireplace facing the door housed a basket of artificial flowers. The rectangular table was lengthwise in front of the fire close enough to the opposite wall to allow two chairs enough space for a body to slide in.

The slender low modern sideboard facing the large window to the back garden displayed an assortment of glass and porcelain objects. The large mirror over the fireplace reflected the portrait of Pope John that hung on the wall over the table.

Donal raised his head from the carpet and nodded a smile at Betty who was sitting at the table with her back to the door. He didn't remember ever talking to her when he used to live around the corner. But he knew she was Jack's mother and whenever he saw her in the village they always exchanged friendly gestures of hello. He shifted uneasily in his chair when Betty returned his smile, but he still couldn't think of anything to say to her.

Betty's high cheeks protruded like small pale oranges when she smiled back at Donal.

Out in the hall Liam was helping Freda to put the vacuum cleaner under the stairs. 'That door is too small,' he said. 'Ours is much bigger and we have a light.'

'It's in now, Liam,' Freda said giving the box a push, then eased her body backwards from the small space into the hall. 'Just the same you are quite right, it's only big enough for a child.'

'The next time I'll put it back for you,' Liam said, smiling up into his aunt's red face.

'Liam's talkin' about under the stairs,' Betty Byrne said. 'I have never been able to get right into the back of it.'

'It gets very narrow in at teh back,' Donal agreed, recalling when he used to hide things right under the first step of the stairs in Plunkett Road when he was a young boy. While he listened to Liam advise Freda how she could cut the wood at the front of the stairs and make another door, he was delighted that the young boy hadn't been his brother when he was Shea's age. 'I wouldn't be able te get inte teh back of er own one now,' he confessed.

Betty raised both of her hands up to the back of her neck

and shoved her net-enclosed hair towards the crown of her head. Her hair dropped down and rested on her neck again when she lowered her arms, leaned on the table and said, 'We were behind Joan's car in the bus yesterday for a while on the way into town.'

Donal nodded a smile as if to say well done.

'We were lucky with the weather,' Una said. She was more anxious than her brother to leave as soon as possible. She felt ashamed for Jack since she knew that, because Donal didn't bring his car into the driveway, Jim Byrne wouldn't put his head in the door. And Betty would have less to talk about than their mammy on a good day. She also felt guilty about wanting to be away from Betty because she used to like her before, and for a while after she was married to Jack.

Freda nodded a smile at Donal from the doorway. She held the door open until Liam came in, then closed it sharply as though she was shutting out something unpleasant.

'Well Una,' Freda said, 'how did the rest of the wedding go?' She walked to the other end of the table and sat down. 'Joan looked lovely.'

Una was now feeling confused, and pleasantly surprised because Freda had come back into the room so quickly. She had never warmed to her sulky sister-in-law, and Freda had always taken every opportunity that came her way to be rude to her.

The same age as Joan, Freda used to play out on the street before the Malones moved to Ballyglass. Both Jack and Freda resembled their father and up until now Una always thought their small eyes and long nose suited a boy more than they did a girl. She noticed today that Freda had learned to use makeup. Her eyes were bigger and brighter. But she knew Freda's new warm manner and attitude hadn't come from a tube or a bottle.

Although Una wondered at the reason for her sister-in-law's warmer attitude, she was happy to return Freda's friendship so she smiled brightly as she said, 'It was the biggest small wedding I have ever been to, and we all had a great time. We were so busy enjoying ourselves that we never found any time to fight or argue.'

'A good argument has made more friends that enemies,' Freda said, recalling hearing Cathy argue with her supervisors.

Una was sitting at the middle of the table with her body twisted sideways towards Donal. She was facing Betty and she didn't want to turn her back on her mother-in-law so she stretched her hand out tapped Freda's arm and said, 'Thanks for looking after the boys for me.'

'Any time, Una, any time,' Freda said, putting her other hand on top of Una's and giving it a light squeeze. 'We had a great day,' she added, glancing over at Shea.

'We were in Eason's and Bewley's,' Shea said.

Donal chuckled.

Pleased to have something to talk about, Una leaned over and poked her brother in his arm. 'You can laugh if you want to, but they are a must for a visit when you don't live here all the time.'

Liam slipped off his chair, slid his hands in the pockets of his trousers and stood in front of his uncle and asked, 'Do you want to see what Freda bought me?'

Donal smiled and held out his hand.

'Not here,' Liam said, lowering his blond head so he could see his hands while he withdrew two small boxes from the pockets of his trousers. He glanced at Donal and said, 'Come over to the table and I'll show you.'

Shea had seen what was in his brother's boxes every half hour since Liam had brought them home. His granny had seen them once and she didn't want to see them again so they both stayed where they were.

The boxes were the same length and twice the depth as a Swan Vista matchbox. When Donal went to pick up one

Liam put his hand over them and said, 'I'll show you.' He then shoved Donal's hand away and opened the boxes very carefully and pulled out two miniature carts. One was a horse with a milk cart attached, and the other was a horse with a trap attached to it.

Donal's stared in amazement at the little objects while his mind flashed back to when he was a boy and the toys he used to get for Christmas. The little objects he was looking at were not the least bit like the toys he used to play with. The cars he remembered had been made from tin and they spurted out whizzing sounds when the wheels were rubbed backwards along the ground to make them go on their own. They were always broken or stolen before the New Year.

Liam moved the little boxes nearer to his uncle and asked, 'Do you not like them?'

'They are very small,' Donal said, recalling the bus conductor outfits that lasted a day, and the cowboy hats that drooped over his ears when it rained. The silver and gold paint that was shining on the miniature carts reminded him of the guns he used to have, and that they didn't last very long either. He wasn't used to children so he didn't know what to say. He had never played with any of his nieces or nephews, or taken them out.

'You can pick them up now,' Liam said, moving back from the table, nodding and smiling his permission.

Though he was charmed with the little toys, Donal hesitated. To his mind children were fed, taken to the doctor when they were sick, went to school and played out in the streets. They did what they were told and they didn't ask questions or tell adults what to do. And they were never given little fragile things to play with because children didn't know how to look after them.

'Go on,' Liam urged his uncle while he put his hand behind the milk cart and pushed it gently along the table.

'Te tell yeh teh truth, Liam,' Donal confessed, 'I'm afraid te touch them.'

'Spread your hands out then and you can hold them for a minute,' Liam encouraged. He then used his small fingers like they were delicate little cranes and placed the toys on Donal's hands. He moved away from the table and said, 'Freda knows how to put them back in their box. I'm going to get what she bought for the girls.'

When Liam was running up the stairs Freda covered her face with her hands. She was both delighted, and embarrassed. She knew she had always been rude and disagreeable to her sister-in-law. She also felt sorry for all the times she had taken her jealousy out on her two nephews because they were Una's children.

Other than her ma and her da, the only family that Freda could remember knowing was her brother Jack. She had some vague memories of living in a country village before her family had moved to Dublin, but she didn't remember any other people. Her ma washed her clothes and cooked her food. Her da went to work every day. He cut the grass and swept the paths on Saturdays and he cleaned the cooker on Sundays. But it was her brother Jack that had fixed her dolls' pram, her bicycle, and her skates. He brought her to the pictures, he brought her to see Santa Claus, and he took her out to the seaside in the summer.

Although Jack hadn't stopped taking his eleven-year-old sister to the pictures on Saturday afternoons when he started going out with Una Malone, Freda didn't understand why her brother wanted to be with someone who had a house full of friends.

'Here he comes,' Una said, nodding her head to Donal when she heard the creak on the top of the stairs that had always annoyed her when she had stayed in the house. The nasty side of her still thought that Jim Byrne loosened the floorboard himself so that he could count the number of times that the toilet was flushed during the night.

Donal lowered his tired arms down to Freda so that she could take the toys out of his hand. She had slid the second cart back into its box when Liam came running into the room holding a small Eason's bag so high that his uncle couldn't see the little boy's face.

The racket from the rattling and banging of the cooker going back together gushed into the room from the kitchen when Liam was stretching his neck so that he could see over the table searching for his uncle, as if he was afraid he wouldn't still be there.

'Take your time,' Betty said, stretching her arm out to stop Liam from running.

Liam ignored his Granny Byrne and walked straight over to the table so he could inspect his little cars. Satisfied that his carts were still there, he smiled at Freda and said, 'Can I show him?'

Freda moved the two boxes so that Liam could put the bag on the table.

'What girls?' Donal asked, although he suspected they were Maurice's daughters, he was enjoying the attention that Liam was giving him so he thought it would be fun to tease him.

'Our cousins,' Liam said, looking at Freda and adding, 'You saw them yesterday.'

'Oh, yeh mean Eileen and Rory,' Donal said.

'No,' Liam snapped. 'Our Irish cousins who live around the corner from our Granny Malone.' He looked at Freda again and said, 'We have cousins all over the world.' He brightened his smile again when he withdrew two small flat oblong boxes the size of a bar of chocolate out of the bag and put them on Freda's lap.

'Not all over the world,' Shea said, moving back from the

table so that his mammy could see the presents. 'We have three cousins in Canada.'

'It's a Celtic cross,' Una called over to her mother-in-law. A wave of impatience passed over her. She knew that her effort to include Betty Byrne in the excitement of the presents had fallen on deaf ears when Betty stretched her arm down to her leg.

The skins on the front of Betty Byrne's legs were very dry because she always sat close to the fire. Una had already told her that the crimplene skirts she wore were not warm enough for the winter cold weather. But Betty continued to wear them because they were cheap and washable.

'Granny has already seen them,' Shea said. He didn't know that his granny sat too near the fire, or that her skirts weren't warm enough. But he often wondered why she was always rubbing the front of her legs, but it didn't annoy him as much as when his Granny Malone was always searching through her handbag.

'I'd like one of these,' Una said.

'Freda will get you one,' Liam said, raising his face to his uncle. 'You can have one on a pin if you want it. She doesn't have to give the girl in the shop any money.' He closed the lid on the box he had taken from his uncle and he was stretching his arm up to get the second little case from his mammy when he called out, 'Freda tell them about the cards you have.'

Freda slapped her thigh before she covered her face as if she was trying to muffle a scream: 'I had some gift tokens that I didn't use at Christmas,' she said through her fingers.

Una tapped her hand on her sister-in-law's shoulder and said, 'Thanks very much, Freda, Emir and Patsy will be delighted with them.'

'I expect they'll have some darkie cousins in a few years,' Betty said, hitching her hair up again.

'We hope so,' Una said, 'but that won't be a novelty for

them.' She glared into Betty's small, shining, beady unhappy eyes and continued, 'They go to school, and play out with children of all colours in London.'

'I'll make some coffee,' Freda said. Her elbow hit Donal in his waist when she stood up sharply.

Una wanted to slap Betty Byrne across her face, and for Freda's sake she wanted to stay for coffee. She caught Freda's arm and said, 'Not for us, though, thanks all the same.' She wanted to cry when she saw the disappointment in Freda's face but they really had to get to Sean's. 'We're on our way to Sean's,' she said, then nearly changed her mind when she saw the tears in Freda's eyes. To bring some warmth back into Freda's face she said, 'Next time I'll bring the whole family.' When a tear dropped from Freda's eye and she laughed, Una added, 'Maybe not or you won't ask me again.'

'It's been a full weekend, Freda,' Donal said. He was embarrassed for Freda and his sister. He patted the pockets of his denim jacket as he said, 'I'll turn teh car while yer gettin' yer things together.'

Betty's slipper made a sharp slap in the lino floor when she stood up quickly. She was in the kitchen before Donal walked into the hall.

When the boys had gone upstairs to get their things, Freda sat back down at the table, folded her arms across her chest and bowed her head into them. 'Una,' she said after a few seconds, 'that was a nasty thing for my mammy to say.' She brushed her hair back from her red face with her hands. 'She can be so very tactless at times.'

Rubbish, Una thought. Your mother is a very unhappy woman. For a moment she wondered if Betty's nasty tongue was worse than her own mammy's silences. She sat down again and put her hand on her sister-in-law's arm. She tried to join up some of the dots she felt were connecting Donal, and the friendly behaviour from Freda. She closed her ears to the sounds of Shea and Liam on the stairs, and the rattling of the cooker that was still coming from the kitchen and patted Freda's arm again. 'Your mammy's not the only one to say things like that. And you know as well as I do that there are many more who think and talk the same way.' Her head was bursting with things she wanted to know about Jack's family. For the first time since she had known her sister-in-law she wanted to sit and talk to her but right now she didn't have the time.

Freda said, 'I am very sorry, Una. Will you apologise to Donal for me?'

'You work with Tony's Gran Bella, don't you?' Una said, coughed a giggle and continued, 'I met her yesterday for the first time. I think she's great. In fact I wish my own mother was more like her.'

'And Cathy,' Freda added.

'Of course, and Cathy,' Una said, throwing her eyes up at the ceiling. 'Now tell me, Freda if you can, who in Ballyglass doesn't know Cathy?' She then raised her hand quickly and added, 'No, not now. That'll have to keep for the next time. We really do have to be in Sean's soon.' She stood. 'I might be able to tell you why it's so important for us be at Sean's next time I see you.'

'Cathy's terrific,' Freda said, then added quickly as though she was afraid she wouldn't get a chance to say it again, 'I hope it's not too late, Una, to tell you that I think you're all great.'

'No, Freda, it's not,' Una said. She could hear Jack and Betty Byrne running down the hall and she didn't want to leave Donal on his own with them. 'But we do have our moments. And don't worry about what your mammy said, it's not her fault.' She squeezed Freda's hand. 'And don't worry about Donal either. He may be quiet and shy but he's smart enough to know your ma was talking for herself.'

'Liam's a real winner, isn't he?' Freda said. She brushed and straightened her skirt. 'I'm not surprised that Jack is so proud of them.' Her eyes were shiny and she tilted her head back when she added, 'Jack should have come home with you. And tell him I said that.'

Again Una wanted to sit and tell Freda about her family. She nodded her head in agreement. 'I can see Liam being a right handful for Jack in a couple of years. We have Jack who knows everything, and by the time Liam is ten he will know absolutely everything.'

'Nobody's perfect,' Freda said, laughing through her tears.

Una embraced her sister-in-law for the first time then said, 'I'll have some of those money cards that Liam thinks you have when you get bored with them.'

Chapter Sixty-six

By the time Una was at the gate, Donal was standing on the pavement side of his car, holding the door open. He waved up to his sister to show that he hadn't needed to turn the car at all. He had turned his back on the small group by the time that Jim Byrne had raised his fist and swung it in a circle towards his own face. When Jim Byrne had made the third demand with his fist for Donal to bring the car down to his gate Donal had opened the boot for Una to put the small cases in.

Sean and Flo lived on another housing estate about twenty minutes drive from Ballyglass. It was north of the city on the same spreading arc of Dublin's housing development. Like with Ballyglass, Ballymore, and all the other new housing estates, the corporation and purchased houses now blended with new shops, schools and small factories.

By the time Shea and Liam decided which seats they would take in the back of the car, Una was closing the boot on the small cases. Five seconds later she was sitting in the front seat searching for the ashtray.

'Have yeh everythin'?' Donal asked, turning round to check there were no other cars coming before he raised his foot off the brake and the car began to ease away from the kerb. He didn't want to go back if Una had forgotten something. The road was clear but he continued to move the car slowly so that Shea and Liam could return their grandparents' wave. He then pulled away sharply without a nod or a smile to Jim or Betty Byrne.

Apart from Bella and Tony the only families Donal knew were some of the siblings of the boys he played football with. Most of them were large families and they lived in Ballyglass. He had been in their houses and he had never felt uncomfortable or unwelcome. By way of apologising to Una for wanting to leave Jack's parents' house he said, 'We didn't have teh time fer coffee.'

'I've never known them to make coffee before,' Una said. 'It must be Freda's idea. I bought a jar of instant the last time I stayed there because I couldn't drink their tea any more. They boil it on the cooker for ten minutes before they pour it out.'

Donal always put his tea pot on the gas. It was the only way he knew how to keep it hot. 'Ten minutes is a long time,' he said.

'No Donal, it's not,' Una laughed. 'It's what the Irish have always done so they could get twelve cups of tea out of three spoonfuls.' She was taking her packet of cigarette out of her handbag while she added, 'I have also grown to like a decent cup of tea since I went to England.'

Donal talked to Shea and Liam about England, school and soccer. He soon forgot about Freda, and he was surprised and pleased at how informed Shea was on all the English leading football teams, and stars.

'I don't like football,' Liam said, poking his head between the two front seats.

'Is that right?' Donal said. He couldn't imagine a world where young boys didn't like football. Until half an hour ago he thought it was the only thing that young boys talked about.

'I like swimming,' Liam said, expecting his uncle to be impressed like Freda had been.

'Is that right?' Donal said again. Apart from having a bath the only time, Donal was ever in water was when he was at the seaside and he hated having to get into the sea because he had been told to.

'Of course it's right,' Liam said, pulling on the back of his uncle's seat and shouted, 'I wouldn't say it was if it wasn't.'

Una patted her young son on his hand. 'Donal didn't mean that he didn't believe you. It's what he always says when he doesn't know what else to say.'

'The thing is, Liam, I don't know about swimming,' Donal apologised.

'It's more important to be able to swim than it is to play football.' Liam continued moving to make room for his brother to lean over into the front of the car. 'Shea can swim eight lengths without stopping.'

'Is that right?' Donal said. He gripped the steering wheel like it was a chicken and he was going to wring its neck and said, 'That's great, and what about yerself?'

For two minutes Liam told his uncle about everything he did, and everything he knew about Dagenham. Donal had never heard a young boy talk so quickly and about so many things. He wondered if the child slept when he went to bed. 'That's great,' he said.

'I don't think it's great,' Liam objected.

'And neither does your daddy,' Una said, easing Liam's hand off the back of her seat. 'And Donal is entitled to his opinion on Stansted Airport as much as you are.' She had been half-listening to what her son had been saying because she was immersed in her own thoughts about her in-laws and her husband. But she also knew that Liam would talk forever unless he was stopped.

'To tell yeh truth, Liam, I don't know much about it,' Donal said.

'I don't think anyone does,' Una said, moving her head about at the traffic that was just crawling along both sides of the road. There was nothing interesting for her to see like gardens, or porches because they were driving through a building site. Her vision of the houses was blocked with cranes, tractors, lorries and other vehicles sneaking in and out of openings along the road. Liam and Shea soon became more interested in the turmoil that was going on outside the car than talking to their uncle.

Worried about the time, Una tried to see over the car in front of them. 'Do you know what the hold-up is?' she asked, rubbing the face of her watch again as though she could make time stop until the traffic moved on; they had to get to Sean's soon.

Donal rolled down the window on his side of the car, stuck his out to see what was going on. 'I think it's the water and sewage for the new school up ahead.'

'You're very calm about it,' Una giggled. 'Jack would be going mad by now, he can't stand traffic hold-ups at any time.' She lowered her voice. 'But then you are always calm whatever is going on. Nothing gets you down.' She couldn't remember a time when her brother had lost his temper. He was always undemanding and unspoilt.

But some things worried Donal and right now he was ashamed because he had not said goodbye to Freda and he felt he had betrayed Jack, and he would never want to do that. When Freda and Liam were putting the vacuum cleaner under the stairs he remembered when Jack had given him his first pair of real football shoes, and Jack wasn't even married to his sister at the time. He still felt the same joy whenever he thought about the time he had opened the bag and found three pairs of real football boots. They were three different sizes, and although they had been used they had been polished to look like new.

He recalled that one pair of the boots fitted him, and he had wrapped the other two pairs in newspapers and kept them far back under the stairs until he needed them. 'Yeh were right about cuttin' a door in teh hall te get te teh back of teh stairs, Liam,' he called into the back of the car.

'I know I was,' Liam called back to his uncle.

'It's too far back fer te see teh things that are in there.' Donal felt he was saying thank you to Jack for his football boots with praising his son. He still never felt guilty about not giving Maurice either of the bigger pairs of boots.

'I'm going to ask my daddy to put a light in there for Freda the next time he comes home,' Liam called over his shoulder and went back to examining the trucks and cranes.

'I never thought about Freda bein' Jack's sister,' Donal said, 'she never said anythin' about knowin' yeh.'

'I tried to get on with them, Donal,' Una said, 'but it is very difficult to get on with people when they don't talk to you. That's the first time Freda has ever been friendly with me. I noticed her face when she saw you. I don't want to pry but is there something I should know about.'

The traffic started to move along so Donal slid the clutch into gear while he said, 'Freda has a boyfriend.'

'She is old enough.'

'And so is he, but he is a Protestant,'

'Poor Freda,' Una said.

Chapter Sixty-seven

When Donal turned his car into Sean's driveway Una was delighted when she saw Tony's car parked on the road because it told her that Josie and Mike were already there. She didn't care if Maurice came.

'It was thoughtful of Mike to leave the space in the driveway fer us,' Donal said when they were walking into Sean's house through a very smart porch.

Una didn't care where the cars were parked. She was dreading she would find her mammy smiling at her from an easy chair beside the fireplace. She walked through the large living room to the back of the house. She was looking around the kitchen when Josie called out, 'The children are out in the back garden with Liam.'

Relieved that her mammy hadn't changed her mind about staying with her friend Ena, Una sat down beside her sister and for something to say she asked, 'Did you have much traffic on your way out, Josie?'

'There is always traffic,' Josie murmured. She couldn't recall any truck, bus or car she had seen, and she didn't want to remember, or talk about her journey to her mammy's friend, or the journey to Sean's house. She wanted to go back to her family home and finish packing her cases.

The streets seemed narrower, the houses smaller, and the small shops closer together than Josie remembered as Mike turned the car into Manor Place two hours earlier. Josie had

closed her eyes at the narrow pavements, and shut her memory
to the children that used to play out on them until Eileen
started asking her so many questions about when she used to
live in one of the houses that didn't have a garden.

'If it's all right with you, Josie, I'll take us out to Portmarnock instead if Howth,' Mike had said when his wife was
moving to get into the front seat of the car after he had helped
her mammy out.

'Why?' Josie asked. She used to hate her days at the seaside
when she was a child. And the family always went to Portmarnock.

'Eileen wants to see it,' Mike said. He waved to Ena.

Still afraid that her husband would go to Limerick without
her if she objected to anything he wanted to do, Josie said, 'In
that case she can sit in the front seat.'

By the time Josie had given her children a brief summary
about the long walk from the train, and the bags they had to
carry, or drag along the ground when her daddy used to take
her family to Portmarnock for the day when she was a child
her and patience was exhausted. She didn't want to think about,
or talk about her Aunt Sue, or cancer. The excitement with the
wedding and her panic over her husband going to Limerick
drove all thoughts about her Aunt Sue from her mind.

Assuming it was because of Mike's sister that Josie looked
so wretched, Una said, 'I'm sorry to hear about Theresa,'
Then hearing a commotion at the front door, then the voices
of Maurice and Maeve Una thought that by the time Josie
learned about the letter in her handbag she wouldn't want to
talk to her for months.

'So am I,' Josie returned. She wiped her face with her hands
as though she could wash the guilt in her heart before she said,
'I never liked the girl.'

It was the first time Una heard Josie say anything about
Mike's family. She recalled sitting beside Theresa at Josie's

wedding and how she had struggled to engage the tall girl in conversation. 'Neither did I, Josie,' she said. She waited a few seconds to say, 'Anyway it is Mike you're married to and not his sister.'

Josie raised her eyebrows, then nodded her head.

Una continued, 'Just like I married Jack and not his awful father.'

Deprived of sleep, Una's body was tired, and her mind was exhausted. On top of learning what had happened to Joan she was worried about her mammy cutting her hand. She wanted to hold on to the warm feelings that had developed with Josie so she thought it would be better to give her sister the letter now before they sat with their brothers to decide what to do about it.

Withdrawing the letter from her bag, Una said, 'I'm sorry to have to spring this on you now, Josie, but I found this yesterday among Joan's cards.' She gave her sister the letter. While Josie was reading the letter she said, 'This is why we are all here.' She withdrew her cigarettes from her bag and continued, 'I intend to tell the boys about the others. I wanted you here as well but that was before I learned about Theresa. I can manage if you want to go.'

Curtains, and beds danced on the page of the letter Josie was reading. She had never had to worry about the price of anything she bought for the house. In fact she didn't know what a fridge cost, but she was sure that two new beds, and curtains for a couple of windows didn't cost seven hundred pounds.

'We have to think about Cathy,' Una said when Josie was folding the envelope.

'I know,' Josie nodded. She folded the letter, put it back in the envelope and handed it back to Una, saying, 'I will stay.'

Weighing the advantages and disadvantages of telling her brothers about their mammy, Una was sure that she was doing the right thing. She also knew she couldn't speak for Josie,

'What about Mike?' she asked. 'Do you want him to hear about Joe O'Mara, and why we had to leave Ballymore?'

'Does Jack know?' Josie asked.

'Yes,' Una nodded, 'he probably knows more about the family than you do. Jack married me, not my mammy. And anyway his lot are not much better. I sometimes believe that his da is so mean that his ma has to darn her knickers.'

Josie managed a smile then said, 'Tell them everything.'

The family sat around the dining table. Una took the letter out of her bag and laid it on the table and asked, 'Where's Maeve?'

'Out in the garden with the children,' Maurice replied.

Liam placed a deck of card on the table and said, 'Then tell her to hurry up. Una has a plane to catch.'

'This doesn't concern her,' Maurice replied.

Una laid the letter on the table and rubbed it with her fist to remove the creases Josie had murdered into it. She stood and placed the crumpled little packet in front of her handsome brother and said, 'Either Maeve comes in here or you go into Barnet's on Monday morning and pay at least a hundred pounds off this.' She sat down then added, 'You can tell Maeve what you like.'

Liam picked up the letter, read it and said, 'I'll take care of it.'

'Give Josie the letter,' Sean said, stretching his hand towards the table. He picked up the deck of cards, gave Liam one sharp nod and repeated, 'G-give teh l-letter te Josie.'

Josie read the letter, put it down on the table and covered her face with her hands.

Maurice picked up the letter opened it slowly and read it. He slid the letter without the envelope down the table to Donal, then left the room and went out to the garden.

While Donal was reading the letter, Josie and Una exchanged concern with their eyes. One was forced to remember what was probably best forgotten and the other was reliving bitterness that she could do without right now. Josie struggled to remember while Una fought to forget. For the first time in her life Josie wished she were in Limerick.

'Seven hundred pounds.' Donal read the last line, folded the letter and said, 'That's a lot of money.'

Maurice came back with Maeve.

'The money is the least important,' Una said. 'We can pay that at a pound a week each for the next thirty years.'

Elbows shifted and titters died before Una said, 'Barnet's would accept that rather than go to court.' She then raised her eyes from the centre of the table to Josie who was now sitting up straight with her arms folded tight across her waist and added, 'Mathews had to accept a weekly amount when they took her to court.'

With the memory of her drive around Arbour Hill still fresh, Josie closed her eyes and whispered, 'It was a long time ago now.' She glanced over at her husband in time to see him lower his head to his entwined fingers and squeeze them tightly.

'How long ago?' Maurice asked, 'I never heard about it.'

Certainly not the first time Una recalled because it would be another ten months before Maurice was born. And he was probably too young to remember when the other bills came pouring in.

Now that they were assembled Una worried if her brothers really needed to know about how their mammy ran up bills for other people to pay. With such an age difference between them, they probably knew a different mammy, and perhaps she was nicer to them.

Maurice opened a window.

Four cigarettes were lit, and while ashtrays were being found Una's mind went back the six years to the last time when all the family were together for Maura's twenty-first birthday party. She recalled how much the younger family had grown to be part of Ballyglass. Ballymore meant nothing to them and she wondered if they would understand, or believe her. After all even Sean was hard pushed at times to remember when the family had lived in Arbour Hill.

'Yeh only have te tell us what concerns teh letter,' Maurice said.

'If Una doesn't tell you about the others, I will,' Josie said.

Two hours earlier when Donal had been sitting in his car waiting for Una to come out of Byrnes' house some long dead memories from when he used to live in the area floated across his mind. He was now curious about why the family moved to Ballyglass. 'Tell us as much as yeh can remember, Una,' he said.

Una glanced quickly around the table, then sat up straight in her chair, crossed her legs and rested her hands in her lap.

The family were silent while they nodded at their hands as if they were all saying the rosary. Una prayed that Josie would forgive her. 'Mammy has run up large bills before, and no-body knew about them, or even suspected there was anything money owing until there was a final demand.

'Like t-this one?' Sean said, nodding his head to the letter.

Josie's brief tour of Arbour Hill, and Portmarnock stirred memories she had suppressed since before she had started working. When she opened her eyes and saw her youngest brother's permed hair she wanted to turn the clock back to yesterday afternoon and feel his arm around her shoulder again. She knew that was not going to happen so she said, 'We were never told about the first one.'

Una wanted to spit out what she knew and get on her plane back to her own home before her family told her to go. She inhaled deeply and said, 'We lived in Arbour Hill and one Christmas mammy bought us all expensive toys in Barents. She also bought a lot of other things there as well, clothes, shoes, perfume, and presents for her friends.'

'Wait a minute, wait a minute,' Maurice called out. He put his hand into the table and demanded, 'How did she get teh stuff in a shop like that without payin'?' He glared at Una as if he was policeman conducting an enquiry.

'She opened an account,' Josie snapped.

'I d-didn't know that big shops like that gave accounts te p-people like us?' Sean said.

'They do if you are with someone like Pam O'Mara,' Una said.

Three images collided in Josie's memory: her mammy's friend Pam, her mammy's garish outfit, and the house where she used to live when the first time she saw her mammy crying.

Una placed her hand in front of her sister and asked, 'Are you sure you don't want to tell any of this, Josie?'

'No. No. You're doing fine,' Josie said, removing one of her hands from under her chin and waving it into the centre of the table as though she was swatting a fly.

Torn between the stricken face of Josie and the need to continue, Una said, 'Josie, I don't want to go over all this any more than you do.' She prayed her sister would continue to remember, because she wondered if her family would believe her. 'We have to think about Cathy,' she said softly.

'I know,' Josie whispered; she nodded her head and repeated, 'I know.'

Una thought back to the evening a couple of months before Pauline had made her communion. She had come downstairs to go out to the toilet. She knew the body that was sitting by the dim fire in the dark was her daddy because there was enough light coming in from the street lamp to identify his curly hair. The sting she was feeling now was that her daddy hadn't asked her if she was all right when she came back in from the back yard. He hadn't said anything at all to her. It was like one of them had been a ghost.

God almighty, Una thought now, if she hadn't fallen over her brother's tricycle she wouldn't have hurt her leg, and if she hadn't hurt her leg then she would have been asleep when her mammy came home with Pam and Joe O'Mara. Her memory was so clear now that she imagined she could hear the loud buzzing from the engine, and the beam from the lights of Joe O'Mara's car. Clearest of all was the voices and what they had talked about. She turned her head to Sean and said, 'That was the first big spend that I remember.'

'Did yez have te give yer skates back Una?' Maeve asked remembering the skates she used to share with her sister.

'They were worn out by the time anyone knew that they weren't paid for,' Una said welcoming the chance to laugh.

'Joe O'Mara paid the bill,' Josie said.

No he didn't,' Una said. She wondered if her sister knew why he had offered to, but she was pleased Josie remembered. 'You're right Josie in that he offered to pay, but there were strings attached.'Daddy was very upset and went to his mother for the money.'

'What were the strings?' Donal asked. He had never asked his sisters anything about his mammy before. He had no memories of her caring about him. He never missed her when she wasn't there and he hadn't wondered where she was. The first pangs of concern he felt about her was when Sue insisted that his mammy was not to be told why Joan was going to England. Then when Joan agreed with Sue he smothered his anxieties about his mammy and concentrated on helping his young sister.

Forcing his mind not to think about what he would do if Maeve spent that much money without telling him Maurice asked, 'did daddy know she had bought all them things?'

Liam wasn't concerned about the money. He wasn't married and he didn't have a girlfriend to worry about running up any bills for him to pay. What Una had told them was a shock to them all. He understood that of all his siblings that Maurice was the least well of. At the same time he also knew that Maurice was the meanest. He smiled at his miserable brother and said, 'He did when the bill cam in.'

If feelings of shame made a sound Liam would be scream-ing. And all his screams would be for the years he had hated Josie for bullying him into humouring his mammy. He recalled the evening after his sister Pauline went back to Canada, and he told his mammy that he knew about his sister's troubles with her husband and how Harry was getting his money. He had felt shame then, because when he told her he knew that she knew, she had signed his papers for the Air Force and it had been blackmail. 'What strings were involved with Joe O'Mara paying the bill?' he asked.

'It doesn't really matter now,' Una said, 'the main thing is that the bill was paid.'

'G-go on,' Sean urged, 't-tell us anyway.'

Una sat back in her seat, rested her hands in her lap and said, 'Mammy was pregnant when the final demand came in, and Joe O'Mara wanted the baby.'

Maurice shot his head into the table, glared at his oldest sister and shouted, 'Josie! Is this true?'

Furious with her brother, Una stood and shouted back, 'Don't you ever again shout at Josie. There was never any rea-son to tell anyone, and you wouldn't be told now if it wasn't for this letter.' She picked the letter up off the table and placed it in front of him and said, 'You sort it out.'

'Who was the baby?' Flo asked, patting Una's shaking hand.

'The baby was Maura,' Josie said.

Donal wasn't worried about the bill, or the history of any other bills. All he wanted right now was keep his family to-gether. He had no intention of moving back into his family home and he was concerned for his youngest sister living on her own with his mammy now that Joan would not be there any more. 'We have te think about Cathy,' he said.

Think about your older sisters, Mike wanted to shout at his wife's brothers. They have given half of their lives to caring about you. He felt as sorry for Una as he did his wife. But he was more concerned with how Josie would cope when she learned everything about his own father. There was nothing he could do so he worried about how selfish he had been with his own sister.

'Go on, Una,' Liam encouraged. 'If yeh don't tell us teh rest then we'll have te make it up erselves.'

Yes, Una thought, just like I decided about Joan and Sue before I came home. 'As you probably all know already, we moved to Ballymore with the money that daddy inherited when his mother's brother died.'

Other families also moved away from Arbour Hill. Josie remembered the Corporation gave cheap loans and grants to people who would move out of the city. She closed her eyes to the memory of her mammy complaining about her Grandmother Malone not giving her daddy the money until the deposit on the house had to be paid.

Una continued, 'It was after our first Christmas that Mammy wanted more money to pay the rates. At Easter she wanted more money for the electricity, then by the summer the telephone bill. Josie, Pauline and myself paid the telephone bill between us, and Mammy knew that we would do it, so we frequently paid twice.'

Josie nodded agreement and added as though she was living the days again, 'She also told us not to tell Daddy.'

'We've never had a telephone,' Maeve said, smiling at Liam.

Maurice scowled at her.

'All in good time, Maeve,' Liam said smiling back at her, and staring hard at his brother. He knew Maurice more than he had ever known, or wanted to know his daddy. He expected that Maurice was mortified because his wife was listening to unpleasant stories about their mammy. He smiled at Maeve again and hoped she was enjoying herself.

'Let's not argue over phones right now,' Flo suggested.

'Josie always paid more than Pauline or me,' Una said.

'That's not important,' Josie said. She didn't want to remember any more that she had to, but she recalled the fights and arguments, and the shame of having to move to a Corporation estate.

'Then one day the final demand came in from Mathews for over a hundred pounds for coal,' Una said. She rested her cigarette in the ashtray and covered her face with her hands.

Sean laid a hand on Una's back and asked, 'Josie, have you a–anythin te add?'

Josie kept her chin in her hands and raised her face from the table, 'Una is right. We had paid enough, even at that time I wanted to go to London to learn about tinting and colouring.'

'Are yeh sayin' that we moved from Ballymore because of two hundred pounds?' Maurice moaned.

'If you want to, you can see it that way,' Una returned. 'On the other hand it could have been because the loan for the house hadn't been paid for three months, or the rates, or the ground rent, and the electricity was also due.' She dropped her hands to the table. 'But the real reason was because neither, Pauline, Josie or myself had any more money to give Mammy.' She slid the letter up towards her brother and said, 'It's now your turn.'

'Anyhow, who told Daddy?' Liam asked.

'The Dublin Corporation,' Josie volunteered. 'He got the Court Order for the rates; they hadn't been paid for six months. When he went over to see them about paying the bill he found out that the loan hadn't been paid either.'

'What was she doin' with all her money?' Maeve gasped, her voice low and her eyes smiling like she was listening to a fairy story.

'I don't think that concerns you,' Maurice snapped.

'It concerns us all,' Una snapped back and slapped the table. 'That is why we are all here.'

'She goes to the pictures,' Josie said. She saw Mike cover his face with his hands. She continued as though she was reciting a poem: 'She has also spent some money on the house since last year. The beds, and the curtains in the bedrooms are all new. She also has her tea in Jury's when she goes to the pictures.'

Una put her hand on the white envelope and said, 'If you have to pay this, Maurice, or see your mother in jail it will concern Maeve every bit as much as it will you.' She slid the letter down to him and added, 'It's not Maeve's fault that our mother is a lazy selfish bitch.'

'It's none of our faults,' Josie said.

Donal was astonished on learning about his mammy and his older sisters. He knew that what he had heard was true because some memories of when he was a child surfaced while Una and Josie were talking.

Paper always makes a crinkling sound when it is folded, so apart from the laughing of the children in the garden the only sound in the room came from Liam as he slowly folded the letter and said, 'Yer not payin' this one, Josie.'

'We can all pay this bill between us, Liam, Una said, 'but how do we stop Mammy doing it again?'

'Fer a start yerself and Josie are not goin' te pay anythin',' Liam said. He moved his hand across the table to his eldest sister and rested it on her arm, 'Josie, I have never ever told yeh what te do because I never thought I needed te. At the same time I never saw all the things that yeh have done fer the lot ev us. And I'm not talking about doin' any ev er hairs.'

Mike covered his face with his hands when he saw tears roll down his beautiful wife's face.

When the first drop of water fell on Liam's hand, he wondered how long Josie's tears had been boiling her in her head because the small drop of water was so hot. 'I'm askin' yeh now te stop spoilin' er mammy,' he said. He patted her hand and added, 'Now have a good cry. God knows yeh have paid enough fer it.'

Sean didn't remember the Christmas before his sister Maura was born, but he did remember when she was a baby and he had a three-wheel bicycle with a chain that had allowed him to pedal backwards. Before Una had told them about the outstanding bills about when the family had moved to Ballyglass he had suspected there had been money problems but he had never asked about them.

Maurice struggled between excusing his mammy for spending money she didn't have, and paying his share of the bill Una had opened. He refused to believe that his mammy had left it for Una to find. He leaned into the table, stared accusingly at her and said, 'How can we be sure that Mammy wanted you to open her letter and read it?'

'I wasn't meant to open it, or read it, Maurice,' Una said coldly. She held his nervous stare and continued, 'I was meant to find it and give it to her in front of Josie. It was Eileen that opened it, and Flo that read it first, she then gave it to me and I kept it until after the wedding and showed it to Sean.'

Maurice lowered his face to his hands.

Mike wasn't surprised at what Una and his wife had revealed about their mother. He had never liked the selfish woman and although he had never objected to Josie sending her money he had resented the way his mother-in-law expected Josie to give her more. He reflected on his own small family and concluded that his father had been as big a bully as Sheila Malone. They had both failed and harmed their children. He wiped his face with his hands as though he could clear the vision of the stricken face of his sister when the Garda had called to the house to tell his mother his father was in prison.

Reflecting on Una saying that they had to stop their mammy from running up more bills she couldn't afford to pay, he wondered if he could have done anything to stop his father from drinking so much. He had often wondered if his father had been lucky because he hadn't been killed in the fight. Or if his sister and his mother would have been better off. He had heard from a neighbour that the wife and family of the man that had been killed had been relieved of a burden because they no longer had to suffer from the drunken man finding fault with them all.

As far as Mike knew, Theresa had never visited their father in prison. Now sitting through and listening to the drama of his mother-in-law he decided that his sister was wrong. No matter what their father had done he was still their father. His mother was as much to blame as his father was for allowing him to bully her, and her children. 'You should all confront your mammy with this bill,' he said in his usual quiet voice.

Until now the family had forgotten Mike was sitting with him, and they all looked at him as though he had given them an order.

Mike continued, 'My father was a selfish mean bully, and his behaviour eventually got him ten years in prison.'

The shouting of the children in the garden seemed to double in volume with the silence.

'What fer?' Maeve gasped.

Maurice poked his wife in her arm and said, 'It's none ev er business.' He didn't want to hear Mike say it was for not paying his bills.

'He killed a man,' Mike said, then added quickly, 'He got into a fight with another bully that was also an alcoholic.'

'Did he die in prison?' Liam asked.

Mike realised he had said his father was a bully. 'No,' he said. He raised his face from his hands and ran his eyes over the stunned expressions of his wife's siblings. When he saw tears, and sympathy in their eyes he knew he had been wrong not to have told Josie before. He joined his hands again and said, 'I haven't seen him since he came home a couple of months ago but Theresa told me he is a changed man.' He felt free from feeling ashamed of his father and this gave him the confidence to continue. 'I believe that if my mother, my sister Theresa and myself had stood up to him together he might have changed.'

'Not all of us,' Liam said. 'Una has a plane to catch, and Josie has done enough.'

Sean nodded agreement.

Una shoved her chair back and said, 'I have to make a move if I want to catch my plane.' She didn't care what her brothers told their mammy. She looked at Maurice and said; 'I have always found it cheaper in every way to tell the truth.' She went out to the garden and called her children.

Chapter Sixty-eight

Back in her own home in Dagenham, Una lifted her cup of tea off the small table. 'Make sure you put them back into their right boxes,' she said to Jack.

Jack turned one of his son's little boxes over to read the side of it again. 'They are very nice,' he said.

'They're made in England,' Una said, stretching her hand over to the table for her lighter. 'Freda brought them into town after the church on Saturday.'

'I know,' Jack replied. He sat back on the sofa as though he was very tired and added, 'She phoned me after you had left the house.'

'Did she tell you that you should have come home with me?' Una asked after she had lit her cigarette.

'She did, but it's too late now.'

'I'm glad you didn't,' Una returned, tapping her cigarette in the ashtray. 'You wouldn't have liked to have heard what was said about your ma.'

'What on earth did your sister's wedding have to do with my ma?'

Una inhaled deeply. 'Her name is Joan,' she said curtly, 'and you were wrong about her being pregnant but she has had a baby.'

For two minutes after Una had told him about Joan, Jack sat in silence and rubbed his chin, then said, 'I'm sorry, Una.'

'We are all sorry,' Una said. She decided not to ask him what he was sorry about. 'You were also right about them managing without me.'

Jack sat forward on the settee as though he wanted to get closer to Una and said, 'The family were right about my ma, but I would never have told her.'

This was the first time Jack had admitted his ma was a gossip. 'I know that,' she said, 'but they didn't. At least they didn't want to take the chance.' She was mentally exhausted so she thought she would wait a few days to tell him that her Aunt Sue had really wanted to keep the baby.

'She is only a child,' Jack said.

Una was annoyed he hadn't called Joan by her name, 'If you are talking about Joan,' she said, 'she is the same age as Freda.'

Jack leaned into the coffee table and picked up one of his son's little boxes again. 'I'm surprised that Josie never told you,'

'I'm not,' Una said softly. She felt more love for her older sister during the afternoon than she had since they were teenagers. 'Josie would never have gone against Sue,' she said, 'and it was Mike who looked after Joan.' She watched her husband nodding his head. 'Josie did what she could. God love her but she has always bullied the lot of us because Mammy always bullied her. At the same time she hasn't done Mammy any favours.'

Jack couldn't imagine what it would be like to be raped. He was always tall for his age so he hadn't been physically assaulted or bullied in school. However, he knew what it was like to be bullied, and he worried that he had been like Josie and had bullied Freda and Una into pleasing his da so he wouldn't complain to his ma about leaving their hometown twenty years ago.

Lights from a car shining through a gap in the drapes told Jack that it was nearly eleven. He guessed it was his neighbour coming home from the bingo. He also saw that Una was tired. 'You go on up to bed,' he said, 'I'll wash up the cups.'

'The boys slept well,' Una said, 'Freda gave them her bed and she slept in the box room.'

'You stay in bed in the morning,' Jack said. He wanted to talk about his sister and tell her about why his parents had moved to Dublin from Ulster but it would take too long and he could see that she was tired. 'I'll take Shea to school.'

Una wiped her face with her hands: 'Liam has his playgroup in the morning as well.'

'I know.'

'Talk him out of wanting to take his cars with him,' Una said.

'Don't worry,' Jack picked his empty mug off the coffee table. 'You go on up.'

'He has a couple of jobs for you to do for Freda when you go home again,' Una said.

'I am not fixing that bloody cooker again,' Jack said, 'I have already told me da if it was still there when I went home again that I will drag it out to the front garden and leave it there.' He turned back from walking out of the room with the two mugs in his hands and added, 'He has enough money in land to buy a new cooker every year.'

This was the first time Una had heard Jack criticise his da. 'It's a light under the stairs that Liam has promised Freda,' she said following her husband into the kitchen.

'There is a light under the stairs,' Jack said. 'I put it in years ago. The miserable git took the bulb out the second time when me ma forgot to turn it off.' He turned on the water and started rinsing the mugs.

Una's thoughts floated back to the afternoon when Mike had told them about his father. She wondered if Mike would have told them if he hadn't heard about her mammy, and if Jack would have criticised his dad if she hadn't told him about the Barents' bill she had found among Joan's cards.

She looked around her lovely new kitchen and recalled

when Jack had a new damp course put in. He had said the walls would fall down if it hadn't been done. She decided that all the family secrets came falling out because she had kept her mammy's letter – just like her kitchen wall would had collapsed if Jack hadn't had the damp course fixed. 'It's your ma that has to put up with the cooker,' she said.

'No she doesn't,' Jack replied, turning off the water.

'You're not expecting your ma to go out and buy a cooker on her own, are you?' Una said, expecting him to know that his ma wouldn't buy a pot without asking his da.

Jack turned round from the sink and snapped, 'I don't expect that silly woman to do anything, but that doesn't mean that I don't think she should.'

'Your ma doesn't have her own money,' Una said, almost stunned by the way he was talking about his ma.

'Yes she does,' Jack replied. He switched off the light over the sink and added, 'You go off to bed.' He nodded his head to some papers he had left on the table: 'I want to tidy them up.'

'Buying a new cooker is not the same as bringing home a set of pots,' Una said. 'A cooker needs to be piped or wired in. I wouldn't be able to move a cooker on my own and I'm stronger than your ma.'

'The gas board and the ESB deliver and install cookers,' Jack said. He pulled out a chair and sat down at the table. He didn't have any work to do on his papers. He wanted to be on his own for a while.

'Can't you do them in the morning?' Una said. 'You don't have to be in work until two this week.'

'I only want to check that I have done something,' Jack lied. He was afraid that Una would continue to ask him about his ma and da. 'You go on up,' he encouraged, 'I'll only be a few minutes.' He had expected that she would stop thinking about her family when she came to London like he had ceased to wonder about the family he had left in Derry when he was ten.

'It's the time of the month,' Una said, 'and we only have about three days.'

'Three days for what?' Jack asked, looking into her smiling eyes.

'To make a baby,' Una replied. When she saw him blush she decided to tease him so she said, 'Cathy told me.'

Jack lowered his face to his papers.

Una continued, 'She told me about the three days.'

'I suppose Cathy would know,' Jack said, closing his folder. He stared intently at the blue soft card but, no matter how hard he tried, he couldn't bring an image of Una's young quiet sister into his mind. All he could see was Cathy's bright smile and her mass of dark brown hair.

Una said, 'What Cathy doesn't know she makes up.'

Jack shoved his papers away from him and said, 'If I had known about Joan I would have gone with you.'

Una saw sadness, and a plea for forgiveness in his eyes. 'I know,' she said, 'and if I had known I wouldn't have haggled about going either.' She closed her eyes at the memory of how she had felt when she was leaving on the Friday. 'But we are all like Cathy.'

Jack smiled and said, 'There is only one Cathy.'

'I mean when we are not told about something we make it up ourselves.'

'I never thought about that,' Jack lied. He turned off the light in the kitchen and he was walking over towards Una when he said, 'Remind me to tell you about the family I have in Derry.' He thought that by telling Una it would help to recall enough to be able to tell Freda everything she wanted to know.

Chapter Sixty-nine

Mike returned the telephone receiver to its cradle and walked into the living room where Josie was sitting at the table with Cathy. 'Time to get the children up,' he said and sat down at the table.

'It's grand fer yeh that it's not rainin' fer startin' out,' Cathy said.

'I expect it will rain sometime,' Josie said, 'it always does.' She shoved her chair back and was about to walk away when Cathy caught her hand.

Cathy also stood and put her arms around her sister hugged her tightly and said, 'I'll miss yeh, Josie.'

After yesterday afternoon in Sean's house Josie was cried out. But tears shone in her eyes when she embraced Cathy's hug and said, 'I'll miss you too, Cathy.'

'I want to get petrol in the village,' Mike said to Cathy, 'so if you are ready I will take you to the factory.'

'I'm ready,' Cathy said. She gulped down the last of her tea and left the room to get her jacket and bag.

Mike was waiting in the car when Cathy came out of the house. 'Yeh can take yer time,' Cathy said as she closed the door. 'I don't want te give me supervisor a heart attack with bein teh first in teh queue te clock in.'

Mike smiled. He could picture Cathy standing in a queue of young girls, some of them as pretty and smart as herself, to clock into a factory to work eight hours at a job few of them liked. 'Do you still like the job?' he asked.

'I have never liked teh job,' Cathy replied quickly, 'and before yeh ask if I am sorry I didn't stay on at school teh answer is no.'

With Cathy's reply Mike didn't know whether to ask her about her job or why she didn't stay on at school. He was curious about both. After a few seconds' silence, he chose the job and said, 'Josie told me you have a great time in the factory.'

Delighted that Josie had talked about her, Cathy smiled and said, 'I do, but that doesn't mean I like me job.'

Mike nodded his head as though he understood. He didn't, he had never worked in a factory.

Cathy had always liked Mike and she was sorry she had been flippant with him. It wasn't his fault he had to go to Limerick so soon, and it was proper that Josie should go with him. 'We make our own fun in the factory,' she said, 'and as fer school it just wasn't fer me.'

Mike nodded his head in agreement again, and this time he understood. The best apprentices Josie had ever had were the girls who had left school without taking any exams. 'School doesn't suit everybody,' he said.

This time Cathy nodded her head in agreement. 'I intend to have me own business some day,' she said with more confidence than when the idea had come into her head.

Mike nodded his head in approval and said, 'let me know when you are ready and I will help you with the accounts.'

Overwhelmed with Mike's offer of help and encouragement, Cathy felt tears come to her eyes. He hadn't laughed, or told her she was being silly or stupid. A vision of her planned business swam into her head like a swan gliding across a pond.

They were coming to the traffic lights onto the main road. The petrol station was to the left, and Cathy's factory was to the right. 'Yeh can let me off when yeh turn teh corner fer teh petrol station,' she said, 'I have plenty ev time te walk down to teh factory.'

Mike had promised her brothers he would wait outside the factory until Cathy went in. 'Are you sure?' he asked. He thought that if she came home while her brothers were there she was tough enough to cope with whatever happened. He could only do his best to keep her away from the house. And he also though that Cathy should be told because it would prepare her for any other bills that might come in.

Cathy sniffed to clear the moisture in her eyes, looked at her watch and said, 'I'm in plenty ev time.' She didn't know what time it was because her eyes were too misty to see her watch. There were few cars going north so when Mike turned the corner to the left he pulled into the kerb.

Cathy had her left hand on the handle to open the door when Mike was pulling on the hand-break. She opened the door then turned her head back to Mike and said, 'I'm sorry about yer sister, Mike, and I will pray fer her.' She swung her feet out onto the pavement and was out of the car before Mike had said goodbye.

Liam and Donal were sitting in Liam's car waiting for the traffic lights to turn when Cathy passed them on her way to the factory. She didn't see them because she had her head bowed so that her tears would fall on the pavement and not run down her face.

Eileen and Rory were at the front gate when Liam pulled into the kerb of his family home.

'Daddy is not back yet,' Rory said to his uncles.

'Cathy won't be back until after six,' Eileen said, 'and we are all going to Limerick when my daddy gets back.'

Chapter Seventy

Sheila Malone woke to sound of bouncing on the stairs. Her bedside clock told her it was getting on for eleven. She assumed the noise on the stairs was Josie getting ready to go to Limerick. It was nearly half past eleven when Sheila heard the gate rattle. She had dozed off again so she hadn't heard Mike's car drive off. She worried when she heard the hall door open and close, then the living room door open and close.

Downstairs in the living room Maurice nodded his head by way of greeting to his three brothers who were sitting at the table playing cards. He glanced at the clock and said, 'I take it Mammy's not up yet?'

'Yer in time,' Liam replied. He moved the cards he had in his hand about, then placed three in front of him and said, 'I'll open fer a shillin'.'

Upstairs Sheila could hear male voices, but she couldn't identify any of them so she got out of bed, opened her bedroom door and listened for a few seconds. There were definitely two or more male voices. A brief moment of terror swept over her body because the only words she could make out were numbers, and they were arguing like they were betting against each other.

A brief wave swept over her because she thought they were men who had come to select furniture to pay her Barents' bill. She wrapped her dressing gown around her and without putting anything on her feet picked up her handbag and went down the stairs. She was about to open the door when she heard one of them say, 'I think it's time we woke her up.'

'Go ahead,' Liam said, 'bring her up a cup of tea and tell her we are waitin' te talk te her.'

Maurice wasn't going to bring his mammy up a cup of tea and he wasn't going to tell her to do anything. But he would make the tea so he rose from his chair like a child who was obeying orders. He had reached the door when his mammy walked in.

Still suffering from the panic of expecting to find strange men in her house, Sheila stared at her son as though he was a ghost. When she saw her other three sons sitting at the table she walked quickly out of the room and down the lobby to reach the toilet before she peed in her knickers.

'Will I make tea for everyone?' Maurice asked.

'Not fer me,' Liam said, 'I won't be here long enough te drink it.' He showed his brothers his hand of cards and said, 'I'm out.' He then stood, walked out into the hall in front of Maurice and sat on the second last step on the stairs and waited until his mammy came back up the lobby. She was about to mount the stairs to go back to bed when he said, 'We want te talk te yeh inside.'

Sheila closed her eyes and walked into the living room like she was a schoolgirl obeying a summons from a headteacher.

Donal and Sean were still sitting at the table but they had put the cards away.

Liam went into the kitchen. The smell of tea boiling on the cooker made him want to heave. 'Come into teh livin' room now,' he said to his brother.

Maurice followed Liam into the living room. Their mammy was standing at the front window as though she was waiting to be told what to do.

Liam pulled the Barents' letter from the pocket of his jacket and handed it to his mammy and asked, 'Do you have enough money in your bank account to pay this?'

Sheila took her time opening the envelope and withdrawing the letter. She had read it every hour since she had opened it over a week ago but she pretended to read it again, then sat down in her easy chair, placed her handbag on the floor beside her feet and said, 'No.'

'It's a lot of money to spend,' Sean said.

Sheila sat back in her chair and looked out the back window.

Sean continued, 'We know yeh have s-spent similar sums of money before when yeh knew yeh didn't have t-teh money.'

Sheila picked her handbag up off the floor, opened it and pulled out a handkerchief.

Maurice was sure she was going to start crying so he said, 'I'll bring yeh in a cup ev tea.'

Liam moved from standing behind his mammy's chair and stopped Maurice from leaving the room. 'Her tea can wait until we are done,' he said. He turned back to his mammy and said, 'Teh four ev us will pay this bill, but it is to be teh last time yeh buy anythin' if yeh don't have teh money teh pay fer it.'

Sheila brought her handkerchief up to her face and blew her nose. She returned her handkerchief to her handbag, then stood and, keeping her eyes on the floor, walked out of the room with her handbag on her arm and went upstairs.

'That's all we can do,' Liam said.

'How much is that each?' Maurice asked.

Until now Donal hadn't said anything, but he had been thinking. He had been thinking a lot since yesterday afternoon in Sean's and he was feeling guilty about not supporting his sisters when they were all living at home. Also from visiting the Byrnes and hearing about Mike's daddy he saw that his older sisters had another family to think about. He didn't know much about Flo's family but he knew Angie and Maurice had her to look after so he said, 'I'll pay this bill.'

Liam had also been thinking since he had left Sean's house, but he had been thinking about his mammy. Unlike Una, he wasn't angry with his mammy, unlike Josie, he wasn't afraid of her and, unlike Maurice, he had never missed her attention. Still she was an old woman now, and all her children except Cathy had homes of their own. He doubted she would ever change. She would always be lazy and selfish.

Maurice had worried about where he would get the money to pay his share so when Donal said he would pay the bill he smiled gratefully at him.

Sean knew Donal could afford to pay the bill but he also felt he had some responsibility so he said, 'Thanks Donal.' He stood and added, 'If yeh need help let me know.'

Donal nodded his head and said, 'That's all we can do fer now.'

'Except fer Maurice,' Liam said, 'he can bring her up her cup ev tea.'

Chapter Seventy-one

Sheila Malone was already dressed when she heard her sons talking in the hall. She stood at the window of her bedroom and watched Sean, Donal and Liam walking down the path. She expected Maurice would follow them so she picked up her handbag and walked over to the door to go downstairs and phone for a mini cab. She had never been concerned for her health, but when she reached the door it opened. A shiver ran down her body to her feet when she saw that a tall man with a halo of light behind him was standing with a cup of tea; she thought she was having a heart attack. She stepped back and dropped her bag on the floor.

Maurice was so shocked by the look on his mammy's face he spilled the tea on the floor. 'I brought yeh up a cup ev tea,' he said, bending down to pick up her handbag and spilling more tea. The bag was heavy and the handle was on the far side of him and as he had the cup of tea in one hand he could only use one to lift the bag. He dragged the bag towards him by the bottom and some of the contents stayed on the floor.

'Leave the bag,' Sheila shouted as another shock struck her body when she saw a small piece of paper lying on top of the other envelopes that had slipped out of the bag. When Maurice was stretching his hand out to pick up the papers, Sheila shot her foot out, moved her son's hand away and shouted, 'I said leave them.'

Maurice stood. It was a long time since his mammy had

shouted at him like that. But he had avoided her wrath since he was a young boy. He still had the cup of tea in his hand and the only places he could put it was on the windowsill or his mammy's bedside cabinet. His mammy was blocking his way so he said, 'Where do yeh want yer tea?'

'Bring it downstairs,' Sheila replied, turning her back on her son and moving so he wouldn't be able to insist on picking up the papers that had fallen out of her bag.

Maurice left the room and descended the stairs faster and more noisily than he had mounted them, left his mammy's cup of tea on the draining board and almost ran out of the house.

Liam and Angie were standing at Angie's front gate when Maurice was running down the road. 'That didn't take long,' Liam said. 'I suppose it would be too much te expect that he threw teh cup of tea over her.'

Angie nodded her head as though in agreement and said, 'Cathy will some day.'

Five minutes later when the church bells were ringing out the angelus, Sheila was in the hall making a phone call. Fifteen minutes wait, the girl in the mini cab office had told her so she went into the living room, sat down at the table and emptied her handbag. She returned two cigarette lighters, two packs of playing cards, three lipsticks, four small bottles of perfume, six pencils, a nail file, a hairbrush, a bottle of nail polish, and a packet of cigarettes. The remainder of the contents of the bag were an assortment of bits of paper.

She spread and shuffled through the papers and picked out the white small crisp cheque. She smiled at the memory of telling her sons that she didn't have the money to pay the Barents' bill in her bank account. The remainder of the papers were receipts for the items she had bought in Barents, and her afternoon tea in Jury's hotel. She went through them all and kept some to give to Joe O' Mara even though he had told her he didn't want them. She tore up the rest and put them on the embers in the fire grate and set fire to them.

Black smoke oozed from the burning papers when Sheila put the match to them. She watched the ends of the paper curl and turn to grey while she recalled Joe O'Mara giving her the cheque to buy anything his wife wanted. She would buy what she wanted, knowing that Pam would tell her keep it for herself. She looked at the clock, then used the poker to mess the burning paper about to be sure they were all burnt.

While Sheila was putting on her coat, Liam was sitting with Angie Dolan talking about Cathy.

'I promise I'll get in touch with Donal if she's not copin' with yer mammy, or anythin,' Angie said as the familiar grinding of the brakes on a bus passing at the top of the road sounded.

Liam stood and said, 'I'll get that one on teh way back.'

Angie walked over to the door with him and as was her habit she looked out the window and saw his mammy coming out of her house. 'Yeh will have yer mammy's company,' she said, nodding her head over to his family home.

Liam turned back and looked out the window. His mammy was standing under the concrete shelf looking up the road. 'I'll wait fer teh next one,' he said.

'Yeh might be better going fer teh one that's just gone up.' Angie suggested. 'Yer mammy looks like she's waitin' fer teh next one te go up. If she was goin' fer teh one that's up there she'd be walkin' up teh road now.

Liam was nodding his head in agreement when a mini cab pulled up outside the gate. Instead of getting out of the car the driver hooted his horn and made a hand gesture up to the woman who was at the door of the house.

Sheila Malone ignored the driver and turned her head down the road.

'Good fer her,' Liam said, 'the lazy bastard should get out ev teh car and knock on teh door.' He then walked out of Angie's house and up the road to get the bus into the village.

www.ingramcontent.com/pod-product-compliance
Lightning Source LLC
Chambersburg PA
CBHW070539120726
47909CB00007B/2186